"It's not every day a man spies a peeping princess hovering overhead," Granger said. "Perhaps your royal duties include palace surveillance?"

Emmaline shrugged. "Perhaps they do."

"In that case, wouldn't it be prudent for you to conduct an up close and personal interrogation as well? I'm perfectly willing."

Emmaline mused.

It certainly was an inviting offer.

And she was feeling a bit naughty.

What would Remi say if he saw her flirting with another man?

Well, she wasn't married to him yet. But she would be, in a matter of weeks. After that, improper conversations with men like Granger Lockwood would be out of the question.

This might be her last chance for a bit of innocent fun.

Or not-so-innocent fun . . .

Wendy
Corsi Staub

A
Thoroughly
Modern
Princess

AVON BOOKS
An Imprint of HarperCollinsPublishers

This is a work of fiction. Names, characters, places, and incidents are products of the author's imagination or are used fictitiously and are not to be construed as real. Any resemblance to actual events, locales, organizations, or persons, living or dead, is entirely coincidental.

AVON BOOKS
An Imprint of HarperCollins*Publishers*
10 East 53rd Street
New York, New York 10022-5299

Copyright © 2003 by Wendy Corsi Staub
ISBN: 0-380-82054-4
www.avonromance.com

First Avon Books paperback printing: November 2003

Avon Trademark Reg. U.S. Pat. Off. and in Other Countries, Marca Registrada, Hecho en U.S.A.
HarperCollins® is a registered trademark of HarperCollins Publishers Inc.

Printed in the U.S.A.

10 9 8 7 6 5 4 3 2 1

For Mark,
my own Prince Charming . . .
For the young heirs to the throne,
Morgan and Brody . . .

And for my dear childhood friend,
the girl next door:
Shari Gilson Roof
who is queen of her own castle
filled with charming princes.

I also acknowledge with gratitude my editors,
Carrie Feron and Lucia Macro;
my agent, Laura Blake Peterson;
her assistant, Kelly Going;
and, as promised, Alana Bryant
at 10 East 53rd, who rescued my cell phone.

Prologue

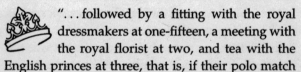 "... followed by a fitting with the royal dressmakers at one-fifteen, a meeting with the royal florist at two, and tea with the English princes at three, that is, if their polo match doesn't . . . Your Highness?"

Princess Emmaline sighed, admiring the way the spring sunshine illuminated burnished highlights in Granger Lockwood's tousled dark hair, three stories below her sitting room window.

"Your Highness?"

Was Granger Lockwood aware that Papa—the king—was running late at the charity golf tournament and wasn't due back at the palace for at least another half hour?

If he did know, he certainly didn't seem to care. He looked as though—

"Your Highness?"

"Yes! Yes, Fenella, what is it?" Turning away from

the window, irritated by the distraction, Emmaline noted that Fenella's sharp nose, close-set eyes, and thin lips had taken on even sharper, closer, thinner characteristics. The older woman appeared to be quite vexed. Well, imagine that.

Emmaline's social secretary possessed precisely two moods. Irritation. And shrill hysteria.

Aware that shrill hysteria was certainly far more unpleasant than Fenella's current state of mind, and could be brought on by the slightest change in plans, Emmaline smiled cheerfully and said, "Yes, Fenella, I'm listening. And it all sounds quite agreeable."

It didn't, of course. Fittings, meetings, teas . . .

All familiar. And not the least bit agreeable on this fine Thursday morning in June.

No, all that was agreeable at the moment was the view from Emmaline's window, three stories above the palace rose garden, where Papa's visitor now lolled on a carved stone bench in the sunshine.

Emmaline had met Granger Lockwood IV several times in passing.

Well, twice, to be exact. And she recalled both occasions with far more clarity than a betrothed princess probably should.

Their first encounter was in the palace drawing room, where he was meeting with Papa. Upon their official introduction, Granger's gaze had fleetingly locked with Emmaline's in a more than professional, businesslike way.

Or had she merely imagined it?

She certainly hadn't imagined the quickening of

her own heart as she looked into his eyes—or the unusual quiver, low in her belly, a sensation that made her blush.

"It's a pleasure to meet you, Your Highness," he had said in flawless French, with a proper bow. "I've heard so much about you."

"I've heard about you as well," she had informed him, hoping that he hadn't noticed her flushed cheeks—and that if he had, he attributed them to the warm, crowded room.

"Oh? What have you heard about me? All very good, I hope."

"Certainly all very . . . interesting," she had said coyly.

She knew that he was a scion of Manhattan's most powerful real estate baron, the elderly Granger Lockwood II.

She knew about his legendary, self-indulgent appetite for fine wine, for nightclubs, for sporting adventure—and for beautiful women.

She also knew exactly why the notorious bon vivant was in Verdunia, and it had nothing to do with sating his desire for any of those things. He was purely there on business.

For years the tiny country had fought to keep the seaside area wild, rugged, untouched. But in the past decade and a half, the fates had conspired against Verdunia. The once-wealthy kingdom was in the throes of a full-blown economic disaster.

Brilliant, affluent, and opportunistic, the elder Granger Lockwood had come up with a plan to create a tourism industry that could save the country. When, on the eve of his preliminary trip to Verdunia in February, the old man fell from a golf cart in Palm Springs and broke his hip, the grandson had been sent in his place.

Papa had been reluctantly receptive enough to invite Granger Lockwood IV back several times since to discuss the possibilities.

Until today, the only other time his path had crossed Emmaline's was at a black-tie palace reception in April. She had been waltzing with her future husband, Prince Remi of Buiron, and Granger Lockwood had spun past them with a ravishing redhead in his arms. When he caught Emmaline's eye, he gave a little nod, then quirked a brow at her.

She had no idea what the gesture implied, but she was instantly seized by that same inexplicable current of . . . well, *curiosity* was one way to describe it.

Electricity was another.

That this foreigner again had her feeling like a weak-kneed schoolgirl was disconcerting.

So was the fact that he was with another woman, and she was with another man—the man to whom she would, in a matter of weeks, be permanently joined.

But today Remi was at his royal palace in Buiron, a good fifty miles away from Chimera, Verdunia's capital city.

Today Granger Lockwood was alone—at least until Papa finally showed up—and he certainly looked as though he had all the time in the world, Emmaline thought, watching him as her social secretary once again droned on. And on. And on . . .

A fragrant breeze stirred the imported Belgian lace curtains that framed the windows. Emmaline inhaled deeply, concluding that the prized cultivars in Mama's rose garden were more intoxicating than the finest French perfume.

And that brash American Granger Lockwood was—at least for the moment—inexplicably more appealing than . . .

Well, than any man Emmaline had ever seen.

Including Prince Remi, she acknowledged guiltily.

What was it about this Mr. Lockwood that fascinated her?

She pondered the question.

Perhaps it wasn't Mr. Lockwood at all. Perhaps he simply triggered some forbidden longing within her.

After all, he seemed so . . . carefree.

And she was anything but.

She glanced down at the platinum and diamond bauble on the fourth finger of her left hand. Suddenly it felt overly snug, unwieldy, and . . . and cumbersome.

Hmm. Was it cutting off her circulation? The heat must be making her fingers swell, she concluded, twisting the ring until it slid over her knuckle. She slipped it into the pocket of her silk robe and glanced at Fenella to see if she had noticed.

"... has requested your presence for photographs," Fenella droned, oblivious to anything but her pages of notes, "prior to ..."

Resting her elbows on the windowsill and her chin in her deliciously liberated left hand, Emmaline leaned her petite frame forward, the better to scrutinize the man below.

With his long legs sprawled straight out in front of him, Granger defied conventional posture, resting his broad shoulders against the bench. His arms were raised and bent like triangular angel wings framing his upper body, his head resting in his clasped hands. His features—more finely sculpted than a nearby centuries-old marble statue carved by Michelangelo himself—were tilted up to bask in the warm Mediterranean sun. His eyes—blue eyes, she recalled, as blue as the sparkling sea in the distance— were closed.

Granger Lockwood, Emmaline decided, regardless of his well-cut Italian suit and a tie, was the picture of casual relaxation.

Yes, Granger Lockwood was the Anti-Fenella.

The thought made her giggle, thus disrupting the droning flow of the social secretary's monologue once again.

"Your Highness . . . ?"

"Yes?" Emmaline turned to look at Fenella, whose narrow lips were tightly pursed.

"The charity supper?"

"Yes, that will be fine, Fenella. It all sounds perfectly fine. Please leave a copy of my finalized itiner-

ary on the desk in my office downstairs. Now if
you'll excuse me, I must be left alone for a few moments."

*Alone to indulge my visual lust for Papa's unwitting
visitor*, she thought, quite enjoying her furtive spy
game.

"Yes, Your Highness." With a quick, respectful
curtsy, Fenella left the room, closing the door behind
her. Her sensible brown pumps made a tapping
noise in the marble hallway, fading quickly into the
distance.

Emmaline turned back to the window, eager to return to her perusal of the unsuspecting man below.

Granger Lockwood hadn't moved.

She watched him intently, wondering what it
would be like to . . .

To have your way with him? Shame on you, Emmaline!

Yet her thoughts refused to be steered in a more
proper direction. On this glorious day, her thoughts
preferred to linger on a tantalizingly intimate fan-
tasy.

Strange . . .

She never fantasized about Remi this way.

Shouldn't a bride-to-be—particularly a virgin
bride-to-be—find herself perpetually consumed by
lurid daydreams of her wedding night?

She found little satisfaction in the prospect of
Remi making love to her . . . or in the knowledge
that no other man ever would. In fact, all at once,
Emmaline found the thought of infinite monogamy
unbearably dreary.

A dazzling orange and yellow monarch butterfly fluttered about Granger Lockwood's head, yet he still didn't stir.

Perhaps he was asleep.

Imagine that. Imagine falling asleep in the palace rose garden while awaiting an appointment with the king of Verdunia. Only a most bold, confident soul would dare allow such a thing.

Or perhaps only a foolish, disrespectful one.

Hmm.

Her fascination enhanced, Emmaline studied the man, looking for evidence of courage—or folly. Kneeling on her padded window seat, Emmaline leaned farther out the window, speculating.

"I wouldn't do that if I were you."

Startled, Emmaline froze.

The masculine voice seemed to have floated up from below.

Yet only Granger Lockwood was in sight, and he hadn't stirred. He hadn't even opened his eyes, as far as she could tell.

She darted a glance over her shoulder, half expecting to find that some well-meaning male member of the palace staff had entered her chamber. The room was empty, and—

"You might fall out of your turret. And then you'd have to walk down the aisle on crutches, at the very least. That would put a damper on the royal wedding, wouldn't you say?"

Stunned, Emmaline pulled herself back inside, clasping a startled hand over her mouth.

Her cheeks were flaming. Her heart was pounding. Of all the—

She jumped up from the window seat and paced the Persian carpet, her embarrassed befuddlement rapidly giving way to agitation . . . and then fury.

There was no doubt that it was Granger Lockwood who had spoken—in English, of course, rather than French, the official language of Verdunia. She had recognized a distinctly American accent, and was certain she had seen his lips move. He must have been spying on her through cracks in his eyelids.

Why . . .

Why . . .

Why, she ought to march right downstairs and have the palace security detail remove that insolent man from the premises immediately.

Yes, she ought to.

But for some reason, Emmaline wasn't prone to doing what she ought to do. At least not today.

She cautiously returned to the window.

She leaned out once again, though not nearly as far as she had the first time . . . and saw that Granger Lockwood was no longer draped on the bench.

No, he was now standing directly below her window, looking up, as though he'd been waiting for her.

His full lips—Anti-Fenella lips—tilted into a lazy grin.

"You're back. Don't worry. If you fall out this time, I'll catch you."

"That won't be necessary," she retorted in her own impeccable English.

"No?"

Emmaline shook her head and confided, "No, because I have wings. I keep them concealed from all but my closest confidants, lest the press find out."

His grin broadened in pure delight.

"Wings, hmm?" His blue eyes boldly looked her up and as far down as the windowsill allowed, as though he were searching for evidence. "You're a fairy princess, then?"

"Must I show you my wand?"

"If you do, I'll show you mine." He winked.

Her jaw dropped. She quickly dragged it back up into place.

He was absolutely, positively, the most dauntless, imprudent . . . no, *impudent* . . . man she had ever met.

He spoke to her as though their relationship were casual, or . . . or romantic. Or downright libidinous.

"So," he said, rocking back on the heels of his polished Gucci loafers, "how *are* things in the gilded cage these days?"

"I wouldn't know," she shot back. "Why don't you tell me?"

"Oh, I wouldn't know, either."

"Really? Then it isn't true that your grandfather is one of the richest men in America?"

"Oh, that's perfectly true," he said easily. "My life might be a little on the gilded side, but the only cages I've seen are the ones that house my grand-father's exotic birds. And yours."

"I don't have exotic birds."

"I meant your cage."

Of all the . . . !

"I am not in a cage, gilded or otherwise, Mr. Lock-wood," she said haughtily.

"Glad to hear it, Your Highness. And in that case, maybe you're free to come down and continue this conversation face-to-face. The back of my neck is getting sore from looking up at you."

Her ringless hand twitched with an errant urge to massage his aching neck muscles.

"I would dearly love to, Mr. Lockwood, but I'm quite busy at the moment."

"Really? Doing what?"

"It's none of your business."

"No, it certainly isn't. But I have to admit, I'm cu-rious. It's not every day a man spies a peeping princess hovering overhead. Perhaps your royal du-ties include palace surveillance?"

She shrugged. "Perhaps they do."

"In that case, wouldn't it be prudent for you to conduct an up-close and personal interrogation as well? I'm perfectly willing."

Emmaline mused.

It certainly was an inviting offer . . .

And she was feeling a bit naughty.

What would Remi say if he saw her flirting with another man?

Well, she wasn't married to him yet. But she would be, in a matter of weeks. After that, improper conversations with men like Granger Lockwood would be out of the question.

This might be her last chance for a bit of innocent fun.

Or not-so-innocent fun.

"If you aren't willing to come down, you could make like Rapunzel and let down your hair so that I can come up," Granger Lockwood offered.

"That only works for princes," she said affably. "And the one in that particular fairy tale found a witch lying in wait, remember?"

"Only on his second visit. The first time, he got lucky."

Emmaline tossed her head, enjoying herself immensely. "Yes, well, as I said, I only let my hair down for princes."

"And me without an ounce of royal blood in my veins," he said, snapping his fingers and shaking his head. "I'd like to see your hair down. Every time I've seen you—in person or in pictures—it's up. Like that." He regarded her trademark upswept style as though he were tempted to scale the palace wall, pluck the pins out, and send her long, dark tresses tumbling about her shoulders.

Even more unsettling than the blatant longing in his expression was her own reaction to it.

She wanted to be closer to him.

She wanted to be face-to-face . . .

Closer than that, even.

Emmaline! What on earth are you thinking?

She swiftly silenced the prissy inner voice.

Hmm . . .

Did she dare venture down to the sun-splashed garden to visit with Granger Lockwood?

She was seized by an odd sense of urgency—a desperate now-or-never sensation.

But . . . your schedule. Remember your schedule, Emmaline.

Oh yes. She was supposed to be getting ready to go out.

Her hair was already styled, as it was first thing every morning. But she still had to dress for her early luncheon with Mother and Queen Cecile of Buiron, her future mother-in-law. Queen Cecile would be presenting funds to be used to add a new wing to Chimera's Children's Hospital.

Naturally, the event would be well photographed.

Emmaline sighed.

Weren't they all?

Especially now, with the royal wedding mere months away.

Of course, her clothing for the outing had been carefully chosen long before this morning. There were two selections, both neatly pressed and ready to don: a long-sleeved blue linen suit in case the weather was damp or chilly, and a pretty floral dress intended for warm sunshine.

That outfit, with all the accompanying accessories, including a broad-brimmed hat, waited in Emmaline's dressing room next door. It would take very little time to put it on, really.

She checked her diamond-studded platinum watch, which matched the engagement ring concealed in her pocket.

There would be a good ten minutes to spare.

Fifteen, if she hurried.

Nothing scandalous could possibly happen in fifteen minutes.

What a shame, she thought, and was at once taken aback and thrilled by her own bawdiness.

She focused again on Granger Lockwood, whose gaze remained fixed on her.

He raised both his eyebrows and an index finger, palm inward. He wagged the finger at her, beckoning.

Emmaline thought about the clothing that had been laid out for her, and the lunch plans that had been made for her, and the mother-in-law who, along with her offspring, Prince Remi, had been selected for her.

With that, she made her decision.

Her own decision.

One of the first—and, although she didn't know it then, the most important—in her life.

She smiled at Granger Lockwood IV. And she said, "I'll be right down."

One

·················

"Can somebody please turn on the air-conditioning?" Emmaline asked peevishly, her voice muffled as two seamstresses, aided by Tabitha, her longtime lady-in-waiting, pulled the heavy silk gown over her head.

"I'm afraid the air-conditioning is on already, Your Highness," one of the seamstresses informed her as the dress settled around her with a deafening rustle.

"Well, can somebody turn it on full-blast?" Emmaline asked, reaching up to wipe a trickle of sweat from her hairline.

"It *is* on full-blast," came the maddening reply.

"I sincerely doubt that." Emmaline brandished her sweat-streaked fingers.

Tabitha caught hold of Emmaline's hand. "Oh my goodness, Your Highness, your makeup is running! Quickly, somebody, please . . . before it drips onto the dress!"

A mad bustle erupted in the designer's studio as both seamstresses and both their assistants rushed for towels.

Emmaline stood motionless, captive hand in the air, feeling additional beads of sweat popping out on her brow.

They *must* be lying about the air-conditioning. It was so bloody hot in there, and it couldn't be blamed only on the fact that she was swathed in layers of silk, wired undergarments, and petticoats that were to give her wedding gown its distinct lines.

Within moments, Emmaline's fingers had been swiftly cleaned with a damp cloth and her face was well blotted with a dry one, lest the beige foundation trickle down and smear on the white confection she found herself wearing.

She certainly would have preferred to forgo her usual heavy makeup on this hot and humid late summer morning, but it would never do to have the photographers who now followed her everywhere capture the bride-to-be looking anything less than radiant.

She would also have preferred a much simpler wedding dress than this frou-frou number—complete with a twenty-five-foot train—that had been created for her by Porfirio, one of the world's foremost fashion designers, who now hovered fussily at her side, emitting troubled moans at the prospect of tinted perspiration spurting forth from the bride-to-be.

And Emmaline certainly would have preferred a far simpler wedding day than the vast state affair that had been painstakingly planned for her and Remi, and now loomed less than a week away.

In fact—and here was a novel concept—she would have preferred to chose her own groom.

But that, of course, was out of the—

"All right, ladies, now the buttons. The buttons," Porfirio ordered, clapping his hands in a brisk staccato. "Quickly, please. We haven't got all day."

As the seamstresses and their assistants began fastening the elaborate rows of buttons at her back, Emmaline's gaze met Porfirio's in the mirror. He flashed her a synthetic smile. She expertly returned it.

What a silly man, she thought, continuing to regard him as he turned his attention back to the dress. That outfit he had on seemed positively clownish. Were purple suede gauchos worn with a lime green tank top and lime green espadrilles really the height of Buironese fashion?

She had no idea whether Porfirio was his first name or his last—not that it mattered. It was the only one he used. Here in Buiron, only the royals and Porfirio were known by a single name, and the latter was far more regal and eccentric, if that was possible, than most members of Remi's family.

Emmaline had hoped to use one of her favorite designers in Paris or Milan to create her wedding gown, but Queen Cecile had insisted—

"Ouch!"

"I'm so sorry, Your Highness!" a seamstress said behind her. "I was just trying to pull the seam together while Giselle fastened the button, but it seems to be—"

"Ouch!" Emmaline squealed again, as the seamstress gave another tug and the fabric dug into her waist.

Another profuse apology ensued, followed by the timid suggestion that Emmaline hold her breath.

She inhaled, detecting the faint and unpleasant scent of something deep-fried hovering in the air.

The tugging resumed.

She watched herself in the mirror, noting that her alabaster skin appeared paler than usual beneath the mask of makeup. What she wouldn't give for a healthy tan. But those carefree days were long gone. For the past few years, Mother—backed by Dr. Estrow, the royal dermatologist—had insisted that Emmaline coat herself in SPF 45 sunscreen and a brimmed hat every time she ventured into the light of day.

"You must protect yourself," Mother had said. "Skin cancer can kill you. And what about freckles?"

Freckles.

Yes, to the queen's way of thinking, freckles and cancer were equally malignant.

Surveying her reflection, Emmaline noticed that as the dress came down over her head, a few tendrils of long dark hair must have escaped her updo and now dangled about her face and shoulders. She rather liked the look, and for a moment toyed with the idea of wearing her hair down on her wedding day.

But that, of course, would never do. For one thing, she hadn't appeared in public with her hair flowing in an undignified manner since her mouth was full of baby teeth. For another, her personal stylist had already concluded that her customary topknot would best suit the diamond-encrusted tiara head-piece and veil—the icing on the cake, as it were.

Herself being the cake.

After giving herself another head-to-toe once-over, Emmaline scowled into her own wide-set green eyes in the mirror.

This was simply too much dress, too much lace, too much—*everything*—for one petite princess. Barely over five feet tall, even in these heeled satin pumps, she was awash in a cloud of white, yet this getup was anything but light and airy. It weighed a ton.

Help! she silently begged the diminutive woman in the mirror.

The woman gazed back, unable to come to her aid.

Claustrophobia set in.

She was being crushed by her dress, not to mention roasted alive.

The brick-walled, hardwood-floored studio was positively stifling, despite the so-called air-conditioning and the ceiling fans swirling over-head. Of course, it was August, and August was notoriously hot and humid in Buiron. This room was unbearable.

Emmaline began to exhale.

"Oh no, Your Highness, not yet. Please take another deep breath and hold it."

Emmaline obliged, again noting the unappetizing deep-fried aroma.

"Is there a restaurant in this building?" she asked, her voice strangled and breathless.

"I'm afraid there isn't," Porfirio said, "but if you're hungry, Your Highness, I would be happy to—"

"No, I'm not hungry," she protested, beginning to feel terribly dizzy. Food was the last thing she wanted right now.

She had eaten her usual light breakfast at the palace earlier, before leaving Verdunia for the drive to Buiron. But today the low-fat yogurt and fresh fruit didn't seem to be sitting well with her.

"There we go," Tabitha said, giving Emmaline's silk-encased arm a little pat. "The bodice is all fastened now."

Emmaline exhaled in relief. "Thank goodness. I was beginning to feel a bit faint. I was going to ask if you could stand in for me—after all, we're precisely the same size."

"I doubt that would be possible," Tabitha said, and added reassuringly, "They just have to gather the train and then bustle—"

She broke off in mid-sentence as a clattering sound, reminiscent of corn popping, suddenly erupted in the room.

At Porfirio's horrified shriek, Emmaline's bodyguard Clyde, who had been stationed just outside the door, burst in, pistol drawn.

In the commotion that followed, Emmaline found herself gripping a chair back for support. Her thoughts—and her breakfast—whirled into an inner spin cycle.

She heard Tabitha assuring Clyde that there was no reason for alarm; heard Porfirio barking orders at the seamstresses, who scrambled about on the hardwood floor gathering up the pearl buttons . . .

The buttons that had popped when Emmaline's bodice suddenly gave way.

If she could focus on something other than her inner maelstrom of nausea, this would be positively humiliating.

Finally Clyde resumed his position outside the door, and Porfirio and the seamstresses launched a harried conference in the far corner of the room.

Emmaline looked at Tabitha. "I don't suppose I can sit down in this garment?"

"I don't suppose you can." Tabitha offered a wan smile.

Emmaline's attempt to return it only made her tummy churn harder. "I thought he was supposed to be one of the world's finest dress designers," she muttered under her breath. "Surely he's capable of sewing a row of buttons tightly enough?"

Tabitha offered nothing but a tactful shrug.

Emmaline knew what she was thinking. That

Emmaline must have gained weight since the last fitting.

But it didn't seem possible. If anything, wedding jitters had killed her appetite. She had been so distracted, so exhausted . . .

So preoccupied by thoughts she had no right to be thinking, about a man she expected never to see again.

Well, with any luck.

"Surely it won't be long before they have the dress ready for you, Your Highness," Tabitha was saying. "Then you can rest and get something to eat."

"I've a feeling it had better be celery sticks," Emmaline said wryly, surveying herself in the mirror. Was it her imagination, or was her bustline spilling almost indecently from the neckline of the gown? It must be this push-up brassiere. It certainly worked wonders for her figure.

"Celery sticks?" Tabitha echoed. "Surely you'll need more than—"

"Tabitha, do you think I've put on weight?" Emmaline asked abruptly.

"No," Tabitha said loyally.

"Tabitha, you and I are both fully aware that I seem to have burst the seams of this dress."

"I wouldn't use the word 'burst,' Your Highness."

"Well, I would," Emmaline said.

Tabitha sighed and shook her head.

She was Emmaline's age exactly, the daughter of Papa's longtime valet.

As toddlers, Emmaline and Tabitha had bonded in the palace swimming pool and gymnasium, establishing a steadfast friendship that began with little regard for bloodline or peerage.

As Emmaline grew into her royal role, she continued to nurture her relationship with Tabitha, until her friend formally became part of her staff as a lady-in-waiting. The arrangement suited them both. Tabitha was required to curtsy before her and address Emmaline by her official title, but she never seemed to mind. And Emmaline relied on Tabitha's faithful listening and calming skills whenever something went awry in her life.

As now.

"Are you sure you don't smell something horrid in here?" she asked, sniffing the air through a wrinkled nose.

"Something horrid?" Tabitha echoed.

"Something deep-fried. Fried clams, or fried fish, or . . ." She shook her head in distaste.

"We passed a seafood restaurant a few doors down when we arrived," Tabitha said. "But the windows are closed and surely you can't smell the odor from here."

"Surely I can," Emmaline retorted. "And it's making me feel quite . . ."

She trailed off as another wave of queasiness swept over her.

This time it didn't ebb as quickly. In fact, it didn't seem to be ebbing at all.

"Your Highness . . . ?" Tabitha watched her, full of concern.

"Tabitha, I believe I'm going to—"

"—and then she threw up."

"Really!" Granger wrinkled his nose and shook his head. "What did you do?"

"What could I do?" The man—whose name, Granger recalled, was Stan or Steve—something with an *St*—gave an exaggerated shrug, nearly knocking his empty glass off the bar. "I brought her to the vet. And the vet said, well, you shoulda known better than to give a dog six Hostess chocolate cupcakes. Lemme ask you somethin'—How the hell was I supposed to know that? Did you know that?"

"Hell, no." Granger took a big gulp of his beer.

Not imported lager or microbrewed ale or even bottled brew.

No, the mug in front of him held good old draft beer straight from the tap of this dive bar somewhere in the East Village, a good fifty blocks—and a world—away from Granger's uptown apartment.

He had wandered in by chance, after checking out a real estate site across the street. The site wasn't going to work out, but the bar had what he needed: airconditioning, a place to sit down, and cold beer.

It had to be a hundred degrees out, and a hundred percent humidity—typical dog-days-in-Manhattan weather. The kind of weather that made a man crave an ice cold beer, even before noon on a weekday.

"Me neither," the unshaven stranger seated on the stool beside him was saying, stifling a hiccup. "I di'n know that. What was I s'posed to do? Eat the cupcakes in front of her? She was begging, up on her hind legs. So I gave her some. Okay, six. But I di'n know it could make her sick. They should make that kind of information more public, tha's all I'm sayin'. That way, nobody ge's hurt. Nobody vomits."

"So what happened?"

"To the vomit? I cleaned it up."

"Geez. That's rough." Keeping one eye on the television set above the bar—the noon newscast was on and he was anxious to check whether the Dow was still up—Granger shook his head in sympathy, feeling for his new friend . . .

Stash. That was it. His name was Stash.

The bartender placed another round in front of them.

"Nah, this one's on me," Granger said, putting a hand on Stash's arm as he reached for his wallet.

"The las' one was on you, too."

"It's okay," Granger said. "Really. Put your money away."

"You're good people, Gallagher."

"Granger."

"Ranger?"

"Granger."

"Granger?" Stash squinted, clearly befuddled, having lost track of the conversational thread.

"My name. It's Granger," Granger said patiently,

as the televised newscast went to a commercial. "So what happened next? After you cleaned up the vomit?"

"What do you think? I paid the vet. Figured tha' way, my girlfriend wouldn't get the bill. Figured she'd never hafta know. But the damn vet sent her somethin' in the mail anyway. And when she got it, she threw me out. Said I shoulda been more responsible."

"That's a damn shame."

"A damn shame," Stash agreed. " 'Cause I never asked to baby-sit her damn dog in the first place, y'-know what I'm sayin'? It was her idea. Not mine. She asked me and I said sure. As a favor. 'Cause I'm the kinda guy who likes to do favors. Y'know what I'm sayin'?"

"Absolutely."

"But jus' between you an' me?" Stash leaned closer on his stool.

"Yeah?" Granger could smell the liquor fumes on Stash's breath, mingling with garlic and brine, courtesy of a recent indulgence from the jar of pickled eggs on the countertop.

"I never liked that dog in the firs' place. It was a real girl dog, y'know what I'm sayin'? All kitten-sized and white and curly, jus' a real yappy little thing. You got a dog?"

Granger nodded. "Two dogs."

"What kin'?"

"A black Lab and a German shepherd."

His new friend slapped the bar so hard that his new drink sloshed over. "Tha's what I'm sayin', Ranger! A Lab and a shepherd. Real dogs. Man dogs. Not yappy little girl dogs. You give a man dog a coupla chocolate cupcakes, and it's not gonna spew all over the place."

"True."

"How 'bout a girlfriend? You got one?"

"A few," Granger admitted.

Stash slapped him on the shoulders, nearly knocking him off the stool. "Good for you. Good for you. Don't settle for one. Especially one with a girl dog."

"I'll keep that in mind."

Stash drained his glass in a gulp. "Hey, Johnny. 'Nother round. This one's on me."

"Sorry, Stash. Gotta cut you off," the bartender said, his gaze intent on a televised commercial for hemorrhoid suppositories.

"Johnny, you know I'm jus' gonna go down the street an' give my business to McBrien's Pub if you won't serve me."

"Sorry, Stash."

"Yeah, yeah." Stash hoisted himself off the stool. "You comin', Gallagher?"

"Nah. I've got to get back to the office," Granger said.

"Well, it was good talkin' to you," Stash said, offering a heartfelt handshake. "Stop in again sometime. I'm here every day."

"I'll do that," Granger promised.

Stash shuffled out the door, leaving only Johnny and Granger in the bar. The hemorrhoid commercial gave way to the helmet-haired anchorwoman again. Granger decided to wait for the financial report, which should be on any minute now, then head back uptown.

"Hey, Johnny," he said, "Would you mind turning up the volume for me?"

"No problem."

As the bartender reached for the remote, Granger raised his mug to his lips, took a sip—and nearly choked on his beer.

There she was.

In living color on the television above the bar.

It was stock media footage he had seen many times in recent years, since long before he met her in person. The camera had captured her exiting a white Rolls-Royce in front of a Chimera restaurant, surrounded by her entourage, pausing to smile and wave at the camera.

Granger had always thought she was beautiful, especially in this footage, wearing a summer suit in a shade of jade that precisely matched her wide-set eyes, her dark hair tucked up beneath a broad-brimmed hat that accentuated her delicate features and high cheekbones. But the camera didn't come close to capturing her spirit. There was no evidence here of the flash in her eyes that had so captivated him in person; no sign, in her demure smile, of the dry wit that had caught him so off guard.

Yet Granger stared at the television, mesmerized anew.

Princess Emmaline of Verdunia . . .

The woman beside whom all others paled.

At least for Granger.

At least since that night a month and a half ago.

It had just been one night.

Not even a *whole* night. Just a few stolen hours.

But here he was, unable to shake the memory of her.

It didn't help that every time he picked up a newspaper or magazine, or turned on a television set, she was there. She, and her fiancé, and their upcoming royal wedding, dammit.

Johnny raised the volume.

". . . reports that the princess is resting comfortably in the hospital and is expected to return in the morning to the palace in Chimera, Verdunia's capital city and home of the kingdom's ruling family," the anchorwoman said. "Through a palace spokesman, the royal physician has attributed the princess's collapse, during a fitting at the Buiron studio of famed dressmaker Porfirio, to heat exhaustion . . ."

Collapse?

The princess had collapsed?

Granger's heart stopped.

Was she all right?

". . . expected to make a full recovery and resume preparations for the upcoming royal wedding. We go now to our correspondent Debi Hanson, who frequently covers the Verdunian royals."

As the camera shifted to a smiling, overly made-up blond, Granger scowled. This woman made a living hunting down personal details about people's private lives, and making them public. To her, a foreign princess was nothing but prey.

Granger clenched his jaw so hard that it ached, overcome by the need to protect Emmaline from predatory so-called journalists. Of course, it was a ridiculous urge. The steel-willed princess had made it quite clear, in the few fleeting hours they'd spent together, that she didn't need protection from him— or from anyone else.

Including her husband-to-be.

Which was fortunate, considering that the slightly built, anemic-looking Prince Remi of Buiron didn't particularly strike Granger as the type of man who would see fit to sully his manicured hands or silk and cashmere wardrobe defending his future wife.

"Thank you, Jane," Debi Hanson said on TV, flashing bloodred lipstick and a mouthful of artificially whitened teeth. "Well, the palace is blaming her collapse on the blistering August heat. But sources close to the princess claim that, just days away from her fairy-tale wedding to charming Prince Remi, Her Royal Highness seems to be suffering from a classic case of bridal jitters . . . or something more serious. Perhaps cold feet?"

Cold feet?

Hope mingled with worry as Granger gaped at the television screen.

"The match between the wealthy heir to Buiron's

throne and Verdunia's eligible princess, the second of King Jasper's and Queen Yvette's three daughters, is rumored to be little more than a business arrangement."

Granger barely listened as the woman recapped information about the once-thriving Verdunia's dismal economic situation. The marriage between Emmaline and Remi would link their formerly feuding families and bridge the long-standing gap between coastal Verdunia and land-locked Buiron, which had long sought access to the Mediterranean for exporting purposes.

That was where Lockwood Enterprises came in. Working with both countries, Grandfather had come up with a viable plan to develop a rugged stretch of Verdunian coast. He had assured the concerned royals that it could be transformed into a tourist mecca and seaport without compromising the region's natural resources and pristine beauty.

The plan would necessitate financial backing from both Buiron's government and Lockwood Enterprises. But the latter wasn't mentioned at all in the mudslinging journalist's brief discussion about what she termed the "royal merger." So far, the Lockwoods' role in the project had been kept under wraps from the media.

Gossip reporter Debi Hanson was far more interested in regaling the American public with details about the wedding's vast financial tab, which included everything from $25,000 worth of engraved invitations to flocks of pure white doves to be released outside the Chimera Abbey after the ceremony.

"What a waste of money, huh?" Johnny the bartender asked, shaking his head in disgust.

"You can say that again." Granger glowered at a televised image of Emmaline beaming on Prince Remi's arm at an engagement reception several months ago.

"You know, when I got married, we had the reception at the Moose club—I was grand pooh-bah back then. But it was a simple wedding. My wife's sisters and my mother-in-law made some trays of lasagne. And you know what? Marie and me are still together after twenty-five years. I don't give those two fools more than a few months, tops."

"I'm with you on that one," Granger muttered.

Fools.

He had no problem finding that an apt description of Prince Remi, whom he had met on a few official occasions.

But Emmaline didn't strike him as the least bit foolish. She had come across as a woman who was firmly in charge of her own mind, if not her destiny.

Maybe they're really in love, Granger thought, watching Remi plant a chaste peck on his fiancée's cheek at the urging of reporters. Emmaline smiled up at him, her eyes hidden behind designer sunglasses. Granger wondered what expression the lenses masked.

Perhaps ill-concealed displeasure?

Or true affection?

For her sake, Granger hoped it was the latter. But he doubted it.

The scene switched to a press conference in front of familiar stone and wrought iron gates, where a throng of reporters surrounded several official-looking royal handlers. A caption at the bottom of the screen read *Royal Palace in Chimera, Verdunia, Earlier Today.*

The man standing behind the podium calmly stated, "As the royal wedding draws near, the princess, like any other bride, is incredibly busy finalizing the details, along with her usual official duties. But she is doing very well and is eagerly looking forward to marrying Prince Remi on Saturday as scheduled."

She was doing very well.

Thank God.

The wedding would go on as scheduled.

Granger muttered a curse and drained the rest of his beer in one gulp.

Back to the anchorwoman, who reminded viewers that the network would have full, live coverage of the royal wedding beginning at four A.M. on Saturday.

Granger slammed his mug on the bar.

Johnny glanced up, startled.

"Sorry," Granger said.

"Hey, it's okay. I understand. I've got stocks myself."

"Stocks?" Granger realized that the financial report had begun.

The Dow had plummeted.

And so, in the wake of the latest news about Princess Emmaline and her royal wedding, had Granger's spirits.

"Are you sure you don't want me to stay with you for a while, Your Highness?"

"No, thank you, Tabitha." Emmaline sank back against the goose-down pillows. "I'd just like to be alone for a little while."

"Of course." Framed in the doorway, Tabitha made a little curtsy and smiled, but she looked worried. "I'll check in again later."

"Thank you. And please don't allow anybody else to come in." Emmaline closed her eyes. "I'll ring if I need anything."

With a slight creak, the door closed behind the lady-in-waiting.

Emmaline heard hushed voices echoing in the cavernous hallway outside her suite as Tabitha relayed her wishes to the concerned members of her staff who were huddled there.

Finally several sets of footsteps retreated down the hall.

Emmaline waited to be sure they had gone.

Finally all was silent.

Emmaline bolted frantically from her bed.

The swift movement unleashed a wave of nausea.

She grabbed the bedpost, waiting until it subsided to mere queasiness.

Then, without stopping to pull on a dressing gown or slippers, she rushed barefoot across the carpeted floor to one of her bureaus. She opened the top drawer and removed a leather-bound datebook.

She didn't use this one to keep track of official engagements or social functions. That was Fenella's job.

Instead, the pages of this calendar were for her personal use, to keep herself organized and jot notes and dates she wanted to remember.

She flipped back to June and scanned the month from the beginning, page by page, past notations about a television program she had wanted to watch and about remembering to personally select a birthday gift for Tabitha . . .

There it was. She found a circle around the date on the first Thursday of the month, and began counting forward from that date.

Precisely fourteen days afterward came the page that was inscribed with a pair of initials.

G.L.

That was all she had dared to write there.

But it was all she would ever need, she knew, to remind her of what had happened on that third Thursday in June.

Truth be told, she didn't even need the initials as a reminder. She knew that she would never forget the significance of the date.

Just as she would never forget the wine-flavored warmth of Granger Lockwood's lips on hers, or the way he had looked at her in the moonlight that spilled in the window of his hotel suite as he plucked the pins from her hair, one after another, until the whole wavy mass tumbled down to graze her bare shoulders . . .

Fourteen days.

Emmaline began counting again, moving hurriedly ahead to the beginning of July.

Nothing.

Her pulse began to pound.

She began flipping the pages of the datebook rapidly, looking for another circled date.

There was none.

None in July . . .

And none in August.

Emmaline felt her knees turning to liquid beneath her. She steadied herself by placing one trembling hand on the dresser as the other one flipped the pages back to June.

And then forward to July.

To August.

Counting.

Searching . . .

Flipping.

June . . .

Counting.

July . . .

Searching.

August . . .

Emmaline's world seemed to be careening out of control.

Where was it?

Where was the circled date?

The nausea edged in again, as if to punctuate the lack of evidence.

There *was* no circled date.

That meant only one thing.

Emmaline hadn't had her menstrual period since the beginning of June.

Precisely fourteen days before she recklessly abandoned her virginity in Granger Lockwood's suite at the Traviata Hotel in Chimera.

Two

·················

 "Granger!"

"Yes, Grandfather?"

"Come in here, please," barked the voice on the telephone intercom.

Granger's eyes rolled skyward. "I'll be right with you, Grandfather."

He swiveled in his leather chair, turning away from his cluttered desk and the three paper Starbucks coffee cups he had drained in the past two hours. The caffeine had been merely a temporary fix. He still felt weak and light-headed, and his skull was pounding. Glancing at his watch, he saw that he had to wait two more hours before he could safely take another dose of ibuprofen.

Two more hours of this headache—and a meeting with Grandfather for added pleasure.

Well, this was shaping up to be one hell of a day. He wouldn't be surprised if the Dow sank even lower than it had the past few days, or if the perfectly blue summer sky suddenly gave way to unforecast storm clouds.

Granger's gaze fell on the floor-to-ceiling windows behind his desk. From here—the fifty-second floor of Lockwood Tower, the midtown office building his grandfather had built two decades ago—he had a sprawling view of lower Manhattan.

His penthouse apartment three floors above provided just as spectacular a view, but of the verdant rectangle that marked Central Park, with upper Manhattan beyond. His living quarters were on the building's north side; his grandfather's on the south side . . .

And never the twain shall meet, he thought dryly, rising from his chair and making his way across the plush carpeting.

In the corridor outside his office, Delia, his secretary, looked up from her computer screen. Her perfectly manicured fingers stopped their rapid-fire dance over the keyboard.

"I'll be in with Grandfather," Granger told her. "When you have a moment, Delia, would you mind sending out for two more double espressos, a large bottle of water, and a large ham and cheese hero?"

"Right away," Delia said with a knowing glance.

A glance that said, *Pretty badly hung over, are you?*

Well, yes, actually, he was. And certainly not for the first time in his life.

Not even for the first time this week.

Yet contrary to popular belief, this wasn't necessarily typical for Granger.

He had always appreciated a night out on the town. Fine wine, exclusive nightclubs, Manhattan's most elite social crowd. Yet despite the rumors about his wild ways, he had always known where to draw the line. Especially on a week night.

Then came June, and his stolen interlude with the unwillingly—or so he suspected—betrothed Princess Emmaline. When he looked into her claustrophobic, denial-ridden gaze, he was struck by the troubling realization that he might as well be looking into a mirror.

The princess's whole life was about confinement and constrictions, about royal duty, about fulfilling other people's expectations.

And so, Granger had suddenly comprehended, was his.

After that fleeting, magical night, he left her behind. Because he had no choice.

He returned to New York. Because he had no choice.

But he promised himself that from there on in, there would be choices.

As he redirected toward himself the disdain with which he had regarded Emmaline's gilded cage, he found himself questioning everything about his life. Everything. All at once, he doubted the paths that had been chosen for him, and the ambitions he had worked so hard to fulfill—ambitions that weren't his own.

That night they were together, he had chastised Emmaline for never having dared to follow her heart. Now he saw that he was no more admirable in his position than the princess was in hers.

But he was going to do something about it.

"How are you today, Mr. Lockwood?" Susan, his grandfather's longtime secretary, asked pleasantly as he arrived in front of her desk, a few yards down the carpeted corridor from Delia's.

"Very well, Susan, thanks," he lied, striding toward the closed door.

He knocked, of course. One simply did not barge in on Granger Lockwood II. Not even when one was a blood relative who had been personally summoned.

"Come in," growled the familiar voice.

Granger stepped into the large corner suite. Plush furnishings, fine artwork, dazzling view.

Of course, Granger had his own furnishings, artwork, and view. But this was all just a notch above. Just enough, he had always suspected, to give Grandfather the psychological upper hand—even though he was always saying that he was phasing himself out of the business, paving the way for Granger to take over.

That would never happen.

Not while Grandfather was alive.

And since the crusty old man showed no sign of impending death—and since Lockwood men traditionally lived century-spanning lives, barring reckless youthful mishap—chances were that Granger was destined to spend the next few decades just as he had the last one: as a glorified yes-man.

"Good morning, Grandfather."

"Good morning."

Clad in one of his trademark three-piece suits, Granger Lockwood II turned away from the window, where he stood puffing on his pipe and gazing out over the skyline he had helped to create. The room was infused with the familiar scent of vanilla tobacco. Normally Granger rather liked the scent, but today—courtesy of one wicked hangover—he found it repulsive.

"We'll sit over there," his grandfather declared brusquely, leading the way to a cluster of black leather recliners in the far corner, beside the black granite-topped wet bar lined with crystal decanters.

A few feet away, a sulphur-crested cockatoo in an ornate cage ruffled its snow-colored feathers. Grandfather was a devoted ornithologist—his sole hobby that wasn't in some way tied to his business. As a child, Granger had often resented the old man's attention to his feathered pets—attention he neglected to give his grandson.

Granger sank into a chair. He wondered whether this was to be a formal meeting. If not, perhaps he could safely lift the footrest and lean his throbbing head back against the cushion.

He regarded his grandfather, trying to gauge his mood. The elder Lockwood wasn't the kind of man who typically tolerated overtly casual posture in a business setting, even when only the two of them were present. Yet there were times when he unexpectedly allowed himself—and Granger—to relax.

Without betraying a hint of his physical frailty, his grandfather sat in the opposite chair, both feet on the floor and his spine just as he drank his aged single malt scotch—straight up. His wrinkle-etched features, beneath a thatch of white hair, were stern.

Okay. So Granger wouldn't bother to reach for the recliner button.

"It has come to my attention," Grandfather began, "that you have canceled three meetings in the last three days."

Oh. So that was what this was about. Granger steeled himself for the battle that loomed inevitably. "That's right."

"Why?"

"I couldn't squeeze them in."

"You couldn't squeeze them in," Grandfather echoed ominously. "You couldn't squeeze in a corporate CEO, a software billionaire, and the deputy mayor of New York?"

"I've been swamped," Granger said mildly. "And I've already rescheduled all three meetings for—"

"We don't *do* rescheduling," Grandfather exploded. "That's not how Lockwood Enterprises is run. If we say we're going to be somewhere, if we are *supposed* to be somewhere, then we are there. Period. For God's sake, Granger, I thought you learned that lesson when you started kindergarten."

Hell yes, he had learned it. Learned it in the most torturous way possible.

Granger's thoughts slammed back to Labor Day weekend nearly twenty-five years ago. The weekend his father, Granger Lockwood III—known, of course, as Trey—drunkenly steered his yacht into a piling on the Long Island Sound, not far from his Rye estate. The accident killed Trey; Trey's younger brother John; and Granger's mother, Elizabeth, who had been eight and a half months pregnant. Granger's infant sister, Charlotte, was delivered stillborn after the accident.

Somehow, that hurt more than anything else. He was devastated by the loss of his mother and father, of course. But Trey and Elizabeth were hardly doting, hands-on parents. It wasn't until Granger reached his teens that he was old enough to understand that his ruggedly handsome father had been an alcoholic, cocaine-addicted philanderer.

As for Granger's beautiful, distant mother—well, he suspected she had battled her own demons. He remembered that she was often in tears, and that she fought bitterly with his father whenever he was home. When he wasn't—and Trey frequently vanished for days at a time—Elizabeth spent a lot of time making phone calls, trying to track him down.

Granger spent most of his time in the care of the household staff: the maids, the gardener, the cook, the chauffeur. Yet there was no nanny.

Trey, who had been in the care of governesses from the moment he was born, had insisted that Elizabeth raise their son herself. Her method of mothering him consisted mostly of staring off into space, brooding, while Granger quietly played with his blocks, building ever-taller towers—just as Daddy and Grandfather did.

When his mother told him, at some point that last summer, that he would soon have a little brother or sister, Granger was overjoyed. At last his solitary childhood would come to an end. He would have a companion, somebody to play with. Somebody who would look up to him, the big brother. Somebody who would want to hug and kiss him.

His mother told him early on that if the baby was a girl, her name would be Charlotte. She said that Grandfather insisted that the baby be named after Charlotte Lockwood, some important family ancestor. But Granger liked to pretend that she would be named after the spider in *Charlotte's Web*. Naming a baby for a fictional arachnid was far more appealing, to a small boy, than naming her for somebody he knew only from an unsmiling oil portrait in Grandfather's study.

The Charlotte Granger conjured in his mind wouldn't be afraid of spiders, or of worms, or of climbing trees. She would ride on the back of his bike, when he was old enough to ride a bike, and she would bake cookies for him, when she was old enough to bake. For Granger, Charlotte existed long before the terrible day when she suddenly ceased to exist.

Shortly after the accident, Grandfather—who was little more than a formal and infrequent visitor to their Rye household back then—appeared and delivered the shocking news about his parents and uncle in the usual stiff, decorous manner. He told the child about his dead infant sister, Charlotte, almost as an afterthought. The old man was completely caught off guard when that piece of information—unlike the earlier bombshell—plunged Granger into inconsolable hysteria.

In retrospect, of course, Granger understood that Grandfather was also grieving that day. He now knew, too, that because Trey and John had been raised by their governesses, Grandfather was ill-equipped to dispense comfort to a suffering child. His method of helping Granger cope with the crippling losses was to advise him to be strong and carry on the Lockwood name in a way that would have made his father proud.

So, immediately following the tragedy, five-year-old Granger found himself plucked out of the familiar Rye estate where he had been raised thus far, and plunked down in Manhattan, in the gruff custody of the grandfather he barely knew.

The quadruple funeral—a vast, public affair held at a Park Avenue cathedral—was held on Tuesday. On Wednesday, Grandfather insisted that Granger start kindergarten as planned. Because it was too late to gain access to Manhattan's most esteemed private schools, Granger remained enrolled at the country day academy his parents had selected in Westchester county. One of Grandfather's chauffeurs delivered him to and from school each day in a black stretch limousine.

The staff of the Rye household was promptly dismissed, of course. Granger would never again see the kindly cook who used to drizzle honey on his fingers for him to lick, or the old gardener with the twinkly eyes, who let the little boy sit on his lap and steer the riding mower over the rolling green acres of lawn. Nor would Granger ever again see that lawn, or that house overlooking the blue water of the sound, where he liked to count sailboats on summer days.

Nor would he see his beloved kitten, Miggs. The feline was dispatched with a member of the household staff, as she'd have posed a threat to Grandfather's exotic birds.

Granger's new residence was the mausoleumlike Lockwood mansion on the Upper East Side. His swiftly hired new nanny was a humorless British spinster who believed that honey rotted little boys' teeth. And his new guardian was a moody tycoon whose main concern was that the future of his dynasty would one day be in the hands of his orphaned only heir. Grandfather was determined to see that Granger would grow up worthy of his future role.

Even now, after all these years, Granger remembered in great detail the daily battles he had waged with his grandfather in the wake of his parents' deaths. Every morning he would whimper, and sob, and beg not to be sent to school. But his grandfather insisted that it was for the best—that going to kindergarten was his duty.

Just as going on to his grandfather's prep school

alma mater and later to Yale, where all Lockwood men went, was his duty.

Just as taking over Lockwood Enterprises some-day was his duty.

Or, as Grandfather preferred to call it, his *destiny*.

A destiny that now felt as smothering as the cloud of tobacco smoke wafting from Grandfather's pipe.

"Yes, well, I've learned a lot of lessons since kindergarten, Grandfather," Granger heard himself say boldly. "One of them is that there are only so many hours in a day."

"True. And each hour must be filled wisely, and efficiently. Time must not be squandered on indiscreet and self-indulgent activities." Grandfather leveled a stern look at him.

Uh-oh.

"It has come to my attention," Grandfather said, "that at two o'clock yesterday afternoon, while you were supposed to be meeting with the deputy mayor, you were in Sheep's Meadow, flying a box kite with a European supermodel who has recently been released from a rehabilitation facility in Minnesota."

Granger nearly choked on his own spit. How on earth . . . ?

"The spectacle made Page Six in the *Post*," Grandfather promptly answered his unspoken question.

The *Post*? As in the *New York Post*? Since when did Grandfather read the tabloids?

Granger was well aware that the old man's daily newspaper perusal was limited to the *New York Times* and the *Wall Street Journal*.

Of course, Granger also read both those papers. But he usually picked up a copy of the *Post* for balance. Today, however, he had been too dizzy to read—unwittingly sparing himself being blindsided by the Page Six account of his Central Park frolic with the breathtakingly beautiful and mind-numbingly stupid Millicent du Bois.

Then again, he was certainly blindsided now.

Grandfather had rested his pipe in an ashtray and steepled his gnarled hands beneath his square chin, leaning forward in his chair to regard Granger through narrowed, buckskin-colored eyes.

"Page Six, hmm?" Granger found himself saying. "Well, at least it didn't make the front page. I suspect that honor was reserved for some other errant blue blood."

"This is not something you should take lightly, Granger. I have looked the other way in the past, whenever rumor floated back to me about your . . . indiscretions. Until now, you have always managed to keep your personal life from interfering with our business. But I cannot allow you to—"

"*What* personal life, Grandfather?" Granger cut in. "I have never had a personal life. You haven't, either. For us, Lockwood Enterprises has been everything. We're no better than . . . no better than . . . than those ridiculous Verdunian royals. All they care about is their kingdom. All you care about is yours."

For a moment Grandfather seemed speechless.

Then, in an arctic tone, he said, "My kingdom, as

you call it, has provided you with everything a man can possibly desire."

"Not everything," Granger said, marveling that his grandfather could possibly know so little about a man's desires. About *this* man's desires, anyway.

This man desired . . .

He desired . . .

Hell, he might as well admit it, if only to himself. He desired an incongruously delicate powerhouse of a woman whose hand belonged to another man—but whose heart, Granger surmised, never would.

Nor would it belong to him.

No, he could never have Princess Emmaline . . .

But surely there were other worthwhile things in this world—not that he could think of any of them at the moment. He *would*, if he only had the time.

He supposed that he could make time . . .

But there was only one way to do that.

And he couldn't possibly . . .

Or could he?

His gaze fell on the caged cockatoo. The bird seemed to be looking back at him from behind the wire bars.

"Grandfather," Granger said, standing abruptly, before his hastily made-up mind could waver. "I'm leaving."

Grandfather checked his pocket watch, left to him by his father, the first Granger Lockwood, founder of Lockwood Enterprises. "You can't leave now. In fifteen minutes we have that conference call with—"

"No, I mean I'm leaving. The company. Forever."
It felt damn good to say it, even if his heart was
beating nearly as fast as it had the night Emmaline
had gazed at him with unexpected yet unmistakable desire.

"Granger, I don't find this the least bit amusing,"
his grandfather said with an impatient wave of his
hand.

"Nor do I. I find it liberating."

"Liberating?" Grandfather appeared incredulous.
"Is that what this is about? You feel the need for free
time?"

Among other things, Granger thought. He merely
nodded, knowing it would be futile to try to articu-
late to his grandfather all that was missing from his
life.

Not that the old man was waiting around for explanations. He strode across the room to his desk
and purposefully grabbed his leather-bound calendar. "If that's the case, then perhaps we can arrange
for you to take some sort of vacation in a few . . ."

"A few what?" Granger asked when Grandfather
trailed off, intent on flipping pages and scanning
dates. "A few weeks?"

"*Weeks?*" Grandfather snorted, looking up.
"*Months.* Not weeks. Months. After all, I'd need
enough notice to—"

"No," Granger cut in. "This isn't going to work."

"Perhaps if we look at the week after Thanksgiv—"

"No, Grandfather. Put your calendar away. A vacation won't be enough, whether it's in a few weeks or a few months. I need more than that. I need . . ." He trailed off.

His grandfather stared, clearly waiting for an explanation.

"What, Granger?" the old man asked at last. "What do you need?"

Not *what*, Granger thought, glimpsing a vision of a green-eyed brunette in his mind's eye. *Whom*.

Aloud, he said only, "I don't know. But I'm sure as hell going to find out."

"No, no, no, I need Granger *Lockwood*," Emmaline repeated impatiently, pacing across her office with the cordless phone in hand. "He's that American who has been here several times to speak with Papa. His office is in New York City."

"Lockwood?" echoed ancient, partially deaf Prudence, the palace telephone operator who would happen to be on duty now, of all times. "L-O-C-H-W-O-O-D?"

"No, not *Loch* as in Loch Ness. I need *Lock*. As in locksmith."

"Locksmith? You need a locksmith? Whatever for?"

Hearing the voice just over her shoulder, Emmaline spun around. Her sister, Princess Josephine, stood behind her.

"Never mind, Prudence. I'll get in touch with him later," Emmaline said into the receiver. She slammed it down and glared. "Don't you ever knock, Josephine?"

"Never," the younger princess said cheerfully. "Why on earth do you need a locksmith? Has poor dear Remi gotten cold feet, locked himself in a tower somewhere, and swallowed the key?"

Remi? Remi!

Why, in her tizzy to track down Granger Lockwood in the States, Emmaline had nearly forgotten her fiancé existed.

Clearly, Josephine had not.

Josephine, Emmaline suspected, would gladly trade places with her when it came time to march down the aisle at the abbey on Saturday. She had seen the way her sister stared at the dashing prince, had heard the coquettish tone Josephine used whenever she spoke to Remi.

Of course, Josephine flirted with virtually every male who crossed her path. But Emmaline was certain her sister was particularly attracted to her dashing brother-in-law-to-be.

Perhaps Remi was even secretly drawn to Josephine as well.

What man wasn't?

Graced with a professional model's height and cheekbones, a crown of untamed black curls, and seductive green eyes, lithe, lovely Josephine had trailed a string of broken hearts from Verdunia to Vermont. She had graduated from Bennington College in May, with a degree in visual arts and absolutely no intention of putting it to use.

Josephine's goal was to become a royal bride as quickly as possible. And of course not just a lowly anybody's bride—but Somebody's bride. With the English princes a bit on the young side and Prince Remi spoken for, she had recently set her sights on the unwitting Prince Lars, the dashing heir to a Scandinavian throne. Her rationale: at six-four, he still had a few inches on her when she wore heels, and besides, those rugged New England winters had seasoned her for life in the frigid north, where she would make a smashing fashion statement in elegant head-to-toe fur.

"I thought you'd like to know," Josephine said, "that you've received more wedding gifts. The sultan of Bekistan has bought you and Remi a pair of Thoroughbreds, and Wyatt Jackson—he's that Texas oil baron we met at the American president's barbecue, remember?—has sent a Monet."

"How nice." Emmaline smiled briefly, making a mental note to write personal notes of thanks for both those extravagant gifts.

Of course, Fenella had hired extra staff for the sole purpose of cataloguing and acknowledging the thousands of gifts and congratulatory messages that had poured in from all over the world. But some gifts—like the quilt that had been painstakingly hand-embroidered by a ninety-year-old French-Canadian woman—deserved a note from the bride herself. The prospect was daunting. Emmaline resolved to worry about it after the wedding . . . then remembered that she had quite enough to worry about at the moment. She had almost forgotten.

Noticing that Josephine seemed to be peering intently at her, Emmaline took a wary step backward. *"What?"*

"Oh, nothing." But her sister's gaze didn't waver, and seemed to have settled somewhere around Emmaline's midsection.

"Why are you looking at my stomach?" Emmaline demanded. Surely Josephine couldn't possibly suspect—

"I heard that you've gained fifteen pounds and burst out of your gown in the designer's fitting room yester—"

"Josephine! Why would you say such a thing?" Genevieve, their elder sister, materialized in the doorway, frowning behind her owlish glasses.

"Where did you hear that?" Emmaline asked in dismay, grabbing a manila envelope and clasping it in front of her to conceal her barely bulging tummy.

Tabitha and Porfirio's staff had been sworn to absolute secrecy about the dress disaster—and about Emmaline's gastrointestinal episode. All that had been reported to the press, once she had landed safely in the hospital, was that she had fainted during her dress fitting due to stress. No mention of the button-bursting nightmare. Or of vomit.

"It was in the morning paper," Josephine said. "One of those blind items in that horrid Annabella Winfrey's gossip column."

"You said you would never again believe a word

Annabella Winfrey wrote after she ran that piece about you canoodling all over Cannes with that German pop star," Genevieve reminded her sister.

"Well, that was preposterous," Josephine said. "Nobody could possibly canoodle with Dolph Schumer without wearing a nose plug. The man has the worst case of halitosis ever."

Genevieve and Emmaline rolled their eyes at each other. Josephine, who was inspecting her reflection in the glare on the window, didn't notice.

"I actually saw you canoodling with Dolph," Emmaline couldn't resist saying. "And you didn't appear to be wearing a nose plug."

"Nonsense. We were talking. We had a lot in common."

Genevieve prodded, "Such as . . . ?"

"Well . . . my personal trainer, Pierre, and his personal trainer, Jean Paul, are brothers."

"Well, that means you and Dolph are a match made in heaven." Genevieve turned her attention to Emmaline, her expression shifting from amusement to concern. "How are you feeling today, Emmaline?"

"Much better, thank you. I'm just trying to take care of a few last-minute details."

"She was calling a locksmith," Josephine said airily, turning away from the glass. "You really should delegate such matters to your staff, Emmaline—especially now, of all times. Next thing we know, you'll be packing your own valises for the honeymoon."

Emmaline sighed. "The next thing I know, you'll

be smuggling yourself into one of them so that you can stow away on Remi's yacht."

"A two-week cruise along the French Riviera does sound divine," Josephine agreed. "But I've no desire to be a third wheel, thank you very much."

Emmaline caught her sister sneaking another glance at her torso. Folding her arms across her middle, she snapped, "Stop that, Josephine."

"Well, *have* you gained weight?" her sister asked. "It's hard to tell in that boxy blazer and those pleated trousers."

"Maybe a few pounds," Emmaline admitted reluctantly. "I'll just have to cut back on all those decadent desserts."

Decadent desserts? Hardly. Despite a blessedly efficient metabolism, Emmaline hadn't maintained her famously svelte figure by allowing herself to indulge in rich treats of any sort. *Ever.*

But she certainly wouldn't allow herself to entertain the real reason behind her weight gain. She had managed to hold it together thus far, and she had every intention of continuing to do so.

"Don't worry, Emmaline. I know how you feel," Genevieve said ruefully.

Startled, Emmaline looked up—then realized with relief that her sister was talking about the weight gain.

Unlike the younger princesses, poor Genevieve had failed to inherit the royal metabolism. Pleasantly plump, the pear-shaped heiress to the Verdunian throne had endured her share of mean-spirited jibes from the press.

As a sensitive teenager, Genevieve had been often reduced to tears by cruel public commentary about her weight. But these days the slings seemed to sail right past her. After all, she was newly betrothed to Reginaldo Caprizzi, a sought-after Italian nobleman who considered her the most desirable woman in Europe—and not merely because of her royal birthright.

As always, thinking about her sister's romantic engagement filled Emmaline with longing.

Reginaldo and Genevieve were so in love . . .

Granger Lockwood's words echoed back to her.

Here's a novel idea: How about marrying for love?

He made it sound so simple. Clearly, the spoiled American knew nothing about duty—or destiny.

Emmaline attempted to shove the thought of him from her mind and get back to the matter at hand—then recalled that he *was* the matter at hand.

"If you two would excuse me," Emmaline said abruptly to her sisters, "I have an important telephone call to make."

"Ah, yes, the locksmith," Josephine said, heading for the door.

"Why on earth do you need a locksmith?" Genevieve asked.

"Why else? Because I urgently need to unlock something, and I don't have a key," Emmaline said simply.

"I hope he can help you," Genevieve told her, leaving the office.

"So do I," Emmaline said hollowly. "So do I."

"Mr. Lockwood! Wait!"

Granger looked down, startled. A sturdy ankle encased in tan panty hose above a sensible black patent leather pump seemed to have wedged itself between the closing elevator doors.

Granger looked up as the doors slid open again. His secretary's anxious face appeared in the gap.

"What is it *now*, Delia?" He had been trying to get out of here for the past few hours. But it wasn't easy, packing up an entire office on a moment's notice and an empty stomach.

The lunch Delia had ordered for him was still in its paper bag, perched at the very top of the brimming cardboard carton in his arms. The first thing he intended to do upstairs—after he took something for his still-raging headache—was eat.

Once his blood sugar was back to normal, Granger figured, he would surely feel more optimistic about his impulsive resignation.

"There's an important phone call for you," Delia said breathlessly.

"You'll have to pass it along to Grandfather." Granger grunted, adjusting the weight of the box in his arms. "I'm no longer employed here, remember?"

"Yes, but I'm sure that you'll want to take this call."

"I'm sure that I won't."

"It's from overseas."

"Please forward it to Grandfather, Delia," Granger repeated, balancing the box in one hand and inserting a key into the security slot above the PH—for penthouse—button with the other. "Let him figure out how to handle it.

So far only Delia knew about his defection—his grandfather had insisted on that.

Well, fine. Granger would show his grandfather—and the rest of the world—that he didn't need another penny of the old man's money. That there was more to life than what cold, hard cash could buy. Wasn't that the whole point of his exodus?

"But Mr. Lockwood," Delia was saying urgently, "this overseas call is from a woman."

"A woman? Is it Brynn?" he asked hopefully.

Brynn Halloway was his closest friend. The fabulously wealthy, fabulously—well, *fabulous*—Manhattan-based heiress usually spent the summer months traveling the globe. He hadn't heard from her in weeks. Granger fully expected her to pop up on his doorstep any day now, but she usually did so unannounced. It wasn't like her to call ahead.

"No, it isn't Brynn," said Delia, a mysterious gleam in her eye.

"Don't tell me it's Millicent?" He was fairly certain he and the IQ-challenged supermodel had exhausted every possible conversational topic last evening. He was also pretty sure she wasn't yet back in Europe. She had, after all, made a point of informing him that her flight back to Paris wasn't until tomorrow, implying that she was free again tonight.

"No, it isn't Millicent. Her name"—Delia paused meaningfully—"is Emmaline."

Granger's jaw dropped.

"*Princess* Emmaline," Delia added, lest there be any chance of confusion.

His chest fluttering as though a flock of Grandfather's exotic birds was trying to break out of his rib cage, Granger bolted out of the elevator, nearly flattening his secretary against the wall.

"I'll take it," he said as he raced by her.

Delia flashed him a smug smile. "I thought you would."

"Let me guess. They've allowed you one phone call and you've chosen me to come bail you out of prison—I mean, the gilded cage you call home."

Granger Lockwood's voice was deeper than Emmaline remembered. But the irony—and the prison-themed crack—were all too familiar.

Seated at her desk, clutching the telephone receiver firmly against her ear, she managed to hold her temper in check. After all, he had almost hit the nail on the head.

"What would you say," she responded, "if I told you that was true? At least the last part."

There was silence on the other end of the line.

Then he asked, incredulously, "You want me to come bail you out? Of prison?"

·

"In a manner of speaking. I've run into some trouble, Granger. And you're the only one who . . ." She trailed off, uncertain how to proceed. Now wasn't the time to get into the full extent of her plight. Not until she knew for certain.

You do know, she scolded herself. *All the pieces fit. The weight gain, the nausea, the missed menstrual period . . .*

But she hadn't yet confirmed the symptoms with a pregnancy test.

How could she?

She could hardly walk into a Chimera pharmacy and purchase one of those over-the-counter test kits. All her life, she had been trailed by reporters who trumpeted her every move. Now, more than ever before, she was conscious of their surveillance, both blatant and covert.

Nor could she ask the royal gynecologist to administer a pregnancy test. Dr. Pratt was, after all, the one who, just prior to her engagement, had examined and pronounced her fit for marriage to Prince Remi. Virginity was a key prerequisite to marrying the heir to the Buiron throne.

Which was why they hadn't even considered checking her for pregnancy at the hospital. Even if the staff had privately suspected the source of her symptoms, it would have been improper for anyone to suggest that the royal bride-to-be was anything but unsullied.

She shuddered at the thought of how Remi—and his parents, and hers, and their subjects, and the press—would react to the news that an American rogue had stolen her precious chastity and left her, to put it delicately, enceinte.

Or, as they said in Granger's corner of the world, knocked up.

But . . . what if she managed to keep her pregnancy a secret? She could go through with the wedding, and pretend that the child was Remi's.

No.

Even if she could bring herself to deceive her future husband—and the rest of the world—the doctors would know the truth. And even if she could trust them to keep her secret, chances were that somebody would figure it out. Remi—if the child looked nothing like him—or, more likely, the media, when the child was born several months "prematurely."

Guilt surged through Emmaline. Her firstborn was intended to be the heir to the throne of Buiron: a careful blend of two royal bloodlines. Not the illegitimate offspring of a seductive American playboy.

"Yoo hoo, Princess," the American playboy said seductively in her ear. "Are you still there?"

"I'm here."

"You were saying . . . ?" When she remained silent, he prodded, "I'm the only one who . . . ?"

"Can help me," she said simply, throwing caution to the wind. "You're the only one who can help me."

"You've got to be kidding."

"I've never been more serious in my life."

He exhaled audibly. To his credit, he rallied admirably. "Well, Your Highness, your wish is my command. After all, you only get to be a bride once in a lifetime. At least, I hope that's the case in your case," he said, without the least bit of sincerity.

Well, it was no surprise to her that he wasn't completely behind her marriage to Remi. He had said as much the night they were together. She knew that he protested out of principle, rather than passion. That he didn't believe in arranged marriages. That it wasn't that he wanted her for himself ... no matter what had happened between them.

Yet she couldn't help feeling wistful. She couldn't help wishing that he would at least try to talk her out of the wedding one last time. That he would give her a compelling, personal, passionate reason not to marry Remi ...

"So what do you need?" he was asking cheerfully. "A lucky sixpence for your shoe? A kick-ass ice sculpture for the reception? Or—I've got it. How about a male stripper with killer abs for your bachelorette party? Because I've been going to the gym regularly and I'm—"

"This isn't about the wedding," she cut in, her voice sounding a little shrill even to her own ears.

"Don't take this the wrong way," he replied, "but from what I gather, these days, even on this side of the pond, *everything* is about the wedding."

"Maybe so, but ..." She lowered her voice, conscious that the stone and plaster palace walls might somehow be thinner than they looked. "Look, Granger, can I trust you?"

The question was moot, she knew. After all, she had already trusted him in a way that she had never trusted another human being. The consequences were that he was now her only ally, willing or not, in the world.

"Of course you can trust me."

That the banter had vanished from his tone gave her the fortitude to continue.

"All right, then." She lowered her voice to a whisper. "I can't marry Prince Remi on Saturday. Or ever."

"Why not?"

"I can't tell you. I promise I will, but . . . not yet. Not until after you've gotten me out of here."

"Out of there?" he echoed. "You mean—"

She took a deep breath and took the final plunge. "I need you to rescue me, Granger. I need you to get me out of Verdunia. Before it's too late."

Three

....

 "You look breathtaking, my dear," King Jasper said as Emmaline entered the enormous drawing room, her gown rustling noisily.

"Thank you, Papa. So do you." She smiled at her father, who was wearing his monarch's purple robe and had placed his gold crown on his balding gray head for the occasion. His green eyes, precisely the shade of her own, twinkled at her from beneath his bushy white brows.

"If you think I'm elegant, you should see your mother," he said with a smile.

As if on cue, Queen Yvette swept into the room, resplendent in gilt and sequins, her auburn hair piled high on her head and ringed by her gold and diamond tiara. Mother was so youthful and ravishing that the press frequently commented on the disparity between the queen and the king, who was nearly two decades older and looked it.

Papa didn't seem to mind, though. He rarely paid any heed to what was said about him, often commenting that it came with the territory in his line of work. It was only when the press took aim at one of his daughters—most frequently pudgy firstborn Genevieve—that he unleashed his royal wrath.

"The girls have gone on ahead," the queen announced, referring to Genevieve, Josephine, and the half dozen other bridesmaids. Earlier, dressed in their periwinkle silk couture gowns, they had joined Emmaline for an endless session with the photographers.

"It's almost time to—oh, Emmaline," the queen interrupted herself, her gaze coming to rest on her daughter. "You look . . ."

"My word for her was 'breathtaking,'" the king informed his wife, who had trailed off, shaking her head slowly as she stared at Emmaline.

"Yes, of course she looks breathtaking," Queen Yvette said with a wave of her bejeweled hand, "but I was going to say wan and pale. Have you eaten, darling?"

Emmaline nodded, all too accustomed to her mother's fussing. "Of course." *And I threw it right back up again afterward.*

"It must simply be nerves," the Queen decided.

You have no idea, Emmaline thought, as she nodded again. She longed to plop herself down on the nearest damask sofa, but Porfirio had forbidden her to sit. He was disturbed enough about her gown getting crushed during the upcoming carriage ride to the abbey.

"Perhaps you'd prefer it if I walked," Emmaline had quipped this morning, as he fretted about how the monstrous train would fit inside the antique coach.

"And drag the hem through the filthy streets?" Porfirio had been horrified.

"I was only kidding," Emmaline muttered, exchanging an eye-rolling glance with Tabitha, who hovered, as always, at her elbow.

Porfirio was not amused. As far as she could tell, Porfirio was *never* amused.

"Every bride has nerves," Queen Yvette informed her daughter. "On my wedding day, I was so jittery that I ran three pairs of silk stockings trying to put them on."

"I only ran two pairs," Emmaline told her mother, mustering a smile.

The queen patted her arm. "The gown looks lovely. Porfirio has outdone himself."

Emmaline glanced at her reflection in the full-length gilt-framed mirror beside the ornate marble hearth across the room. She noted that nothing had changed since she had examined herself in the dressing room upstairs. The gown was positively hideous, a vast, voluminous sea of white awash in baubles and frills. Her billowing layered lace and illusion headpiece was no better, though the jeweled tiara—one of Buiron's most priceless crown jewels—would have been quite lovely alone.

The king retrieved his gold pocket watch on its thick chain from the folds of his robe. "It's time," he informed his wife.

She nodded and took his arm. "We'll see you at the abbey, darling."

Emmaline nodded, swallowing hard over the lump that rose in her throat as she gazed at her parents. This was the last time she would see them before . . . well, before everything changed. Suddenly, all she wanted was to hurtle herself into their arms, dress be damned, and sob the whole story to them.

But she couldn't do that to them. They would be devastated.

Is what you're going to do any better? her inner voice chided.

Yes. Because I'm doing it my way, she told her conscience firmly, lifting her chin a notch and forcing herself to smile at her parents.

The queen appeared hesitant, still looking carefully at Emmaline, as though sensing her inner turmoil. "Are you quite certain you wish to ride alone in the carriage? Papa would be happy to—"

"No, I'd rather be alone," Emmaline said, sticking stubbornly to the drastic change of plans she had implemented just yesterday, much to Fenella's dismay. The social secretary had insisted that it would be more fitting for the royal bride to be transported to the ceremony with her father at her side in the horse-drawn cream-colored wedding coach.

But for once, Emmaline had held her ground. She had told Fenella—and everybody else who tried to sway her—that she wanted to use her last moments as a single woman in reflective solitude.

"But if you're alone, there will be no one to calm your nerves," Queen Yvette said now, her handsome face riddled with uncertainty.

"Well, if I feel the sudden need for company before I depart, I'll convince Tabitha to ride along with me," Emmaline assured her mother.

The queen's eyes clouded at the thought of somebody other than herself or the king accompanying the royal bride to her wedding.

"Don't worry, Mother. The carriage has opaque windows. Nobody will realize she's there."

"But when you get in, you'll be right there for all the world to—

"No, I won't," Emmaline said, and took a deep breath. She might as well inform her mother of the other little change she'd made. Papa already knew, and approved. Fenella, of course, disapproved wholeheartedly. "Mother, I instructed them to bring the carriage around to the side entrance rather than in the front. We'll be out of view of the gates. Nobody will see us getting in."

"The *side* entrance?" Queen Yvette's perfectly arched eyebrows vaulted toward her jeweled tiara. "But Emmaline—"

"I'm sorry, but I don't want to be a public spectacle any longer than I must, Mother," Emmaline said firmly.

The queen opened her mouth to speak, but her husband gave her arm a firm squeeze and said, "I'm sure Emmaline will be fine, my dear. Now let's hurry."

"Shall I help you lower your veil over your face?" Queen Yvette paused once more in the drawing room doorway to ask.

"No, Tabitha will do that," Emmaline said quickly. "She's waiting for me back in the dressing room."

"All right, then."

The king and queen exited the room at last.

A few moments later, Emmaline heard cheers erupt in the throng that had gathered outside the palace gates and knew that the white chauffeured Rolls-Royce, with her parents inside, had left for the abbey.

It was time.

She hurried toward the dressing room, where Tabitha—about to prove herself the most loyal, loving friend a princess could ever wish for—was waiting.

Perched on a wooden press platform beside the palace gates, reporter Debi Hanson was checking her reflection in a small compact, making sure none of her bloodred lipstick had smeared on her teeth.

After landing the plumb assignment to cover the royal wedding for the network, Debi had visited New York's premier cosmetic dentist and raised hell until he squeezed her in for an emergency whitening. After all, this was her chance to shine in the spotlight—and, with any luck, become a front-runner for an upcoming anchor job opening.

Satisfied that her teeth were dazzling, Debi became aware of a helicopter buzzing low over the palace grounds. Resentment stirred. She had no doubt that a fellow journalist was on board, trying to scoop his or her grounded colleagues.

Debi glanced around at the three-ring media circus that stretched from the palace gates to the abbey two miles away. The narrow, ancient cobblestone avenue was jammed with reporters doing live feeds, satellite television trucks, refreshment concessions, vendors hawking royal wedding souvenirs, throngs of well-wishers anxious to catch a glimpse of the bride, even protestors. What they were protesting wasn't clear from where Debi stood—their posterboard signs were obscured by a cart selling Mylar helium balloons sculpted to look like decidedly bloated versions of Princess Emmaline and Prince Remi.

Her eyes narrowed as her gaze shifted from the garish scene skyward. There were other news choppers up there, but this one seemed particularly low as it hovered over the palace grounds. Was it Debi's rival New York network, WGSP? If so, that wench of a reporter Naomi Finkelmeyer would never let Debi live it down.

Seething, she shaded her designer sunglasses using her hand as a visor, and peered at the sky. Dammit! The sun was shining too brightly for her to make out a logo on the copter.

Well, if Naomi thought that this was—

Debi frowned.

The helicopter was practically buzzing the stone

turrets. Surely the Verdunian officials wouldn't stand for this.

A sudden roar went up around her as the crowd erupted in cheers.

Debi turned toward the palace entrance, with its towering, prisonlike black iron gates. Had Princess Emmaline emerged? But . . . she couldn't have. The wedding coach hadn't even arrived at the front entrance to—

"*Noooo!*" Debi shrieked in disbelief. Somehow, she had missed it. All of it. The cream-colored carriage was already trundling away from the palace, presumably with the bride already on board.

"Lenny! Are you getting this?" Debi shrieked at her cameraman, who scrambled for the shot as the team of horses clip-clopped their way toward the gate and the street beyond.

"Yeah! We're going live in three . . . two . . ."

Debi adjusted her sunglasses, took a deep breath, and faced the camera with a smile.

". . . one!"

"We're live from Verdunia, where, as you can see, the bride . . ." she hesitated, cleared her throat, and realized she had to admit to her viewers that she—and they—had missed the big moment, ". . . has already boarded the gleaming, horse-drawn white coach fit for a fairy-tale princess. Princess Emmaline is now departing for her long-awaited wedding at the abbey just a short distance away. And let me tell you, the bride is, uh, a vision in white, in a luscious silk organza couture gown designed by Porfirio."

Debi relaxed a bit, drawing from the information released by the palace in advance. "Of course, Princess Emmaline's face is obscured by her veil, as is traditional, but we can be sure that she's smiling somewhere under all those layers of tulle and lace. After all, she's about to marry her Prince Charming and live happily ever . . ."

Debi trailed off as the roar of the helicopter overhead grew louder. The chopper was much too low, she thought, gazing upward. So low that the wind from the blades was ruffling her carefully coifed hair. Irritated, she tried to smooth it, but her hand became snagged in the sticky, stiffly sprayed nest.

Remembering that she was on camera, she wrenched her fingers free, forced a bright smile, and said, "I'm sorry, we have a little technical difficulty because of that news chopper overhead. Anyway, one might say of the beautiful princess that today is the first day of the rest of her—Lenny, is he *landing*?" she broke off to ask the cameraman.

He shrugged, his camera panning from the wedding coach to Debi to the suddenly empty sky directly above the palace.

What the . . . ?

Shoving displaced hunks of hair from in front of her eyes, Debi stared at where the chopper had been, puzzled. Why on earth would a news chopper land on the palace grounds just as the bride was leaving the premises?

Belatedly remembering Emmaline, Debi whirled around, just in time to see the carriage, with its tinted window glass, disappear around a corner.

"Ladies and gentlemen, there goes the bride . . ." Debi offered feebly.

And there goes my shot at anchorwoman. Damn that Naomi Finkelmeyer!

"We have about thirty seconds to do this," Granger shouted at his old friend Yogi, who was at the helicopter's controls. A former military pilot, Yogi was the one person Granger trusted to accompany him on this mission—and to carry it off without getting caught—or worse.

As the copter, painted with a fictional network logo and disguised as a news chopper, sank toward the ground, Granger scanned the roof of the stone palace, half expecting to see crouched sharpshooters. There were none.

Nor was there any sign of Emmaline.

"I don't see her," he called to Yogi as they landed, his heart sinking.

Well, what did you expect?

Hadn't he known all along, deep down inside, that she wouldn't go through with it? She might have tried to convince him—and herself—that she was willing to take an enormous risk, but when push came to shove, she—

"There she is!" Yogi pointed.

Granger followed his friend's gesture and spotted a figure streaking across the palace lawn toward the chopper. She was dressed in black from head to toe and carrying a small satchel, like an errant cat burglar rushing from a heist.

For a moment he simply gazed at Princess Emmaline, his jaw hanging in blatant admiration at her sheer guts.

Then he leaped into action, opening the door and reaching out with both arms, beckoning her forward.

She stooped low but didn't slacken her pace as she neared the copter, ducking to avoid the whirling blades.

Granger darted another glance at the palace.

No sign of security . . . yet. Any second now, he suspected, guards would appear. If the timing was right, the commotion involving the carriage's departure for the abbey was stalling them. He hoped that would buy the helicopter enough time to get out of there before anyone realized what was happening.

With a jubilant cry that was audible despite the roar of the engine, Emmaline flung herself into Granger's arms. "I really did it!"

"You really did!" He lifted her effortlessly into the chopper, struck by a sudden sense of how surreal it all was—the garish carnival scene at the front of the palace, and the runaway princess bride quite literally sneaking out the back door, with Granger as her still stunned and most unlikely savior. He'd have pinched himself if his hands weren't busy thrusting Emmaline into the seat beside him and fastening her safety belt.

"She's in!" he bellowed at Yogi, who nodded and promptly lifted the helicopter off the ground.

Granger glanced at Emmaline as they rose over the treeline. Her head was turned, and she was staring out the opposite window, very still. Was she having sudden second thoughts? Well, it was too late to back out now.

"Are you okay?" he asked.

She didn't seem to hear him above the engine's roar. Or maybe she was too upset to reply.

He hesitated, then touched her arm.

She turned toward him.

The expression on her face spoke volumes.

She was radiant. Her green eyes sparkled, and her cheeks were rosy beneath her wedding-heavy makeup. Strands of dark hair had tumbled from the pile on her head, in the most becoming state of dishevelment he had ever witnessed.

Still panting from her exhilarating rush to freedom, she flashed him a big smile and a thumbs-up.

Granger grinned and turned toward his own window, his heart quickening its pace and his brain rushing to keep up.

What now? he wondered. He had been so caught up in hatching the daring rescue plot, so busy planning the details, that he hadn't allowed himself to think beyond this victorious moment.

All he knew was that Emmaline didn't want to marry Prince Remi after all—and that she had turned to him, of all people, to help her escape.

Why?

Because he was rich, and connected—and fool-hardy—enough to help her pull it off?

Or because nobody would ever think to look for her in the States?

Or because . . .

Well, maybe because she had realized she had feelings for him?

He felt her grasp on his arm and turned toward her.

"Look," she called, and gestured toward the window.

They were high above the castle now. But he could see, even from here, that several flea-sized figures emerged from the back of the building, waving their arms and looking up in bewilderment. The belated palace security detail, no doubt.

"They think we're a news chopper," Granger told Emmaline. "We're disguised as one."

He noticed that she was wearing a pair of massive diamond earrings that looked utterly out of place with her plain black sleeveless turtleneck tucked into a pair of black stretch pants. "Nobody would ever dream that you're on board, Emmaline. After all, you were just in the carriage, leaving for your wedding."

"Precisely." She grinned, looking for all the world like a sticky-mouthed little girl who had just convinced her gullible mother that she really did drop the first piece of candy into the storm drain and would need another.

"And what will happen when the wedding coach arrives at the abbey with only poor Tabitha inside?" he couldn't resist asking.

"There's no telling," Emmaline said, almost gleefully. "By then, of course, she'll be wearing her regular clothes again, with a heap of discarded gown and veil on the seat beside her. She'll say what I've instructed her to—that she turned her back for a moment, and I vanished."

"But that's ridiculous," he pointed out. "A person doesn't just vanish from a closed carriage riding through crowded streets."

Emmaline shrugged, as though she couldn't be bothered by that tedious detail.

"Besides," he pressed, "won't they figure out that only the bride boarded the carriage back at the palace? The whole thing must have been captured by a zillion cameras."

"But it wasn't!" Clearly quite pleased with herself, Emmaline said, "I changed the plan so that I was to board the coach at the side entrance, out of view. Wasn't that terribly clever of me?"

"But . . . somebody must have been watching, even at the side door."

"Just some of the household staff," Emmaline said with a dismissive wave of her manicured hand.

"Won't they—?"

She shrugged again. "By the time anybody pieces any of it together, we'll be halfway across the Atlantic. I left a note for Papa, apologizing and explaining that

I'm safe and sound, and telling him and Mother not to worry."

Granger made a face, as though that was unlikely, and asked, "What about Tabitha?"

"Oh, I've got plans for her," Emmaline said with a smile. "As soon as the furor dies down, she'll be joining us."

"Us?" he echoed, finding that he liked the sound of it—yet uncertain exactly what it meant. "Then . . . you're planning on staying in New York for a while?"

She said something he didn't hear. At least, he didn't think he had heard it right.

"What was that?" he called. "The motor's drowning out your voice. It almost sounded like you said . . ."

She raised her voice. "I *said*, I'm planning on staying forever."

"*Forever*?"

Somehow, forever had never entered his mind.

Forever was . . .

Well, it was *forever*.

How could Princess Emmaline possibly think that she could hide in his apartment forever? The place was more than spacious, but . . .

Well, sooner or later, she'd have to go outside. And it wasn't exactly as though she would be inconspicuous when she did. After all, a princess couldn't just disappear into thin air, no matter what she had convinced Tabitha to report when the empty carriage arrived at the abbey.

Didn't she realize the whole world would be searching for her?

And that even if the hubbub died down eventually, she would still have one of the most famous, recognizable faces in the world?

Granger cleared his throat. "Emmaline, we really have to talk."

Some emotion he didn't recognize flickered in her eyes, and then was gone. "You're right," she said, her voice raised above the whirring motor. "We do have to talk. But not like this. Not shouting at each other."

"On the plane back to New York, then," he suggested.

One of Lockwood Enterprises' corporate jets was waiting for them in Paris. Grandfather had no idea, of course, and he would be furious when he found out. As far as the old man was concerned, Granger had lost any claim to such perks the moment he resigned. But nobody at the company knew about that yet, and nobody had batted an eye when he made the arrangement for the round-trip overseas flight.

"Oh, I think our talk should wait until we get settled at your place," Emmaline told him decisively. "There's quite a bit to discuss."

Something about her cryptic expression sent an uneasy ripple through him.

Surely Emmaline didn't think . . .

Well, she had just left one groom at the altar. She couldn't possibly want another right away . . . could she?

Of course not. You told her she should be marrying for love . . . and she isn't in love with you, he reminded himself. Nor was he in love with her.

Not that he couldn't fall in love with a woman like her . . . when and if he was ready for marriage.

But he had just extracted himself from the shackles that had bound him from the day he was born. This was his chance to live life on *his* terms. He was finally free.

And so was Emmaline, he reminded himself.

He was worrying for nothing. The last thing she would want now was to settle down.

The last thing Prince Remi wanted was to see his bride walking down the aisle toward him. Yet the moment loomed ominously closer with every tick of the large clock on the mantel in the minister's cavernous study behind the abbey.

Remi was supposed to be enjoying some solitary, contemplative time here before being summoned to the altar. Instead, he had spent the last half hour feeling as though his white bow tie were a noose. He couldn't breathe, couldn't swallow, and was sure that when the time came to utter his vows, he wouldn't be able to speak, either.

That, of course, would never do. The entire world was waiting to see him marry the fair Princess Emmaline of Verdunia.

And he wanted to marry her . . .

Rather, he wanted to *want* to marry her.

He had assumed that the idea would grow on him. Hadn't Father promised that was what would happen? Wasn't that why Father had shared with him the story about his own arranged marriage to Mother?

King Thierry had told his son that he hadn't been in love with Queen Cecile during their engagement—or even on their wedding day thirty-some years ago. But, Father had said, his lukewarm feelings for his bride had gradually flamed into full-blown love.

As for Remi—he seemed to have gone from lukewarm to full-blown cold feet overnight.

It wasn't that he didn't find Emmaline lovable. She was beautiful, and intelligent, and charming. In fact, they got along very well, unless they were discussing music or literature, where their tastes differed dramatically. He preferred classical composers and the classics, while Emmaline adored rock music and best-sellers.

Certainly those differences wouldn't doom a marriage. In fact, their disparate artistic tastes had sparked some of their livelier conversations, and invariably led to laughter and good-natured teasing.

But Remi couldn't imagine that mutual affection ever transforming into any semblance of passion.

And a marriage without passion was . . .

Well, it might have been acceptable for previous generations, or for future monarchs in other parts of the world. But Remi and Emmaline were modern young royals, graced with the many privileges bestowed by their bloodlines. Why couldn't true love be among their blessings?

Why, indeed?

Because you must do your duty, Remi reminded himself with a sigh, looking out the window at the small graveyard filled with centuries-old stone monuments. *And so must Emmaline. You owe it to your parents, and to your countries, and to each other.*

If only . . .

Remi sighed again, as an image of the beguiling Princess Josephine flitted into his mind.

If only they had selected the youngest of the three sisters as his intended bride. He had no more in common with Princess Josephine than he did with her sister—far less in common, perhaps. But something told him there was more to Josephine than met the eye.

Not that what met the eye wasn't incredibly pleasing.

Remi was promptly consumed by the thought of Josephine's mop of untamed black curls that just begged a man's fingers to—

There was a knock at the door.

It was time.

"Come in." Remi swallowed hard and turned expectantly toward the doorway.

King Thierry stood there, resplendent in his purple robe. Behind him was his security detail—and none of the three bodyguards made eye contact with Remi. That was odd.

"Father, what are you doing back here?" Remi asked, striding toward him. "Shouldn't you be in your seat waiting for . . . ?"

Seeing the inscrutable expression on his father's face, Remi trailed off. Clearly, something was wrong. His heart began to pound.

"Remi, I'm afraid I don't know how to say this," his father began. "It's Emmaline."

"Oh no. She isn't . . . ?" Dread surged through him. Had there been some kind of accident on the way to the abbey? A terrorist bomb, or an assassination, or—

"She's gone," King Thierry said flatly.

"Gone?" Remi echoed, thoughts racing. "Gone where?"

"Nobody knows. The abbey is in an uproar. She seems to have vanished into thin air en route to the ceremony. Either she met with foul play somewhere between the palace and here, or—"

"Or she decided she couldn't go through with the wedding," Remi said, somehow knowing instinctively that his intended bride was safe.

He closed his eyes and exhaled, wishing Emmaline well, wherever she was—and silently thanking her for sparing them both. Now perhaps he could convince Papa that Josephine—

His father said, "You'd better hope that isn't the case."

Remi opened his eyes, startled. "What do you mean?"

"I mean that if your bride has left you at the altar, she's disgraced you in front of the entire world."

"I hadn't thought of it that way," Remi said slowly.

His initial elation at having been spared a loveless marriage promptly gave way to sheer humiliation.

Of course his father was right. There was nothing worse than being jilted with millions of people watching. Was there?

"Perhaps Emmaline has been abducted," Remi suggested optimistically.

"For her sake—and for Verdunia's sake—I sincerely hope she has," King Thierry said darkly.

"Maybe I should have at least told Remi," Emmaline said, as guilt seeped in somewhere over the Atlantic.

"You couldn't have." Granger looked up from his shrimp cocktail. "You couldn't tell a soul."

"I told Tabitha," she pointed out.

"You had to. She was your accomplice. Although you could have come up with a better story for her, other than—"

"I told you to stop bothering me with that," Emmaline snapped. "Tabitha's story was sufficient."

"But people don't vanish into thin air. Nobody's going to believe her when she—"

"It doesn't matter who believes her! I keep telling you—what matters is that I've managed to escape Verdunia. And, of course, that Papa and Mother know that I'm safe and that I didn't meet with foul play. But I can't help feeling sorry for poor dear Remi."

Granger scowled as he dredged a fat pink shrimp through a pool of cocktail sauce. "If he was so dear, maybe you should have married him after all."

"You were the one who told me I shouldn't marry him," she reminded him, rather enjoying his child-ish, jealous tone.

He looked up in surprise, the piece•of shrimp poised midway to his mouth. "Is that why you're doing this?" he asked incredulously. "Because I told you that you should be marrying for love?"

Oh dear. What was he thinking?

"Don't flatter yourself, Granger," she said abruptly. "I have a mind of my own, and I made it up without any help from you."

Well, that wasn't entirely true, she reminded her-self, watching him polish off the plump, oversized shrimp and reach for another.

If only Granger had never started harping on her about her arranged marriage, she would never have felt the need to prove anything to him—or to herself. She would never have stolen out to meet him that moonlit, rose-scented night, would never have al-lowed him to kiss her, would never have . . .

Well, it was too late for if-onlies now.

And anyway, if none of that had ever happened, she would be dancing at her wedding right about now—which was the last place on earth she wanted to be.

And what about this? she thought. *Is this where you want to be? Single, and pregnant, and on a private jet bound for New York City with a man you barely know?*

A man who was now, she noted, eyeing her un-touched shrimp cocktail as though he wanted to devour it. Which was precisely the manner in which he had looked at her that fateful evening.

"Aren't you going to eat that?" he asked politely.

"No, thank you." Actually, the smell of shellfish was making her queasy, and the ginger ale the galley attendant had brought her wasn't helping.

"Do you mind if I . . . ?" He was already reaching for her plate.

She sighed. "Not at all." She did mind, though she wasn't sure why.

Perhaps because, thanks to him, she was tormented by this so-called morning sickness round the clock.

"I haven't eaten all day," he said unapologetically, digging in. "How about you? Aren't you hungry?"

"Not for shrimp."

"Well, Ambrose will be bringing the steaks out in a few minutes."

"Steaks?" The thought of red meat nearly made her gag. She tried to force the image away, but it persisted. A hunk of char-broiled meat, marbled with fat and oozing blood . . .

"Uh-oh," Granger said, "Don't tell me you're a vegetarian."

"Actually . . ." Emmaline swallowed hard, her stomach churning. Maybe she should just tell him the truth right here and now and get it over with.

"Because I'm sure Ambrose can whip up some kind of pasta for you if you'd prefer it."

"Pasta?" Her stomach reverberated—this time out of hunger rather than nausea. She realized she hadn't eaten since the breakfast she had thrown up just before donning her wedding gown.

"The galley's fully equipped," Granger said, and added, "You can have anything you want."

If only that were true. Emmaline smiled wistfully at his words.

Then she caught herself, and realized that everything had changed. Now anything was possible. She was free at last to follow her heart.

The only trouble was . . .

"What do you want?" Granger was asking.

What *did* she want?

A quick soul-searching yielded only "Pasta. I want pasta."

That was the best she could do for now. But it was a start.

All other decisions would have to wait until she had some food in her stomach. After all, she was eating for two. And, judging by the way Granger had polished off both shrimp cocktails in a few minutes flat, she had her work cut out for her.

Imagine that.

Awestruck, she went completely still.

Until this moment, she had been so caught up in the escape plot—and the exhausting charade as she went ahead with the flurry of wedding details back home—that she hadn't stopped to contemplate the human life growing within her.

Now the wonder of it all hit her full force.

She was going to have a baby.

Granger Lockwood's baby.

For the rest of their lives, they would be bound together by the child they had created.

What would the baby look like?

Would it be a little boy with Granger's clear blue eyes?

Or would it be a little girl who looked like Emmaline herself—a daughter, she vowed fiercely, who would never be confined by the boundaries of public palace life that had so severely restricted her mother's childhood.

This child would be free to live life to the fullest.

And so will I, Emmaline vowed.

"What are you thinking?"

Startled by Granger's voice, she found him watching her intently.

"That I can't quite believe this is happening," she said truthfully.

"You're not having second thoughts?"

Was she?

Emmaline looked into Granger Lockwood's eyes. Something stirred deep within her.

Not the baby . . . it was too early, she reminded herself, for that. But someday soon, she knew she would feel their child squirming and kicking in her womb. And in the spring, she would cradle a newborn in her arms.

Yet that was all that was certain about the future. For the first time in her life, she had no idea what tomorrow could bring.

Emmaline realized, as she stared at the man who

had inadvertently started all this with an enticing invitation to chat in the garden on a warm June day, that what she was feeling was a gush of happy anticipation.

This was uncharted territory . . . and she wouldn't trade it for the old life—or the new one she had been about to launch with Remi.

An image of his face flashed before her, but she pushed it away. She didn't want to worry about the man she had jilted. He might be hurt now, but she had done what was best for both of them. Someday he would know the truth, and he would understand.

She simply couldn't marry Remi carrying another man's baby. She would never be able to hide the truth. He would know. The whole world would know. And her blatant betrayal was something no man in Remi's position would ever be able to—or expected to—forgive.

"No," she told Granger. "No second thoughts."

"Good."

"How about you?" she asked him. "Do you have second thoughts about your role in any of this?"

"Nope. I'm always up for an adventure . . . and I'm assuming we're about to embark on one."

Emmaline looked him squarely in the eye and smiled. "You have absolutely no idea."

four
·················

As the limousine pulled up in front of Lockwood Tower's spot-lit rosy marble fa-cade, Granger spotted Carlos, the long-time Saturday evening doorman, at his post. This wouldn't be the first time Granger would whisk a high-profile female companion into the building after dark on a weekend, and Carlos could always be counted on for his discretion.

Still, Granger wasn't taking any chances. Before landing in New York, Emmaline had donned the blond wig he had brought along for her, and she was wearing a pair of oversized sunglasses despite the fact that the sun had set almost an hour ago.

"Good evening, Mr. Lockwood," Carlos said gal-lantly, as Jimmy, the chauffeur, opened the limo's back door.

Jimmy was also a longtime Lockwood family em-ployee, hired by Grandfather half a century ago. At this late stage, Granger had serious doubts about the old man's eyesight—which wasn't very reassuring when you were a passenger and the old man was tooling along the FDR Drive at eighty miles an hour, but came in handy when you were sharing the backseat with a princess who very much needed to remain incognito.

"Good evening, Carlos." Granger stepped out onto the street and looked around.

This block of Fifth Avenue was, as he had anticipated, all but deserted at this hour on a steamy Saturday evening in August. Most of the residents who could afford to live in this neighborhood could also afford beach houses or country estates. Virtually no one remained in this part of Manhattan but a couple of stray tourists.

The Lockwoods were no different from their neighbors. Grandfather was spending a few days at his estate in South Hampton, and Granger—before he had quit the family business and before Emmaline had beckoned—had intended to head to Seaside Serenade, the family's Newport mansion, for a typical weekend of sailing and tennis.

But here he was, and there she was, Princess Emmaline, stepping out of the car and gazing up at Lockwood Tower, her expression masked behind the oversized sunglasses.

Granger saw Carlos glance discreetly at her as he accepted her bag from Jimmy.

Inner alarm bells clanged.

Emmaline was virtually unrecognizable in the

wig and glasses, and her clothing—those slim black pants, the figure-hugging sleeveless black top, and black flats suitable for sprinting—now seemed less cat burglaresque than urban casual chic.

Still, Carlos wasn't nearsighted, or farsighted. Nor was he the kind of man who would neglect to give a beautiful woman a thorough once-over. Since Saturday nights were slow, he seemed to spend a lot of time reading the tabloids at his post—and Emmaline's face was invariably plastered all over them.

Granger took Emmaline's arm and swept her toward the building so quickly that Carlos barely beat them there to open the door for them.

"Have a nice evening, Mr. Lockwood. You, too, ma'am," Carlos called after them as he handed her bag over to Granger.

"Thank you," Emmaline returned in a flawless American accent—flawless, that was, for someone who'd been raised in the outer boroughs. Or Jersey.

Impressed nonetheless, Granger waited until they had crossed the air-conditioned lobby, passed the stoic night security guard, and were on board the express elevator. He removed his bulging Tiffany key ring from his pocket and jabbed a key into the slot above the PH button.

The moment the doors had slid silently closed behind them, he turned to her and said, "What happened to your accent?"

"What accent?" she asked in her usual accent—a regal, lilting inflection reminiscent of her native tongue, which Granger happened to speak fluently, though they had always conversed in English until now. And she had wisely remained silent through Customs—where she showed the fake passport he'd obtained for her—and during the drive from the airport, as Granger and Jimmy exchanged the usual brief comments about the weather and the evening traffic.

"*That* accent," he said, pressing the button marked PH and raising an eyebrow at her. "But when you spoke to Carlos back there, it was gone. You sounded like—"

"Like a New Yorker?" she asked hopefully in that nasal-sounding American accent again, as the elevator began to rise.

He grinned, echoing, "A *Noo Yawkah*? How'd you learn to *tawk* like that?"

"We get your television programs in Verdunia," she informed him, obviously quite pleased with herself. "Of course, they're mostly reruns of older shows, but I've been watching them and studying the characters' speech patterns."

"Oh yeah? Which programs? *The Nanny*? *The Sopranos*?"

"Both of those. Some others, too. How did you know?"

"Lucky guess," he told her. How was he going to break it to her that she wasn't going to blend into his world speaking like a cross between Fran Drescher and a hit man? "Listen, Your Highness—"

"You shouldn't call me that."

"I won't, in public. But nobody's—"

"Don't call me that in private, either," she interrupted again. "Just call me Emmaline. Please."

For a moment there was silence, except for the jaunty, piped-in Muzak version of Jimmy Buffett's "Margaritaville."

Granger cleared his throat, suddenly aware that she was standing close enough for him to smell her floral French perfume.

And to kiss her. If he wanted to.

Not that he *didn't* want to. But that wouldn't be a good idea . . . even if they were alone. After all, she wasn't there because she wanted to be with him. She was there because she wanted to get away from the man she was supposed to marry. The man she no longer wanted to marry because—

Well, who knew why she had changed her mind about Remi and the royal wedding? He doubted it had anything to do with what had happened between the two of them that June night. He was no fool, and she had made it clear that they could have nothing more than a few stolen moments in each other's arms. And he didn't want anything more than that, then or now . . . did he? Did *she*?

He looked at her, wishing he could see her eyes behind those damn glasses.

"Emmaline," he began.

A smile curved her lips.

"What?" he asked.

"*Your* accent," she said. "Saying my name. It sounds nice, Granger."

"*I* don't have an accent," he protested lamely, his

breath catching in his throat at the unaccustomed sound of *his* name on *her* lips.

"Oh, but you do."

He leaned a bit closer to her. "Can you please take off those glasses, Emmaline?"

"I thought you said before that your housekeeper might be—"

"In the apartment, yes. But she isn't here in the elevator with us," he pointed out, a bit hoarsely.

"No," she agreed, reaching for the glasses, "we're quite alone."

She pulled them off, baring a verdant gaze that told him all he needed to know.

He shifted his focus from her eyes to her mouth. Her lipstick had long since worn off, leaving her lips a pale, natural pink that reminded him of a seashell's satin-soft lining.

No. He couldn't do this.

He closed his eyes and took a deep breath, but the air was abloom with her rose-scented perfume, plunging him back to that heady June day in the palace garden. He recalled the giddy surge of schoolboy exhilaration when she appeared before him, and heard again the ribbon of girlish laughter in her voice as she said, "I'll bet you didn't think I'd take you up on your invitation for a tête-à-tête."

"No," he had replied, "I didn't think you would. Maybe I judged you too hastily when you were up there in your turret."

"Why? What did you think of me?"

"That you didn't have the courage to come down here and hear what I have to say."

Her green eyes had gleamed at him. "Oh, really? And what do you have to say that can't be shouted up to my turret?"

"Sweet nothings, mostly," he had returned. "And it's not so much what I can't *say* from that distance as it is what I can't *do*."

"Oh? What can't you *do*?"

But she had known full well then, in that instant before he kissed her, what he was going to do. Just as she knew it now.

She had wanted it then, just as she wanted it now.

He opened his eyes and looked at her. Her eyes were closed. Her face was tilted upward, her lips moistened and slightly parted. She was waiting for him to kiss her.

Who was he to disappoint a princess?

He reached toward her, placing his hands on her bare arms, surprised at how velvety warm her skin was in the arctic chill of the elevator. He heard her breath catch in her throat as he leaned closer.

"I can't do *this*," he murmured.

"Oh, but you can."

Just as his mouth brushed hers, the elevator bumped to a halt and a soft ding announced that they had reached their destination.

The doors slid open.

Frustrated, Granger removed one hand from Emmaline's arm and pressed the Door Open button firmly. Holding it down, he looked at her.

"I believe we've arrived at your floor," she said, her voice hushed, her mouth mere inches from his.

"I believe we have."

"Aren't we going to get off the elevator?"

"Not until we finish what we started."

With that, he kissed her again, hungrily. As her lips parted beneath his, it was all he could do to control the urge to lift his fingers from the Door Open button and allow them to roam. He remembered the supple heat of her naked flesh beneath his caress that night in Chimera. Shyly tentative one moment, unabashedly ardent the next, she had finally confessed to him, as she fumbled with the buttons on his shirt, that she was a virgin.

He was still as amazed by that revelation as he had been by her impulsive decision to bestow upon him the precious gift she should have been saving for her wedding night. In fact, he had summoned every ounce of self-restraint when she told him, certain that they shouldn't go any further. It was Emmaline who coaxed him onward, undressing him with growing confidence, and trailing fluttering kisses across his naked chest until he groaned and hauled her against him once again.

But they were alone then, in a bed, in his hotel room . . .

This wasn't the time, or the place.

Granger pulled back reluctantly.

Emmaline's eyes opened. She was panting

slightly, her cheeks flushed, her blond wig slightly askew.

"We should go," he said raggedly.

She nodded.

"My apartment is right there." He gestured beyond the elevator at the carpeted vestibule and ornate double doors. "We can go inside and—"

"Talk," she said abruptly, reaching up to straighten her synthetic hair.

"Talk," he said, nodding. "Right. That's what I was going to say. We can go inside and talk. After you."

Granger followed her off the elevator.

The spell was definitely broken . . . and judging by the sudden all-business expression on Emmaline's face, he would be wise to head straight for a cold shower.

A steaming bubble bath . . .

Yes, and a cup of hot chamomile tea.

Those familiar indulgences would calm Emmaline's frazzled nerves and wildly beating heart, if anything could.

Being kissed by Granger just now had almost pushed her over the edge. It was all she could do to keep herself standing upright as she stepped over the threshold into his penthouse apartment.

She was instantly met by a wild barking, accompanied by the thunderous scampering of paws across hardwood and marble. Two enormous dogs materialized, joyously catapulting themselves onto Granger.

"These are my dogs, Newman and Kramer," he announced over the yapping canine chorus.

"Do tell." Emmaline summoned a gracious smile, wondering briefly whether she should ask which was which, before concluding that it didn't matter. She wasn't particularly fond of four-legged creatures—a distaste that Granger obviously didn't share. She watched incredulously as the two enormous animals rested their front paws on their master's shoulders and slurped dog saliva all over his face, to his apparent delight.

Finally he laughed and said, "All right, down, boys. I've missed you, too."

They obeyed. Then, to Emmaline's utter horror, the black dog trotted over to her and sniffed her legs.

"Newman . . ." Granger said in a warning tone.

The dog defiantly proceeded to bury his nose in Emmaline's crotch.

Pretending to pat Newman's head, she did her best to push him away.

"Sorry," Granger said, grabbing hold of Newman's collar. "He does that to guests sometimes."

Speechless, Emmaline could only stare as Granger wrestled the dog away, calling, "Come on, you too, Kramer."

The German shepherd, who had appeared to be on the verge of following Newman's lead, gave Emmaline's lower region a last longing glance before obeying his master's command.

She breathed a sigh of relief when she heard Granger putting them into a room and closing a door, ignoring their protesting woofs.

He returned to the entryway and closed the door, which had been left ajar. "Sorry about that," he said. "The boys miss me when I'm gone. I'll keep them in the other room until they settle down a bit. But you'll get used to them."

Emmaline seriously doubted that. But he was clearly trying to be a concerned host. And as his guest, she had to remember her manners.

"This is very nice," she murmured, looking around the entryway. It was tastefully appointed: marble floor, wainscot and crown molding, and handsome deco-style wall sconces that cast a soft glow.

"It's no royal palace," Granger said, locking the triple dead bolts, "but I like it."

"I wouldn't mind never setting foot in another palace as long as I live," she informed him. "I'm ready to . . ."

"See how the other half lives?" he supplied, when she trailed off.

"Exactly."

"Well, then, Princess, come on in and check things out." He led the way into a large living room. Floor-to-ceiling windows along two walls provided a dazzling view of the glittering Manhattan skyline and the vast dark rectangle that marked Central Park.

The color scheme was—well, lacking in color. Everything was done in shades of white and beige. The furniture was what she would expect to find in a well-to-do American bachelor's apartment: modern and rectangular, glass and leather. A far cry from the fussy European antiques that furnished both the palace back home and Remi's private quarters in the castle in Buiron.

The thought of Remi sent another guilty aftershock through Emmaline. What was he doing right now, back in Verdunia? Or had he left for Buiron as soon as it was apparent that she had left him at the altar?

Poor Remi. How could you have done such a thing to him?

And what about Papa, and Mother? They must be frantic with worry, despite the note she had left behind.

Well, someday everyone—Remi and her family— would understand that this had been her only option, under the circumstances. Better than to marry Remi and publicly humiliate him by bearing another man's child instead of the expected royal heir.

It would have been best of all, she reminded herself sternly, if she had never met Granger Lockwood. He was the one who had gotten her into this mess.

"Are you hungry?" he asked, going around the room, turning on table lamps.

She shook her head, unable to speak, all at once nauseated and exhausted and overwhelmed by her predicament.

"Emmaline?" He turned toward her, catching a glimpse of her face.

She did her best to smile, but hot tears were already spilling from her eyes. She turned away quickly and reached up to wipe them away with the back of her hand.

Granger crossed the room swiftly, beside her before she could make a move to get away.

Where would she go, anyway? She was in a strange apartment, in a strange city, in a strange country, with a strange man. Oh, what had she done?

"Emmaline," Granger said softly, behind her, putting both hands gently on her shoulders. "Are you all right?"

"No," she said, sniffling. "Quite the opposite."

"You've been through so much today," he said, patting her arm. "Once you've had a good night's sleep, you'll feel better."

"I'm sure that I won't," she retorted.

"Of course you will. In the morning everything will seem—"

"Mornings are the worst," she snapped, spinning around to face him. "Thanks to you, I have spent every wretched morning with my head in the—"

She broke off, realizing what she had done. She couldn't tell him like this.

Perhaps she shouldn't tell him at all.

"With your head in the what?" he asked, looking bewildered.

"Sand," she improvised. "With my head in the sand. Thanks to you, I convinced myself that leaving Verdunia and not marrying Remi was the right thing to do."

"Hey, this whole thing was *your* idea," he said, taking a step back and throwing his hands up. "You called me, remember? You asked me to rescue you before it was too late."

"But I never said that I should leave him at the altar!" She shuddered at the thought of how poor Remi must have felt, having to face all those people, and the cameras, and, God help him, his mother, the formidable Queen Cecile.

"It was the only way," Granger reminded her. "You don't plan an escape and cross the ocean and find a helicopter in a few hours. I got there as soon as I could. It just happened to be on your wedding day. You're lucky I managed to get there in time."

"I'm lucky?" She caught a glimpse of herself, blond wig and all, in a large mirror across the room. "I'm standing here in this ridiculous disguise, which I'm probably going to have to wear for the rest of my life, in this apartment I'm never going to be able to leave again, and you think I'm lucky?"

"Listen, I've got news for you, Princess," Granger said, folding his arms and regarding her with an expression that almost seemed smug. "You're going to have to leave this apartment."

Her jaw dropped. "Are you tossing me out on the street?"

But . . . he couldn't make her leave! Panic darted through her. She needed him. He was her only ally.

Again she cursed herself, and Granger Lockwood, and the fateful night that had led to this plight.

His expression softened. "Of course I'm not tossing you out. What kind of man do you think I am?"

"I have no idea what kind of man you are," she admitted, her eyes filling with tears again. "I just . . ." She took a deep breath and forced herself to look him in the eye. "I have nowhere else to turn. I need to stay here. If only for tonight, until I can—"

"Emmaline, you can stay tonight," he said. "That's not what I meant. It's—" He exhaled heavily. "Look, I don't feel like getting into the details right now, but to make a long story short, I'm going to be moving."

"Moving? Moving where?"

"I have no idea."

"When?"

"I have no idea," he said again, with a shrug. "But I'm certain that it will be only a matter of days before my grandfather throws me out of this place. I'm surprised he hasn't changed the locks already."

"But why would he do such a thing?"

"Because he owns the building, and now that I'm no longer working for him, I'm pretty sure I'm no longer welcome to live here."

"You're no longer working for Lockwood Enterprises?"

"I quit a few days ago."

"And your grandfather was upset?"

"Oh, you could say that. In fact, he's all but disowned me. So you see, Princess, you're not the only one who's about to turn your life upside down."

"I . . . I don't know what to say." Emmaline's mind was racing.

She had assumed, perhaps naively, that Granger would take care of her . . . at least until she got herself on her feet and came up with a plan. Now it seemed dubious that he would be able to take care of himself, let alone a displaced princess . . . and a newborn child.

"Look, it won't be so bad. I mean, wherever I go, you can come with me," Granger said. "It'll be fun."

"Fun?"

"Sure. We'll find a place to live . . . maybe downtown, where the rents are cheaper. And we'll get jobs."

"Jobs?" she echoed weakly.

He nodded, his blue eyes alight with enthusiasm. "After all, I've had a free ride until now, and so have you. Don't you think it's time we found out what we're made of? Don't you think it's time we found out how regular people live?"

She was silent, contemplating that. Regular people. As in *commoners*.

All her life, she had wistfully wondered what it would be like to be an unencumbered commoner.

That didn't necessarily mean she wanted to find out firsthand. Especially now, when she would have a baby to provide for.

"Can you imagine what it will be like, not having to answer to anyone for the first time in our lives?" Granger went on. "Not having to live up to anybody's expectations but our own. Free to explore everything life has to offer. No baggage. Nobody looking over our shoulders, or getting underfoot . . ."

Nobody except a small child, Emmaline thought grimly.

She couldn't possibly tell Granger about the baby now . . . if ever.

The best thing to do, she concluded, would be to head home to Verdunia as soon as possible. Her parents would shield her from the press and take care of her.

On second thought, they probably weren't thrilled with her right now. Perhaps they, like Granger Lockwood's grandfather, would disown her.

Well, perhaps she could conceal the pregnancy somehow, and give the baby up for adoption . . .

But even as the thought entered her mind, she discarded it. She not only wanted to have this child, she wanted to keep it, raise it, love it.

There were plenty of single mothers in the world. High-profile ones. Even royal ones.

She could do this, without any help from her parents or Granger Lockwood. Let him go off in search of his cheap downtown apartment and his—his *job*.

"What do you say, Emmaline?"

"I'm exhausted," she said truthfully. "Can I . . . ?"

"Sure. I'll show you where the guest room is. We'll talk more in the morning."

She nodded, thinking that she had no intention of talking to him about anything. By the time he awak-

ened in the morning, she would be on her way back
to Verdunia.

Princess Josephine helped herself to a third blue-
berry scone and reached for the butter.

"How can you eat at a time like this?" Princess
Genevieve demanded.

"I'm hungry," Josephine said simply, spreading
the scone with a generous layer of butter.

The two sisters were seated on the palace terrace,
overlooking the large lawn where Emmaline's escape helicopter had landed yesterday, according to
palace security.

Josephine couldn't help being impressed by her
sister's sheer nerve. But that didn't mean she didn't
consider Emmaline a colossal fool. How could anyone in her right mind abandon the scrumptious
Prince Remi at the altar?

After biting into the rich, crumbly treat, Josephine
reached past a vase of bright red poppies for the
crystal pitcher of freshly squeezed orange juice. She
refilled her goblet, splashing a bit. A few droplets
landed on Genevieve's cell phone, which was beside
her placemat. She was waiting for a call from Reginaldo, as usual. He called every morning, promptly
at eight.

Three minutes to go, Josephine thought, glancing
from her diamond-studded wristwatch to her sister's untouched breakfast: a cup of black coffee and
three plump red strawberries.

Poor Genevieve. How dreary it must be to constantly have to watch one's weight. Josephine had never dieted in her life.

"Perhaps you could sprinkle a bit of sugar on those berries to add extra flavor," she said helpfully around another mouthful of scone. "Sugar doesn't have as many calories as—"

"I'm not worried about calories right now, Josephine! I'm worried about Emmaline. As should you be."

Josephine contemplated that, still munching, then said reasonably, "Emmaline's note said that she's safe and sound, wherever she is. I don't see why we need to worry. She'll turn up sooner or later."

Genevieve shook her head, looking exasperated. She pushed back her chair.

"Where are you going, Genevieve?"

"To see whether Papa has heard anything from Emmaline yet."

Her sister swept through the double French doors into the palace.

Josephine shrugged and helped herself to a strawberry from her sister's plate. She bit in, made a face, and reached for the crystal sugar bowl. As she sprinkled a generous spoonful of sugar over the berry, a telephone rang.

Startled by the proximity of the sound, Josephine saw that Genevieve had left her cell phone behind.

Josephine popped the sugar-dusted berry into her mouth and picked up the phone and flipped it open. "Right on time as always, darling," she said sweetly into the miniature black receiver.

"Genevieve?"

The familiar voice that greeted her didn't belong to her future brother-in-law.

"Emmaline?" Josephine asked, her eyes widening.

There was a pause on the line. "*Josephine?* I thought I was calling Gen—"

"You were." Josephine narrowed her eyes, wounded. "Why aren't you calling me?"

"Why are you answering Genevieve's phone? Where is she?"

"Oh, around here somewhere. More importantly, Emmaline, where are *you?*"

"I'd rather not say."

Josephine quickly lowered the phone from her ear and glanced at the small screen that displayed the call's origination. She instantly recognized the area code—and the name. *Lockwood, Granger.*

"Emmaline, what on earth are you doing in Manhattan with that American playboy?" Josephine asked, again marveling at her sister's spirit.

Emmaline gasped. "How did you—"

"Caller ID," Josephine said brusquely. "Do tell, Emmaline—have you been seeing that delicious Granger Lockwood behind Remi's back?"

"No!"

"Then why—"

"Josephine, you mustn't breathe a word of this to anyone. Do you understand? Not Papa or Mother, not Remi—"

"Not even Genevieve," Josephine said, pleased to be privy to her sister's secret for a change. Honestly, sometimes she and Genevieve acted as though Josephine were a pesky child. It was about time somebody made her a confidante . . . even if it was by default.

"How long are you staying in New York?" Josephine asked, thinking of Remi. If her sister had gone and fallen in love with another man, the prince would be eligible once again.

"I'm not staying in New York," Emmaline replied. "I'm going to rest for a few hours, and then head for the airport. I'll be home before night falls in Verdunia."

"Oh." Josephine deflated. "Then you're coming back to Remi?"

There was a long moment of silence on the other end of the line. "I'm not certain about that," Emmaline said softly. "All I know is that I've made a tremendous mistake . . . and that I can't possibly stay here with . . . with *him*."

"Oh, why not give him a chance, Emmaline?" Josephine urged. "You never know. He might grow on you. And you and Remi are all wrong for each other."

She heard a choking sound on the other end of the line.

"Emmaline . . . are you crying? Whatever is the matter?"

"Everything is the matter," Emmaline said on a sob. "Oh, Josephine, I don't know where to turn. I— I—"

"You can turn to me, Emmaline," Josephine said. "What is it?"

Her sister sniffled. "Can you keep a secret?"

"Of course!" Josephine said indignantly.

"All right. I simply must tell somebody. Josephine, do you remember that night in June when I left the charity dinner early to—"

"Josephine! Are you talking to Reginaldo? Why didn't you tell me?" Genevieve had materialized on the terrace once again.

"Shh! I'll be off in a moment," Josephine said, turning her back on her sister and returning her attention to the phone.

It was too late.

"Don't say a word to anyone, Josephine," Emmaline said, her voice hushed and harried. "Remember . . . you promised."

"But—"

"Goodbye, Josephine. I'll see you tonight." The connection was broken instantly.

Josephine scowled. She flipped the phone closed and tossed it to Genevieve, who scrambled to catch it.

"Josephine! What are you do—"

"It wasn't Reginaldo," she said. "It was just a wrong number."

"A wrong number? But it sounded as though you were chattering to whoever was on the other end."

"Well, one shouldn't be rude to anyone," Josephine replied, impressed by her own quick-thinking duplicity. "Not even a wrong number."

Genevieve seemed satisfied with that.

As her sister marched back toward the palace,

phone in hand, Josephine leaned back in her seat and thought about Emmaline.

And Granger Lockwood.

He was yummier than one of those ripe red berries, Josephine thought, sprinkling sugar over another one and popping it into her mouth.

Who could fault Emmaline for falling in love with him?

And who could fault her younger sister for offering comfort to the bereft Prince Remi in his time of need?

Five

········

Granger was midway through his third cup of coffee, seated in the den in front of the television set with Newman and Kramer dozing at his feet, when he heard the guest room door open.

Both dogs heard it, too, lifting their heads and growling.

"It's okay, guys," Granger said as he quickly reached for the remote. "It's only Emmaline."

Reassured, the dogs settled down again.

Aiming the remote at the television, Granger pressed Mute, then changed the channel from CNN to one of the networks.

No luck.

An enormous close-up of Emmaline's face filled the screen.

He flipped again, to another network. And then another.

Like the Cable News Network, every local station was showing coverage of the biggest story to hit television news in months. Rumors were rampant: that there was some vast political conspiracy involving the governments of Verdunia and Buiron, that the princess had been abducted, that the disappearance was a shameless publicity stunt, or that she had gotten cold feet and abandoned Prince Remi at the altar.

Oddly, from what Granger could tell, that last theory was regarded as the least likely.

There was much talk about what appeared to be a tragic end to a fairy-tale romance, casting Emmaline and Remi in the role of star-crossed lovers. The prince was said to be distraught and in seclusion with his parents back in Buiron.

The Verdunian royals, repeatedly shown in fleeting news footage as they were hustled out of the abbey in their wedding finery, were holed up at the palace in Chimera.

Neither family had issued any kind of official statement. No mention was made of the reassuring note Emmaline said she had left for her father—or, Granger had noted smugly, of the helicopter that had landed on the palace lawn.

He hurriedly turned off the television and removed his feet from the coffee table, sitting up just as Princess Emmaline stepped into the adjacent hallway from the guest room.

Granger frowned, noticing that she was already

fully dressed. As she took a few steps in the opposite direction, he saw that her movements seemed almost . . . furtive? What the heck was she up to?

"Good morning," he called.

He heard her startled gasp as she stopped short, her back to him.

"Going somewhere, Princess?"

She turned around with obvious reluctance. He saw that her handbag was over her shoulder, and she was wearing the sunglasses. And the blond wig.

He hadn't planned to tell her right away about the wall-to-wall media coverage of her disappearance, but if she was planning on going out for a walk or a bagel or something, he had to stop her. If anyone spotted her on the street, she'd be mobbed in an instant.

"You're going to need to disguise yourself more than that if you're leaving the apartment," he warned her, rising from the couch and walking toward her in his bare feet. The dogs trotted along at his side. "A paper bag over your head might do it, but even then, you're taking a chance."

"You're up early," she responded, clearly not thrilled to see him, much less Newman and Kramer.

"Nice seeing you, too," he said dryly, watching as Newman's wet black nose made a beeline for her crotch.

She deftly reached down and headed him off with a firm half pat–half shove against his head.

Panting, the dog made another feeble attempt, but

the princess pat-shoved him again and shot a pointed look at Granger. He noticed that her nose was wrinkled.

Well, okay, the boys could use a bath. He wondered if his housekeeper had skipped the regular Saturday appointment with the pet grooming service.

"Move it, Newman," he said, collaring the Lab and giving him a nudge down the hall. "You, too, Kramer. Out of here. Would you like some coffee?" Granger asked the princess, as Newman trotted back to the den, with Kramer at his heels. "Or are you in too much of a hurry?"

She put a hand against the wall, almost as though she were trying to brace herself. "No, no coffee."

"Tea? Orange juice?"

"No," she said, and he heard her gulp audibly.

"I can make you some breakfast if you'd like," he offered. "Nothing fancy. My housekeeper, Antonia, is off on Sundays. Which is a shame, because she makes the richest, creamiest hollandaise sauce I've ever tasted. But I can do toast, and eggs—scrambled, sunny-side up, poached—fried in bacon fat is my favor—hey, where are you going?"

He stared in disbelief as Emmaline bolted back into her bedroom.

She was actually running away from him.

"Was it something I said?" Puzzled, he followed her.

The bedroom was empty. The cream brocade drapes, which matched the wallpaper and the bed-ding, were open to reveal a sweeping view of the city.

"Maybe she really can vanish into thin air," Granger muttered, seeing no evidence of the princess.

He noticed that the door to the adjoining bathroom was slightly ajar. Then came the most horrible retching sound he had heard since his college days, and he knew what it meant.

"You're throwing up," he marveled, his voice carrying through the crack in the door. He could see her kneeling in front of the toilet.

She broke off, panting, long enough to bite out, "Thank you, I had no idea," before launching into another round of vomiting as she kicked the door closed with her heel.

He cringed. "Are you okay?"

"Go away," she managed.

Granger retreated to the den, where he paced across the navy Berber carpet to the window. The sun was coming up, tinting the charcoal sky pink and casting golden rays over the leafy expanse of Central Park.

Poor Emmaline. She had been through so much. No wonder she was sick to her stomach.

He wondered if she had slept any better than he had. Possibly—since he hadn't slept a wink. He had spent the night tossing restlessly in bed before giving up and brewing a pot of coffee at about four A.M. and retreating to the den, his favorite place to kick back.

It was the only room in the apartment that he'd decorated himself. The rest of the place had been professionally done, but when it came to this room, Granger had locked horns with the designer over everything from the color scheme to the projection screen television and massive, surround-sound stereo system. The woman had proclaimed the media center and the navy and maroon palette too overwhelming for the room. But then, what did he expect? She was monochromatic in every way, from her design style to her personality to her name: Ann Smith.

Granger would have preferred somebody with more flair. But Grandfather had hired the bland Ann Smith and was footing the bill, as usual.

Not that any of it mattered now.

After depositing the princess in his guest room last night, Granger had checked his mail and messages. That was when he learned, courtesy of Deegan, MacDuff, and Hart, Attorneys at Law, that he was expected to vacate the apartment by Monday morning at the latest.

Twenty-four hours from now, he would be out on the street, presumably with the runaway princess bride in tow.

Granger retrieved his cup of coffee and plopped down on the recliner—the most comfortable piece of furniture in the apartment. Naturally, Ann Smith had regarded it with the utmost distaste when she saw it.

"Where did you find *that*?" she had asked. "On the curb?"

"I bought it at Crate and Barrel," he informed her.

Her expression revealed that for her, there was little difference between the upscale retail chain—where *anybody* could shop—and the curb. All of the furniture she had selected was custom-made by renowned artisans.

Leaning his aching shoulders back in the chair and raising the footrest, Granger wearily sipped his coffee and contemplated his situation.

Granger Lockwood II meant business. He had informed his grandson—through his lawyers, of course—that he would no longer enjoy any perks and privileges connected to Lockwood Enterprises.

Granger suspected that the official legal notification was a ploy to convince him to reconsider his resignation. Grandfather must not believe that he had what it took to make it on his own out in the world without the Lockwood fortune.

Well, the old man was sorely mistaken. Granger was determined to show his grandfather—and anyone else who doubted him—that he could survive.

As soon as he finished this much-needed dose of caffeine, he would go out and pick up the Sunday *Times*. He no longer subscribed, as his weekends were generally too action-packed for sitting around reading. But even he knew that if you sought an apartment in Manhattan, your best chance of finding it was in the Sunday classifieds.

Come to think of it, the Real Estate section wasn't all he needed. He'd better check Help Wanted while he was at it.

For the first time today, he felt a renewed flicker of excitement. There were so many interesting careers to choose from. He was eager to try his hand at something new, even if he had to begin at entry level and work his way—

The sound of a toilet flushing jarred him back to awareness.

He lowered the footrest and sat up, setting his cup on the table beside the chair. Poised, he listened as Emmaline's footsteps retreated from the bathroom.

When, after a few minutes, she hadn't reappeared in the hallway, he got up and went to look for her.

Knocking on the guest room door, which was still ajar, as he'd left it, he called tentatively, "Are you okay in there?"

The reply was a barely audible moan.

Alarmed, he pushed the door open and peered into the room.

The princess was curled up on the bed, her back to him.

Granger walked quickly around the foot of the bed and bent over her. A shaft of sunlight streamed in the window and fell across her face. Her eyes were closed, and her skin was pale. She had discarded the sunglasses and the wig. Her own dark hair was tousled on the pillow. He had seen it like that once before, also in the early morning light, in his hotel room.

He hurriedly shoved that image from his mind

and touched her forehead. Her eyelids flew open.

"I'm fine," she said abruptly. "It must be something I ate."

"Last night? On the plane?" He remembered how she had pushed the pasta around on the plate half-heartedly. "But you didn't eat."

"Oh . . ." She closed her eyes again. "Maybe that's it, then."

"You need to eat," he decided, his mind racing. "I'll make you something."

"No!" She stared up at him in alarm. "No, please don't cook anything. I won't be able to take the smell."

Clearly, the palace kitchen was well out of range of her delicate royal nostrils. She certainly was spoiled. Well, Granger decided, now that she was in the real world, it was time for her to wake up and smell the coffee. And eggs and toast.

Not that he was accustomed to making breakfast for overnight guests—or even for himself, for that matter. On the housekeeper's days off, he generally had breakfast delivered from a neighborhood restaurant, caught a bagel and coffee on the run, or went out for brunch.

But he knew that his Sub-Zero refrigerator would be filled with fresh ingredients, and that the cabinets were equipped with frying pans, or griddles, or whatever one needed to cook eggs. He had seen Antonia operate in the kitchen several times. Not that he'd been paying close attention—but he was sure he could prepare a simple meal. He wanted to, for some reason. For *her*.

He headed for the door, then paused on the threshold and glanced back at the bed. The princess was motionless, her arms wrapped around her middle.

Granger was swept away by an unexpected tide of tenderness. She looked so small and helpless, a displaced princess cast adrift on a queen-sized mattress in a foreign land.

She had nowhere to turn but to him—and he was determined not to let her down.

"You'll be okay," he said softly. "Just rest. I'll take care of you."

And he meant it, confident, as he went off to the kitchen, whistling jauntily, that a good, hearty breakfast would surely cure whatever ailed Princess Emmaline.

"What . . . what is it?" Swallowing hard, Emmaline lifted her fork and cautiously poked the congealed substance on the plate Granger had set before her.

"It's an omelet," he said proudly, passing a bottle across the table. "Ketchup?"

"No, thank you."

She swallowed again, watching him douse his own so-called omelet in sticky-looking red goo.

He looked up, and she summoned a halfhearted effort to erase the disgust from her expression.

Apparently it didn't work.

"What's the matter, Princess? I take it you don't like ketchup?"

"I've never tried it, but—"

"You've never tried ketchup? You've got to be kidding me. Here." Again he thrust the bottle at her. "Try it."

"No, thank you, really. I just . . ." She took a deep breath. "What kind of . . . *omelet*"—and she certainly used the term loosely—"is this?"

"Just what I had on hand in the fridge. Goat cheese, tomatoes, and some kind of sprouts. Alfalfa, maybe. My housekeeper does all my grocery shopping. The cooking, too. Though I have no idea what concoctions Antonia's been hiding sprouts in if she's been serving them to me. I never noticed them before. But they're not bad," he added, munching contentedly.

Emmaline set down her fork.

"What's the matter? Are you allergic to eggs or something?"

Perfect. That was a perfect solution. Although she'd better be careful. She didn't want to rule out a whole dairy group, just in case she wound up staying with him longer than this morning, despite her intention to flee as soon as breakfast was over.

"I'm not allergic to eggs," she said. "Just to . . . sprouts."

"Alfalfa?"

"All sprouts." It came out more harshly than she intended, and she made an attempt to smile. "I'm sorry. I should have told you."

"Well, there are plenty of eggs. I can make you an omelet without sprouts," he offered, pushing back his chair.

"No, that's okay. I'll just have some..." She reached toward the heaping plate in the middle of the table.

"Toast?" He pushed it toward her. "Go ahead. I made a lot."

And all of it was positively scorched. "Did you toast the whole loaf?" she asked weakly. It certainly appeared that he had.

"There are a few slices left."

"I'll just have some bread, then, thank you."

"With butter? Marmalade? Peach-mango chutney?"

She gulped. Her stomach was in full spin cycle. The last thing she wanted to do now was eat anything, but some instinct told her to do the opposite of what made sense. Food would ease the nausea. Plain food. Not peach-mango chutney. Or sprouts.

"Just a slice of bread would be fine," she told Granger. "I can get it."

"No, you sit. You still look a little green. I'll get it."

He jumped up and left the dining room.

Emmaline clasped a hand to her mouth, fighting back another wave of morning sickness. This was torture. How long was it going to go on? She didn't think she could bear it another day, let alone for nearly eight more months.

"Here you go." Granger breezed back into the room with a plate that he set in front of her. "Sure you don't want anything to go with this? Peanut butter or something?"

"No, thank you," she said hastily.

He went back to his seat, and to his eggs.

She hesitated, wishing he would go back into the other room and leave her to eat—or perhaps to throw up again—in peace. It wouldn't even be so bad if he were seated at the opposite end of the large rectangular table. But he had insisted that she sit at the head, and he had taken a seat to her right, his plate mere inches from hers.

Well, she couldn't stall all day. She noted, as Granger doused his omelet with a blizzard of salt, that he wasn't going anywhere anytime soon.

Reluctantly, Emmaline picked up the bread, took a bite, and forced it down.

Okay. So far, so good.

Another bite.

Force it down.

Another bite.

Force it down.

Once she got into the rhythm of it, she found the queasiness subsiding. She was so relieved at what was beginning to feel like a miracle cure that she almost forgot Granger was there, until he cleared his throat noisily.

Emmaline looked up to find him staring at her. She noticed that in this light, his navy polo shirt made his eyes look deeper blue. It was rumpled, as were the khaki shorts he wore with leather deck shoes—no socks. His cheeks were shaded in razor stubble.

Emmaline couldn't help comparing his casual style to the perpetually clean-shaven, neatly combed Remi's buttoned-up wardrobe.

Not that Granger didn't clean up quite nicely, she thought, remembering how dashing he had been that night, months ago, at the black-tie reception at the palace.

"You don't look like you're enjoying that bread very much," he commented.

"It's fine."

"But you're so businesslike about eating it."

She shrugged.

"Do you have . . . Maybe I shouldn't ask, but . . . I mean, you're so skinny. Do you have an eating disorder or something?"

"An eating disorder?"

Hmm. An eating disorder.

He kept offering possible explanations for her behavior, and it was tempting to seize this one just as readily as she had the allergy excuse.

But Emmaline reminded herself that she couldn't keep up the charade forever. Sooner or later she was going to have to tell him the truth about the baby.

Unless, of course, she fled the country immediately and never saw him again.

Which had been her plan first thing this morning, before Granger—and a cascade of vomit—intervened.

She took another bite of bread for fortification, then looked him in the eye. "I don't have an eating disorder," she told him firmly.

"You're just a picky eater, then."

She eyed the unappetizing breakfast he had prepared.

Then she reminded herself that he was just trying to be a good host, and that she should be grateful to him for all he had done for her.

But what about what he did to you? a disapproving voice inquired. *If it weren't for him, you'd be . . .*

If it weren't for him, she'd be on a yacht somewhere in the Mediterranean right now.

With Remi, she reminded herself.

Married to Remi.

She didn't want that . . .

Not any more than she wanted . . .

This.

But what she *wanted* didn't matter.

She was stuck with *this.*

Stuck with Granger Lockwood.

At least for the time being.

"Yes," she said stiffly, "I guess I am rather . . . *dis-criminating* when it comes to food."

"Well, you're not missing much. This omelet sucks. The toast, too. I think it's burned."

"You . . . *think* . . . it's burned?" She watched him shovel a charred hunk of toast into his mouth, and found herself laughing, shaking her head.

He laughed, too. "Hey, what can I say? I'll eat anything when I'm hungry."

"In that case . . ." She reached under the table and pulled off her black leather slingback.

"What's this?" he asked, staring at the shoe.

"Dessert. Would you like it as is, or à la mode?"

He chuckled. "That's what I like about you, Princess."

"My shoe?"

"Your sense of humor. You actually have one. And it catches me off guard every time."

"Really?" She regarded him thoughtfully, chewing and swallowing another bite of the deliciously yeasty bakery bread before asking, "Why is that? Aren't princesses supposed to be amusing?"

"None that I've ever known have been."

"Then you've known quite a few princesses, have you?"

"None as amusing—or as beautiful—as you are." The twinkle was still in his eyes, but so was something else. Something that made her heart beat faster and her breath catch in her throat.

She exhaled slowly, staring at him, the smile fading from her lips. "Granger . . ."

He leaned across the table. "You have a crumb . . ."

Her heart raced.

He reached out and brushed her cheek. ". . . right there," he murmured.

"Is it . . . ?" Her voice, when she managed to find it at all, was hushed.

"It's gone." He leaned closer.

Before Emmaline knew what was happening, his fingers had been replaced by his lips. He grazed her cheek, then found her mouth. As tender warmth bloomed with the kiss into blazing heat, Emmaline forgot everything . . . everything but the here and now, and this man.

When he tore his mouth away from hers long enough to say, "Come with me," she allowed herself to be pulled to her feet and went willingly.

If the master bedroom had been any farther from the dining room; if she'd had a moment to collect her thoughts, to realize what she was doing, she might have found the strength—and common sense—to resist.

But mere steps down the hall and precious few breathless seconds led her to Granger's king-sized bed.

There they tumbled; fumbled with buttons and zippers and clasps until at last there was no barrier between them. Cradled in his strong arms as he eased her into a downy heap of pillows, Emmaline felt sheltered in a sanctuary from which she never wanted to emerge.

"Are you okay?" he whispered, his breath hot against her ear.

She nodded and closed her eyes as his warm mouth trailed tantalizing kisses along her skin, delving into the hollow beneath her ear and the one at the base of her throat, and then lower still. She moaned as his tongue encountered one swollen nipple.

"Did I hurt you?" he whispered, lifting his head.

Her breasts had grown increasingly tender these past few days, yet now his touch aroused a curious, pleasurable ache in them.

"No, you didn't hurt me. It's—" She gasped as his mouth once again brushed her delicate flesh.

Her arms tucked beneath his, her hands splayed on his shoulders, she could feel the ripple of muscle beneath his taut skin. Filled with wonder, she stroked his back, his biceps, captivated by his masculinity.

It was all so extraordinarily innovative to her— this exquisite proximity to a man, this ability to touch him, to inhale the intoxicating scent of him, to see, when he lifted his head and looked into her eyes, the undiluted desire in his blue gaze.

Clasping his shoulders, she opened herself to him, and his body melted into hers. This time, unlike their last, she knew what to expect.

Yet it was different, somehow. There was no last-minute concerned hesitation on his part, no discomfort or pain on hers, just an intense rush of pleasure mingling with a closeness unlike anything she had ever felt.

Emmaline was overcome by the exhilarating physical sensation of him moving inside her, of his body encompassing hers. Somehow, it seemed reciprocal, as though she had slipped inside him, too—as though she had become a part of him, and he of her.

She never wanted it to end; yet when she felt him heave a shuddering groan and realized what was happening, she was filled with an electrifying satisfaction. Giddy with newfound sensual power, she marveled that *she* was capable of creating this astoundingly tangible response in a man—in *this* man.

When Granger collapsed against her, spent, breathing hard, she stroked his hair, steeped in contentment.

Then he rolled onto his back and pulled her with him, tucking her head against his chest and encircling her in the crook of his arm. She listened as his breathing slowed and finally slipped into the telltale rhythm of sleep. She told herself that she should get up, get dressed, start making plans.

But she couldn't quite bring herself to leave the shelter of his body. Not yet.

She yawned.

Just a few more moments.

Then she would . . .

When she opened her eyes, the light had shifted.

Granger was stirring beneath her.

They had been asleep. Both of them.

And before they fell asleep . . .

She lifted her head and found him looking at her.

"What are you smiling about, Princess?" he asked lazily.

"It's just . . . it's quite incredible, isn't it?"

"What we did?" He grinned and nodded. "I'd say so."

"I can't believe I never realized . . ." She trailed off, shaking her head.

"And now that you know," he said, seductively tracing her jaw with the back of his finger, "are you content with your choice?"

She stiffened.

It all came back to her.

The wedding.

The escape.

The *baby*.

I have to tell him, she realized. *I can't keep this from him another moment, and certainly not for a lifetime.*

It was Granger's child, too. They were in this together. Suddenly, that once-frightening knowledge was comforting.

"We have to talk," she said.

"You keep saying that. And you're right. We do have to talk. But first . . ." He stretched and rolled away. "I have to run a quick errand."

"An *errand*?"

"Yup." He sat up, swung his legs over the edge of the bed, and bent to look underneath it, presumably for his discarded clothing.

"Can it wait?"

"Absolutely not."

"What can you possibly have to do so urgently on a Sunday morning?" she asked, ire rising within her. Certainly it wasn't more important than what she had to say.

"I have to get the newspaper. We need the classifieds."

She stared at him in disbelief. "That can't wait?"

"This is Manhattan, Princess."

"I'm quite aware of our geographic location," she said tartly, and wanted to add that he was supposed to be calling her Emmaline. At the memory of how she had reacted earlier to the sound of her name on his lips, she held her tongue. She wasn't in the mood to be seduced again. And anyway, he managed to make "Princess" sound like a pet name and not an official title.

"Well, I need to find an apartment, immediately," he was saying. "I don't know if there's an abundance of affordable real estate in Verdunia, but it's not exactly ripe for the picking in these parts."

"But Granger—"

"We're talking cutthroat competition." He was pulling his khaki shorts on as he spoke.

"I need to—"

"We're talking first come, first served."

"Granger—"

"I'll be right back, and then we can—"

"Granger!"

He fell abruptly silent at her shout, then turned to look at her. "What is it?"

"It's . . ."

It's now or never.

She gulped, then took the plunge. "I'm pregnant."

"Pregnant?" Granger echoed.

His initial shred of disbelief gave way to a landslide of conviction.

"Pregnant," he said again.

She was pregnant. Of course she was. Now everything made sense . . .

Sort of.

Her nausea and exhaustion made more sense now.

Yet now, the fact that she was here with him made even less sense.

He looked at her. She was sitting up in bed. Her glorious, passion-tousled dark hair spilled over her naked shoulders, and his hungry mouth had erased every trace of lipstick from hers. She had drawn the comforter tightly over her breasts, clinging to it like a shield, and her eyes bored warily into his.

"You're pregnant."

"I'm quite aware of that."

"But . . . pregnant?"

"Will you please stop saying that word!"

"Does Remi know?"

She shook her head.

"Your parents?"

"No."

"Does *anyone* know?"

"No. Not even Tabitha. Just you."

He was so flattered by the fact that she trusted him, of all people, with her secret, that it took him a moment to remember to wonder why.

"Shouldn't you have told Remi?" he asked, frowning.

"I couldn't. He wouldn't understand."

"Maybe you're not giving him enough credit," Granger said reluctantly. He wasn't an ardent Prince Remi supporter, but that didn't mean the guy was an ogre—or that he didn't deserve to know he was going to be a father.

Emmaline cleared her throat and said delicately,

"Maybe you aren't aware that as his royal bride, I was presumed to be—and medically certified to be—a virgin. That was before I met you."

A virgin.

The word was a high-speed freight train slamming into him.

A virgin.

He had known that. Of course he had. The night they were together . . .

She had been a virgin.

He had been her first.

Perhaps . . .

"Emmaline . . ." His voice was hoarse, but at least he'd managed to locate it. "Was I . . . was I your only . . . ?"

"You were the only one," she confirmed softly.

"Not even Remi . . . ?"

"Just you."

"So . . . it's mine? The baby? It's . . . it's my baby?"

Baby.

The word tasted foreign on his lips. He realized that, quite possibly, it wasn't a word he'd ever even uttered. He'd simply never had occasion to talk about babies, singular or plural.

In Granger's world, babies were . . .

Well, babies just *weren't*. They weren't *in* his world. They didn't belong here, either.

"Granger." Emmaline was staring at him. "You mean you thought . . . you thought it was Remi's baby?"

He nodded mutely.

"But if it was Remi's baby, why would I be here?"

"I don't know. I guess maybe if you were ashamed to be a pregnant bride . . . or if you were feeling trapped . . . I don't know. I guess it wouldn't make any sense for you to be here if it were his, would it?"

She shook her head.

And he found himself thinking that it made even less sense for her to be here, carrying his child. Did she actually expect him to . . . well, to marry her? To be somebody's father?

Father.

A word that had crossed his lips almost as sparsely as the word "baby" had. But his mind— well, that was a different story.

Granger's thoughts darted back along a dim, but familiar path.

He remembered awakening to a shadowy image of a tall man stealing into the bedroom long after Granger had fallen asleep—a tall man, bumping into things, leaning over to clumsily kiss his sleeping child. He had always smelled of cigarettes, and gin, and night air.

Perhaps it had happened only once. Perhaps it was a regular routine.

Or perhaps it had never happened at all— Granger's father stealing in to kiss him good night. Perhaps he only wanted to think that it had.

"Well?" Emmaline asked, jarring him back to the present.

He looked at her.

She was expressionless, waiting.

"I don't know what to say," he said at last. "I—you—this is totally unexpected. What are . . . you . . . going to do?"

He had intended to say, *What are* we *going to do?* He knew it was what he *should* say. Yet somehow the word wouldn't come. He wasn't ready to be a "we."

I haven't even had a chance to be a me, he protested inwardly. Selfishly. But he couldn't help it.

He certainly wasn't ready to be somebody's father. So . . .

What are you going to do?

The words hung heavily in the air, along with all that was unspoken.

"I'm going to have the child, of course," Emmaline announced, eyes flashing beneath that dark fringe of lashes.

"Of course."

"I haven't yet been to a doctor, but I believe the due date is sometime in the middle of March."

"And when you told me . . ." He scrambled to keep up with what she was saying, but his thoughts seemed unable to get past the notion that she was carrying a child—*his* child. He took a deep breath, tried again. "When you told me yesterday that you were planning to stay here forever . . . you meant . . ."

She lifted her chin. The gesture was slight, but telling. "Don't worry, Granger. I only needed you to help me escape my wedding and Verdunia. I had nowhere else to turn. From here on in, you're off the hook."

The words sounded as stiff and unnatural as the blond wig she had worn earlier.

He wanted to tell her not to worry. That he would take care of her. And the baby.

But the truth was, he prided himself on being a man of his word. Grandfather had taught him well. It was the Lockwood way.

Granger wasn't about to make a promise he wasn't capable of keeping.

Perhaps he might have been, before. Before he had defiantly turned his back on his grandfather, the business, and the family fortune.

Now that he had willingly shed his riches for rags, he wasn't even all that certain he could take care of himself. But he was determined to try.

"All I need is a place to stay until I can get settled," Emmaline was saying.

He blinked. "You can stay with me."

"Here? But I thought—"

"I mean, wherever I end up. Don't worry. I'll find us a place before . . ." He had less than twenty-four hours to vacate the premises. "Before the sun goes down."

With that, he pulled his rumpled navy shirt over his head and stood. He jammed his feet into his deck shoes, not even caring that the heels were squished down beneath his feet.

He opened the bedroom door and was greeted by Newman and Kramer, who had apparently been lying in wait in the hallway.

"Later, boys, later," he said, giving them each a hurried pat on the head.

Making his way hastily to the door, feeling rather like someone about to parachute from a burning plane, he called over his shoulder, "I'm going for the paper, and I'll try to start seeing places right away. I don't know how long it'll take, but I'll be back as soon as I can. Make yourself at home. My house is your house . . ."

Except that tomorrow, his house would no longer be his house. Or hers.

Where would they go?

Stepping out into the hallway, he stabbed the Down button.

What would they do?

As he waited for the elevator, Granger rubbed his suddenly throbbing temples.

A baby.

Oh hell.

A baby deserved a father. And not just any father, he thought, frowning at the recollection of his own inadequate paternal upbringing.

A baby deserved a father who would be there. With a checkbook, yes. But with a warm lap and strong arms. With reassurance, and discipline . . .

And love.

Granger swallowed hard, wondering what the

hell he was doing. Maybe he should just swallow his pride; go back to his grandfather and Lockwood Enterprises.

He could turn around, march back into the apartment, and call Grandfather at the house in the Hamptons. He could tell the old man that he'd made a huge mistake. He could apologize. He could beg to return to his old job, his old home, his old life.

Then he wouldn't have to bother with building a new one.

The elevator doors slid open.

He hesitated, rooted to the spot, weighing his options.

The doors started to slide closed again.

Granger reached out, wedged his foot between them, and stepped inside.

Six

....

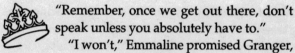 "Remember, once we get out there, don't speak unless you absolutely have to."

"I won't," Emmaline promised Granger, who was holding Newman and Kramer on leashes and had an umbrella tucked under his arm and several bags slung over his broad shoulders.

She nibbled on a saltine cracker as they walked across the polished marble floor of the lobby, the dogs' nails and her heels making a staccato tapping sound that echoed in the deserted space.

She'd suffered her usual bout of morning sickness first thing, before Granger had dashed out to the deli and brought back bagels with cream cheese. The last thing she wanted to do then—and now—was eat. But the bland starch seemed to settle her stomach. Not entirely—but enough so that she had safely made it from the apartment to the elevator to the lobby without vomiting.

So far.

It was too early for the office workers to have started pouring into Lockwood Tower on this gray, rainy Monday morning. A uniformed security guard was at his post, reading a newspaper. He barely looked up as they passed.

A doorman was stationed on the sidewalk just outside the spinning glass doors.

"You're out bright and early this morning, Mr. Lockwood," he said cheerfully. He tipped his cap. "Ma'am."

Emmaline smiled briefly, keeping her blond head tilted down as they stepped out into the drizzle. Would anybody wonder why she was wearing sunglasses on a grim, rainy morning?

Perhaps not. This was New York, after all.

Emmaline adored New York. She had been here on countless occasions, for the theater and the seasonal fashion shows and various charity fundraisers. She always stayed in an elegant midtown hotel, dined in the finest restaurants, and was escorted about town in a chauffeured limousine.

She now realized that for all the time she had spent here, she had never seen the city from this perspective. From a New Yorker's perspective. Before, she had been separated from the masses by tinted glass or velvet ropes or a VIPs ONLY placard.

Not any longer.

Now she wasn't a visiting princess. She was one of them. A New Yorker. At least for the time being.

The hurried commuters rushing along the sidewalk paid little attention to Emmaline and Granger, or to one another. Or even to traffic, she realized, as a few feet from the curb, a cabdriver screeched to a halt, honked his horn, and bellowed an obscenity at a pedestrian who had just stepped out in front of him.

"Walking the dogs yourself today, Mr. Lockwood?" the doorman asked.

"Actually, we're leaving for ... for the day," Granger replied.

"Did you call for your car, Mr. Lockwood? Because I don't see—"

"No, Roger, it's okay. I'm not taking the car today," Granger said quickly, clinging to the leashes, the umbrella, his duffel bag and Emmaline's satchel as the doorman reached out to take them from him.

"Can I get you a cab, then?"

"No, thank you. Have a nice day, Roger." Granger juggled the baggage straps over his shoulders, then put up an enormous black umbrella.

He held it low over Emmaline's head as they walked down the street, effectively shielding her from any passerby who might happen to glance in her direction.

They rounded a corner.

She was afraid to ask, but curiosity was getting the best of her. "Granger, if we're not taking a cab—"

"Your accent," he cautioned, holding a finger to his lips and swiveling his head from side to side, as if to make sure nobody was eavesdropping.

The coast was clear, but she couldn't be too careful. She began again, but lowered her voice and spoke in her practiced New York accent. "If we're not taking a cab, how are we getting there?"

"The subway," he announced—gleefully, for some reason.

"The *subway*?" she echoed weakly.

She had never seen a subway, let alone been on one.

Under the best of circumstances, she wouldn't be thrilled by the idea of descending below the Manhattan street and riding a stranger-filled train through a dark tunnel. Now, as she forced the last sodden bit of saltine into her upset stomach, it was all she could do not to gag.

What she wanted to do was drag herself back into the queen-sized bed in Granger's guest room fifty-five stories above this noisy city street.

But that was impossible.

He was taking her to his new apartment, which he had presumably found last night after hunting for hours. She had been in bed, asleep, when he returned. In fact, that was where she had spent most of the day. She had never slept so much in her entire life.

But when Granger woke her that morning, she had felt as though she could go on sleeping for a few more hours, at least.

No such luck.

Here they were, on their way to the subway to go downtown to Granger's new home on Eldridge Street.

A studio apartment, he had called it. Emmaline had no idea what that meant, but the phrase brought to mind Porfirio's quarters in Buiron. The fashion designer's studio was a spacious network of oversized rooms, all of them adorned with high vaulted ceilings, exposed brick, and hardwood floors.

Emmaline figured that if Granger's studio apartment was anything like that, they would be quite comfortable there—if only until she found a place of her own.

She had been too exhausted yesterday to be able to think coherently about her predicament, but she could no longer put it off. She had to make plans for her future—and her baby's future.

She couldn't go crawling back to Verdunia. Well, she *could* . . . if she were willing to become a public disgrace. But that would mean dragging her family— not to mention Remi—into a full-blown scandal.

It would be far better to remain in anonymity here in New York. Surely Papa would be willing to support her financially. She would call home just as soon as she and Granger were settled in his studio apartment.

"There it is," Granger said, pointing, as they crossed a wide avenue.

"The apartment?"

"The subway," he said with a grin.

"Oh. I almost forgot." She tried to muster an enthusiastic smile.

She supposed the subway looked harmless enough. It was just a stairway that disappeared into the sidewalk. Beside it was a green globed streetlamp-type thing on a tall post.

They crossed the street and walked down the steps. Granger was careful to cling tightly to the dogs' leashes. People rushed past them, heading up and down in a flurry of activity. They reached the bottom of the steps. She saw several vending machines along the wall, a row of turnstiles, and a large map showing a network of colored lines.

Emmaline glanced at Granger, who appeared a bit uncertain.

"Have you ever taken the subway before?" she asked.

"Of course."

"Often?"

He seemed to hesitate before admitting, "Once." There was a pause. He added, "In London."

"In *London*?"

"I'm sure this is exactly the same," he said with what she suspected was false confidence. "We just have to look at the map, figure out where we're going, and then get on the train."

As he spoke, there was an ominous rumbling that shook the floor beneath their feet.

"What is it?" Emmaline clutched Granger's arm. "An earthquake?"

"I think it's the train," he shouted above the roar.

The commuters who were still on the stairway launched themselves downward, bolting for the turnstiles. Emmaline watched in amazement as people shoved cards into slots in the turnstiles. They hurtled themselves forward to another stairway on the other side and disappeared as the air filled with the sound of squealing brakes.

Emmaline looked at Granger.

He was looking at the vending machines.

"I'll get our tickets," he said, reaching into his pocket. He produced a roll of cash.

"Yo, dude, they're called MetroCards," a nearby voice said.

They turned to see a teenaged African-American boy standing there. He was wearing jeans, a T-shirt, and a navy blue baseball cap with the letters NY criss-crossed above the visor.

"If I was you, I'd put that cash away before somebody decides to take it off your hands," the boy told Granger. "Subway ain't no place to be flashing that stuff around."

"You're right. Thanks." Granger hastily peeled off a bill and looked again at the vending machines.

"Ain't you never been on the subway before, dude?" the boy asked, looking from Granger to Emmaline, who shook their heads.

"Yo, you tourists?"

"Yes," Granger said with a quick nod. "We're tourists. From, uh, Kansas. And we would appreciate it if you'd help us get on the subway. We're not sure how to get our tickets."

The boy seemed to consider it.

"Look, take this money, get us our tickets, and you can keep the change," Granger said, shoving the bill he was holding at the boy. "Just show me how it works so that I can do it myself next time."

"Dude, no problem." The boy was suddenly grinning and agreeable. "Guess my mama was right. You do a good deed, you get rewarded. But you know, dogs aren't allowed on the subway."

Granger shrugged. "We're not going far. We'll take our chances."

Five minutes later, Granger, Emmaline, and Newman and Kramer were stepping onto a downtown-bound train. They had to fight their way in, swept along with a sea of other riders, going upstream against a tide of passengers who were disembarking.

Inside, the car was more crowded than the platform had been, filled with stoic-looking people wearing everything from business suits to turbans to skimpy summer tank tops and shorts. They held briefcases, newspapers, babies, Walkmans, shopping bags, paper coffee cups with jagged sections of the white plastic lids torn away for sipping.

There were no seats. There was barely room to stand.

"Hold the pole," Granger suggested as the doors slid closed behind them, sealing them into the car, where the air was hot and close and scented with garlic and strong cologne and sweat.

"What po—"

The train lurched. Granger grabbed an overhead metal strap with the hand that clung tightly to the dogs' leashes, and held Emmaline's arm with the other. Not that she'd actually have fallen to the floor, wedged as she was against the bodies of strangers, the dogs . . . and Granger Lockwood.

She pressed closer to him in an effort to get away from the others, and found herself flashing back to yesterday morning's encounter. She still couldn't quite believe that they had wound up in each other's arms moments after she had every intention of putting an ocean and as much European continent as possible between them.

Strange, Emmaline thought, how a man could infuriate you one moment and the next, leave you breathless with passion.

A disembodied voice crackled overhead on a loudspeaker, its words unintelligible aside from the phrase "next stop."

Strange, Emmaline thought, how you could be a royal princess bride in Verdunia one moment and the next, riding a subway in Manhattan.

Strange, too, how your stomach could be semi-settled one moment and the next, on the verge of—

"Are you feeling okay?"

She looked up to find Granger's face mere inches away from hers, watching her.

"Just a little . . ." She swallowed hard, fighting back the nausea.

"Sick?" His blue eyes were concerned.

She nodded.

The train slowed, then jerked to a stop.

The doors slid open.

People got off, jostling and pushing their way out as others jostled and pushed their way in.

"There's a seat," Granger said, and Emmaline saw

that a spot had been vacated a few feet from where they stood.

A dour-faced businessman made a beeline for it.

Granger stepped in front of him, cutting him off.

"Hey!" the man said, "That's my seat."

"It's her seat," Granger said, and propelled Emmaline into it. She sank down gratefully, wedged between an elderly Asian woman and an enormous man who overflowed past his bench allotment. She took a deep breath of the stale air and rested her elbows on her knees, and her forehead in her hands.

"You can't do that. I was about to sit there," she heard the man say.

"Let the lady sit down." Granger's tone was reasonable, but there was an ominous undercurrent. Newman and Kramer appeared poised to defend their master.

"The lady can stand. That's my seat."

"The lady will sit. She's sick and she's exhausted and she's pregnant."

Pregnant.

There it was, a public declaration made, courtesy of Granger, to a throng of strangers.

Emmaline didn't dare lift her head.

"Yeah? She doesn't look pregnant."

"Well, you don't look like a—"

The loudspeaker blared another unintelligible announcement, obliterating Granger's undoubtedly colorful insult.

Emmaline heard a plastic bag rustling, then felt something poking her arm.

She lifted her head and saw that the elderly woman beside her was offering her something small and pale brown.

"It's ginger root," the woman said in heavily accented English. "You take it."

"What did you call me?" the businessman was asking Granger.

"Peel and grate it. Make ginger tea. It will settle your stomach."

"Thank you," Emmaline said to the woman, her eyes suddenly welling with tears behind the sunglasses.

She wanted to hug this stranger, whose exotic eyes were filled with sympathy and kindness.

And she wanted to punch the rude businessman, who deserved the insult Granger obligingly repeated.

The train slowed again.

Emmaline darted a glance upward and saw the man glaring at Granger. He growled, "If I wasn't getting off at this stop, I'd—"

His words were muffled by another blast of the loudspeaker. This time, Emmaline was able to make out the word "street."

New York was a bizarre, foreign world, she thought, as the train screeched around a curve in the tunnel.

She could never be at home here. She could never

be like that woman who was standing a few feet away, somehow maintaining her balance while holding a fussy infant and a squirming toddler's hand.

But if she stayed here and had her baby, that was exactly what it would be like—minus the toddler. She would be a single urban mother, riding the subway. Living in an apartment, and shopping for groceries, and cooking, and cleaning, and doing all of the things regular people did here in New York.

A regular person?

A single mother?

A New Yorker?

She couldn't be any of those things.

A wave of homesickness washed over Emmaline. Suddenly she yearned for her old life. For the palace and her parents; for Tabitha and her sisters; for a view of the glistening Mediterranean, and freshly pressed designer clothes that weren't snug in the waistband, and healthy meals prepared by the royal chef, served on delicate bone china with citrus garnishes.

The train stopped.

The doors opened.

People got out, including the surly businessman.

People got on, including a group of young boys, one of whom was holding a radio that blasted a throbbing beat.

Granger leaned toward Emmaline and raised his voice to be heard above the hip-hop music. "How are you doing? Okay?"

She nodded.

She wasn't okay, but there was nothing he—or she—could do about that.

"Just a few more stops," Granger said. "Can you make it?"

She exhaled heavily. "I have to make it, don't I? I haven't any choice."

He offered a grim smile.

She bent her head again and focused on her trembling hands clutching the ginger root in her lap.

"At least join us downstairs for dinner, Remi," Queen Cecile urged, seated in her favorite chair, which had once belonged to Marie Antoinette. "The prime minister will be here. He's expecting to see you."

"No, thank you, Mother." Prince Remi turned away from the drawing room window, with its view of the breathtaking Buironese hillside dotted with late summer blooms. "I've no appetite."

"You mustn't let this destroy you," the queen said, narrowing her eyes at her son. "You must keep up your strength so that when the princess turns up, you'll be able to—"

"What if she *doesn't* turn up, Mother?"

"I don't appreciate being interrupted."

"I'm sorry, Mother." Remi sighed and crossed to the sofa, but thought twice about sitting. He knew from experience that the antique upholstery was stiff and uncomfortable, and that if he leaned back, his head would bump the curved wooden trim along the top.

"If the princess has been abducted," the queen went on, "your father will see that the ransom is paid."

"I'm certain King Jasper will pay the ransom," Remi said wearily. He didn't believe Emmaline had been abducted any more than he had on their wedding day, but going along with that theory was far simpler than discussing the alternative.

"He can't possibly pay a ransom without our help," Queen Cecile pointed out. "Now of all times, we must present a united front, Remi, lest anyone think that the future of Buiron—and of course, Verdunia—are threatened."

Remi sighed. How well he knew that the economic futures of both countries depended on the merger—rather, *marriage*—between him and Princess Emmaline.

Apparently she didn't give a damn about either of their kingdoms—much less about Remi's feelings, or his reputation.

Sooner or later, she was bound to turn up alive and well. Then the entire world would regard Remi as the most spectacularly jilted groom in history.

If only he could find Emmaline before somebody else—namely, the media—did. Then he could convince her to . . .

To what?

To help him concoct a believable kidnapping scenario, with Remi as her noble rescuer?

To relocate to some remote location—say, a nearly deserted tropical island—where the natives had

never seen a photograph of the world's most photographed woman?

To create a new identity, complete with plastic
surgery?

As Remi brooded, a butler discreetly entered the
room and cleared his throat.

"I have the palace in Chimera on the telephone,
Your Highness," he informed Remi.

Remi's heart skipped a beat. "Who from the
palace is calling?"

"It's His Majesty himself, Your Highness. Will you
take the call?"

"Of course."

"Perhaps there's been word of the princess,"
Queen Cecile said hopefully.

"Perhaps."

"I shall wait here. Please give the king my
warmest regards."

"Of course, Mother." Remi headed to the adjoining study, where he could take the call in private.

He closed the heavy mahogany doors behind him
and settled himself behind the seventeenth-century
desk. The ancient chair creaked beneath his weight.

Remi looked at the phone.

He cleared his throat nervously, reached for the
receiver, then hesitated.

It was awfully hot in here. Musty, too.

He turned to the window beside the desk and
cranked one of the leaded casement windows open
slightly. A hint of fresh air wafted into the room,
along with the sound of a crowd somewhere below.

Remi leaned toward the window, which faced the palace gates, and glanced at the ever-swelling throng of media, curious bystanders, and security personnel. Seeing food vendors' carts and several tents on a knoll in the distance, he had the sinking feeling that nobody had any intention of leaving until the princess had turned up safely—or quite the opposite.

Reluctantly, Remi picked up the receiver and greeted King Jasper.

"How are you?" the king asked.

"The last two days have been exceedingly difficult," Remi said with unaccustomed candor. "I'm sure you understand—and that you've had a difficult time of it yourself, Your Majesty. I'm terribly worried about dear Emmaline."

"Of course you are."

"Has there been a ransom note?"

"There has been a note," the king responded, somewhat cryptically.

Remi's stomach turned over. Had he been wrong, then? Had Emmaline been abducted after all? His spirits soared. If she had been abducted, his honor would be saved. They could go on with the wedding as soon as she had been safely released from her captors.

"Whatever the ransom is, Your Majesty," he said fervently, "I am prepared to—"

"There is no ransom."

"No ransom? But . . . ?"

"The note was from my daughter, addressed to me."

Remi digested this bit of news, then asked slowly, "What did it say?"

"I'm afraid Emmaline has gone into hiding," King Jasper said. "I've no idea why, or where she is. She simply stated that she is safe, and that her mother and I are not to worry."

"But . . ." Remi frowned. "Did the note say anything about . . . did it say when she would be back?"

"I doubt that she has any intention of coming back," the king said grimly. "Not unless somebody finds her and brings her home."

"Has Interpol—"

"Since there has been no crime, Interpol has no reason to get involved."

"Then who—"

The king cleared his throat loudly, and with unmistakable meaning.

Remi pondered this. "Shall I . . . shall I search for her, then?"

"The royal detectives are searching. The press, of course, is searching. In fact, the entire world seems to be eager to pick up Emmaline's trail." There was a chill in King Jasper's voice as he added, "My daughter was desperate enough to flee rather than become your wife. Have you any idea why?"

"Not the slightest," Remi said truthfully, staring unseeingly out the window. "I have never treated Emmaline with anything other than the utmost respect. As far as I know, she was as willing to begin our life together as I was. *Am*," he corrected hastily.

"In that case, I would suggest that you find her and convince her to come home to you."

It was more an order than a suggestion.

And Remi fought back the urge to contradict what he had just said; to simply tell Emmaline's father that he and the princess had never been more than halfhearted about their proposed marriage in the first place.

But for one thing, he suspected that the news wouldn't be news.

For another, he suspected—no, he *knew*—that it wouldn't make any difference to a man whose life had been steeped in royal duty since birth.

Not that Prince Remi's hadn't. As heir apparent to the throne of Buiron, he had always known—and done—what was expected of him, for the good of the people and the preservation of the royal line.

Did he really have any choice but to continue to do so?

Biting back his reluctance, he asked King Jasper, "Have you any idea where I should begin the search?"

"No, I haven't."

"Then what can I—"

"Surely you can think of a way to reach out to Emmaline without coming face-to-face with her," the king said pointedly.

"But . . ." Remi gazed thoughtfully at the media circus below.

"I'll do what I can," he promised Emmaline's father.

"Well? What do you think?" Granger asked, several steps behind Emmaline as she crossed the threshold of the fifth-floor walk-up.

Somehow, he had managed to wrestle the dogs on their leashes, the luggage, and the umbrella out of the subway, down several blocks, and up all these stairs. He had noticed that Emmaline didn't volunteer to help.

Well, he couldn't expect her to carry luggage in her condition. At least she could have taken the umbrella—but she didn't offer and he didn't ask.

After all, she was royalty. Royalty didn't schlepp.

Still panting from the exertion of all those stairs, she turned her head, apparently looking around. It was impossible to see her expression behind those sunglasses, but her mouth appeared to be puckering rapidly into a tight little slash.

Granger tried to follow her gaze and see the place through her eyes.

Not that he had to go that far. Seeing it through his own eyes, in the grim light of this gray, rainy morning, was more than enough.

It was a dump.

How on earth had he convinced himself that he could live here?

For one thing, pets were allowed.

For another, the single room had somehow seemed almost cozy last night. Of course, he'd toured it in the glow of the building super's flashlight, since the place was vacant and there were no overhead fixtures.

Well, the first thing he would do—after getting Emmaline settled—was go out and buy a lamp.

Granger looked around for a place to set their bags and settled for the dust-ridden floor.

He would have to buy some furniture, too . . .

He wiped a trickle of sweat from his brow.

And an electric fan . . .

His stomach rumbled hungrily as he crossed the short distance to open the window.

And groceries . . .

The window wouldn't budge.

And a crowbar . . .

As he turned back toward Emmaline, something brushed his face. A cobweb.

And cleaning supplies, he decided. They would need lots of cleaning supplies.

Hearing the plop, plop, plopping of water dripping, he walked toward the corner that served as a kitchenette. The dogs followed him, tags jangling.

Hmm. No matter how tightly he turned the lever, he couldn't stop the leak. He would have to tell the super.

He gazed at the stove. He wasn't sure what one would use to get all that charred grease off what might once have been white enamel, but perhaps Emmaline would know how to—

No. What was he thinking? She wouldn't have

any idea, he realized, seeing her nose wrinkle delicately as he opened the fridge and the smell of ancient sour milk wafted out. Emmaline had probably never cleaned anything in her life.

They made a fine pair. The pampered princess and the penniless playboy. How on earth were they going to survive here?

He closed the fridge, stirring the nest of dust bunnies on its top.

Though the window was closed, street noises wafted in to mingle with the steadily dripping faucet. Sirens raced down the adjacent avenue. Horns honked. A jackhammer reverberated. Somewhere in the distance, a car alarm bleated incessantly.

"Where . . ." Emmaline began, then sneezed.

"God bless you."

"Thank you." She coughed, her hand covering her mouth as she asked, "Where is the rest?"

"The rest . . . ?"

"The rest of the studio. *Achoo!*"

"God bless you. This *is* the studio."

"This is it?" She looked horrified. "One room?"

"That's what a studio is. One room. God bless you," he said as she sneezed again.

"Will you stop blessing me?" she snapped. "I've never felt less blessed in my entire life. We simply can't stay here . . . *achoo!*"

"Gesundheit," he couldn't resist saying amiably.

She glared.

"We have to stay here," Granger informed her mildly. "There's nowhere else for us to go. My grandfather—"

"Yes, I know. Your grandfather has thrown you out of your penthouse. But surely you can do better than . . ."

She trailed off, shaking her head as she looked around again.

He looked, too, taking in the grungy linoleum, the battered walls, the scarred porcelain sink, and the laminate countertop that bore rust-colored ring-shaped stains and what appeared to be a cigarette burn mark. There was a litter of what looked like some sort of tiny black pellets, too. Must be coffee grounds, he decided.

Granger turned back to Emmaline. "The truth is, I can't do any better than this . . . yet," he said optimistically. "Until I get a reasonable salary—or figure out if there's a loophole in my trust fund—this is the best place I can afford."

"What about your salary from your old position?"

"I quit . . . remember? No more salary."

"I'm aware of that, but what about the pay you've received until now?"

"I spent it," he said with a shrug.

"Don't you have investments?"

"Of course I have investments. Not liquid—and all tied to Lockwood Enterprises—and retirement. And in case you haven't noticed, I'm nowhere near retirement age."

"Surely you have credit?"

"Grandfather has seen to it that I don't," he said wearily. "Look, Princess, all I have is whatever cash I was able to find in my apartment yesterday."

After searching his wallet, various coat pockets, and the cookie jar where he tossed spare cash to use as tips for delivery people, he had come up with only four thousand and some-odd dollars. It was enough for the deposit and first month's rent on this place, and would buy them the barest necessities. Perhaps the furniture would have to wait.

But not the crowbar, he decided, jutting his lower lip to blow a gust of breath in the direction of his sweaty forehead. It was stifling in here, and the place reeked. Claustrophobia was setting in. If he could just open a window . . .

"Why can't you access your trust fund?" Emmaline asked.

"Because it doesn't become mine until my thirtieth birthday."

"Which is . . . ?"

"A year from next spring. March."

"March?" There was something about the way she said it . . .

Oh.

Yes.

March.

The baby was due in March.

For a brief moment, he allowed himself to fantasize that the baby would be born on his birthday.

He saw himself, a few years down the road, with a little boy on his knee and a candlelit cake in front of them. They were both wearing hats, he and his son . . . pointy party hats with the elastic chin straps that always snapped off the first time you put them on your head.

Granger knew about such hats from personal experience, as he had attended a few birthday parties in his childhood. But he had never had one of his own—Grandfather didn't believe in celebrating being another year older. Age, in his opinion, was the enemy. The best thing you could do was ignore it and hope that it wouldn't sneak up on you.

If Granger's son was born on his birthday, he would throw a big party every year, with pointy hats and cake and presents and maybe even a clown.

In fact, he decided, he would throw an elaborate yearly celebration no matter what day his son was born.

He would do it even if his son was a daughter . . .

A daughter.

A little girl who had pink cheeks and pink bonnets and little pink-cheeked dolls who wore pink bonnets, too.

A little girl who looked just like her mommy, with dark hair and green eyes that sparkled when she was happy and . . .

And turned murky as seawater in a nor'easter when she was angry.

Granger realized that Emmaline had removed the sunglasses at last, and her stormy eyes were fastened on his face.

"What's the matter?" he asked. "Are you feeling sick again?"

"*Again?* I never *stopped* feeling sick."

"Look, I'm sorry you don't feel good," he said, bristling at her accusatory tone. "But that's not exactly my fault."

"It isn't?" she shot back.

"No! I mean, I didn't set out to get you pregnant, Emmaline. And if anyone's to blame, it's . . . it's both of us," he amended hastily, having seen her tempestuous expression grow even more fierce. "Look, Emmaline, we're both responsible adults. We both should have known better. We should never have let anything happen between us that night . . . or yesterday, for that matter."

"I couldn't agree with you more. But there's no going back, is there?"

"No. There's no going back."

And God only knows what lies ahead, he thought bleakly.

Several hours and countless tears later, Emmaline sat cross-legged on the grungy linoleum floor, thinking that she had never been more miserable in her life.

Granger had gone out—where, she had no idea. She had been in the tiny, windowless bathroom, throwing up, when he left. He had called out something, but it was muffled by the closed door and the ever-present street sounds, and she hadn't bothered to ask him to repeat it. She didn't care where he was going, grateful to have some time alone to collect her thoughts.

Alone, that was, except for the dogs. Though Newman still persisted in sniffing her crotch from time to time, he seemed to be getting used to Emmaline's presence. Kramer, too. And she was actually getting used to them, too—though their dog breath was enough to make her gag whenever they exhaled in the vicinity of her nose.

She had decided against calling Papa just yet. For one thing, there was no telephone in the apartment. And Granger had discovered earlier that his grandfather had rendered his cellular phone useless by curtailing service.

For another thing, Emmaline wasn't so certain that Papa would be willing to support her here in New York after all. He might demand that she return to Verdunia to face the disgraceful consequences.

She hugged her stomach as she sat there on the floor, cradling the tiny life within.

"I have to get you out of here," she whispered to the baby. "I have to get us both someplace where we can be comfortable, and safe, and . . . and happy."

But where?

If she couldn't go back to her family in Verdunia . . .

And she couldn't stay here with Granger . . .

Where else was there?

Who else was there?

She longed to call somebody who would know what she should do. She yearned for her father's protective wisdom, for her mother's sympathetic ear, for Genevieve's well-padded shoulder and for Tabitha's sound advice. She even longed for impetuous, irreverent Josephine, who would surely find some humor in Emmaline's dismal plight.

And yes, for solid, stolid Remi, who at least had a strong sense of propriety, not to mention the financial means to support her.

Unlike the disinherited, down-and-out, devil-may-care Granger Lockwood.

Footsteps promptly sounded outside the door, and a key turned in the lock. As though he had been summoned by her disparaging thoughts, Granger stepped into the studio, laden with shopping bags.

"I'm back," he announced, as Newman and Kramer greeted him exuberantly.

"You don't say."

She couldn't help noticing that, try as she might, she couldn't deny that he was infinitely appealing. At least in the physical sense. Far more appealing— five o'clock shadow, rumpled New York Yankee logo T-shirt and all—than solid, stolid Prince Remi would ever be. At least, to her.

"Are you all right?" Affectionately patting Kramer's head, he peered down at her.

"Would you please stop asking me that?"

"By all means. I'll add it to my mental list of your complaints. Let's see . . . I should stop saying the word 'pregnant.' I should stop blessing you. I should stop inquiring about your well-being. Is there anything else I should stop?"

"Yes. Please stop . . . just stop being so . . ."

"So what?" He plopped his plastic shopping bags on the floor and closed the door with a kick of his white Nike sneaker.

"So . . ." She searched, frustrated, and settled for "So American."

"Sure." He looked amused and asked, in flawless French, "What would you like me to be?"

She harnessed a smile that threatened to burst forth and disrupt her steely glare. "Not French," she told him.

"But I'm fluent."

She shrugged, to show him that she wasn't impressed. She was fluent, too. In more languages than French and English. All part of breeding for a future monarch.

"Oh, come on," Granger said lightly, striking a ridiculous pose. "Picture me in a beret, with the Eiffel Tower in the background and a crusty baguette tucked under my arm."

She refused to give way to humor. "You don't look French."

He switched to well-versed Spanish, asking, "Is this better? I could wear a sombrero and make us a pot of chili. Have you ever had chili?"

"Never. And I've no desire to try it," she said primly. In English. *Her* English, not flat American English.

"How about McDonald's? Ever had McDonald's? Burgers, fries, shakes . . ."

"I had a burger once."

"At McDonald's?"

"No. At a pub. In London."

He made a face. "That's not the same thing. Just like the London tube and the New York subway aren't the same thing. Here. See for yourself." He rustled his bags and produced a paper sack, thrusting it at her.

"What's this?"

"Lunch," he said, looking pleased with himself.

She opened the bag to look inside, and a delectable aroma wafted out. To her dismay, she found herself salivating.

The last thing she wanted to do was give him the slightest satisfaction right now, but she couldn't seem to help herself. She was famished.

"Go ahead," he said. "Try a fry."

She reached into the paper bag and took out a french fry.

Newman materialized, nosing his way in with a hungry sniff.

"Get over here, Newman," Granger said. "This is for you. You, too, Kramer."

As Granger dumped a couple of cans of dog food into plastic bowls, Emmaline gobbled down the french fry. And then another. And then two. And then five, all at once.

"They're better with ketchup," Granger informed her, sitting beside her and opening another paper bag. "Here." He passed her several red and white packets.

"Try the Big Mac," he urged.

She was already biting into the burger, and was immediately certain that it was the most delicious thing she had ever tasted.

"I didn't know whether you liked chocolate shakes or vanilla," he said, looking pleased with himself as he watched her indulge, "so I got you one of each."

To Granger's utter delight—and Emmaline's utter shock—she actually drank both shakes.

And in between satisfying slurps through a pair of plastic straws, she ate all the french fries, polished off the entire Big Mac, then worked her way through a cardboard container of something called Chicken McNuggets, which were luscious when dipped into barbecue sauce that came in a small foil-topped packet. For dessert, she had an apple pie out of a paper box, and it was every bit as scrumptious as a slice of the palace chef's apple pie à la mode served on royal china with a platinum fork. Perhaps even more scrumptious.

The more she ate, the better she felt.

And not just physically.

"Thank you for the food," she told Granger, who was sipping the last of his own shake through a straw. "It was kind of you."

"Well, I'm a kind kind of guy."

She smiled. "Where were you, anyway? Besides McDonald's."

"One of those big discount chain stores. There's one over on Broadway. I've never been in a place like that before."

"I haven't, either. What was it like?"

"I'll bring you with me when I go back. They have everything. Cereal, sheets, spatulas, candy bars, televisions . . ."

"Televisions? Did you buy one?"

"No." He shot her a look. "Why?"

She shrugged. "I just thought it might be good to . . . to see if there's been anything on the news about . . ."

"About the runaway princess bride?"

"Exactly."

"And you just wondered about that now?" he asked incredulously.

"I've been distracted," she said. "But I thought it might be on the news—"

"I hate to break it to you, Princess, but you *are* the news. The only news."

"What do you mean?"

"Are you sure you want to know?"

"Of course I want to know!"

She watched nervously as he got to his feet, brushed the crumbs off his wrinkled shorts, and walked over to the heap of shopping bags on the floor. He rummaged through them, pulled something out, and handed it to her.

She gaped at the tabloid newspaper. Beneath the banner, the front page was encompassed by a large photo of Prince Remi, and a single-word headline in enormous bold black type: *JILTED?*

"Oh no," Emmaline murmured.

"Oh yes. If you don't mind my asking . . . what did you expect?"

"I do mind your asking," she retorted.

Conscious of Granger's eyes on her, she flipped to the story on the next page . . . and realized that the coverage didn't end there. The next five pages of the newspaper were filled with articles about her and Remi, her disappearance, and the curtailed wedding. There were file photos of her and her parents, of the castle and the abbey. There were diagrams, too: her family tree, the Buironese line of succession, a map showing Verdunia and Buiron, one showing the route the royal coach had taken from the palace to the abbey for the wedding.

Emmaline flipped back to the first page and scanned the article.

Apparently Papa hadn't leaked word to the press that she had vanished willingly. There had been no official palace statement to that effect. But speculation was rampant, with this particular reporter noting that there was no evidence of a massive police investigation—at least, not what one would expect if a princess had met with foul play.

"Poor Remi," Emmaline said, swallowing hard and gazing at a particularly endearing photo of her former fiancé, wearing a kilt in the Scottish Highlands.

"Yes, poor Remi. That skirt doesn't do a thing for his knees, and the plaid makes him look a bit hippy," Granger said, peering over her shoulder.

Emmaline glared at him. "That wasn't what I meant. And it's a kilt, not a skirt."

To his credit, Granger was immediately contrite. "I'm sorry. I shouldn't be joking about this."

"No, you shouldn't."

"I'm sorry," he said again. "Sometimes I don't know what to say, so I go for the laugh. I guess it's a defense mechanism."

His tone was guileless, but she eyed him suspiciously. He really did appear to be genuine. He reached toward her.

She flinched when he touched her arm, but he left his hand there. To her consternation, the gesture was comforting. It felt right.

She gazed down at the page. Her parents looked up at her, their faces frozen in grainy black and white regal smiles.

"Look, it's going to be okay," Granger said. "They'll forget about you in time."

"Mother and Papa?" she asked, irritated that he could even assume such a thing.

"Of course not. I meant the press. Some new scandal will come along and blow you off the front pages and CNN . . ."

"It's been on television, too?" she asked, dismayed. She jostled his hand off her arm.

"You really do live in a protective bubble, don't you?" He shook his head. "We're talking round-the-clock, wall-to-wall coverage, Princess. At least, as of this morning. I haven't seen a television since we left the penthouse."

"You were watching television this morning? Why didn't you tell me?"

"For one thing, you were sleeping. And for another, I wasn't sure you'd want to see what was going on. You have enough to worry about."

She contemplated that, and tossed the paper aside. "I do, don't I."

He nodded.

She noticed that his hand was on her arm again. His fingers felt warm and reassuring on her bare skin.

Earlier she had been grateful when he left her alone.

Now she was grateful that he was there. She needed him. He was all she had—and the only person on earth who knew her secret.

But for how long?

"What if they find me?" she asked in a small voice.

"The press?"

"Anyone. Everyone. What if they find me?"

"They won't," he promised. "I'll hide you."

"You can't hide me forever."

"Sure I can."

"You don't look very confident," she observed.

"Well, it would be a hell of a lot easier to conceal a fugitive princess if I had money."

"Everything is easier with money," she told him.

"Not everything."

She shrugged. "That's beside the point."

"Not really, Emmaline. Haven't you ever been the least bit curious about what it's like to live like regular people do?"

"Of course I've been curious. That doesn't mean I'm eager to actually go out and do it."

"Well, I am," he said. "Do you know what I bought at that store?"

"Candy bars?" she asked hopefully.

"No." He rattled a plastic shopping bag. "I bought this."

"What is it?"

"You don't know?"

She shook her head.

"Do you care to guess?"

She eyed the mystery object, which was white plastic and consisted of some sort of handle that was stuck inside a circular cylinder with a flat base.

"I have no idea," she concluded.

"Take a guess."

"Please stop playing games."

"You're no fun. It's a toilet brush," he said triumphantly, tugging the handle to remove it from the cylinder, and revealing that one end consisted of rows of bristles.

"A toilet brush?"

"You've never seen one before?"

"Of course I haven't."

"Let me guess. The servants scrubbed the palace toilets and kept the brushes hidden away from your delicate royal eyes."

That was essentially the truth, but she resented his tone. "As if you haven't been surrounded by servants of your own," she retorted.

"You're right. I have been. But not anymore. Now I'm going to clean my own toilet, with this brush and this special cleaner." He held up a plastic bottle, admiring it. "See how the bottle neck is curved? That's so that you can squirt it under the rim of the bowl."

"How positively revolutionary." She yawned and rubbed her aching shoulder blades.

"Are you tired?"

"A bit. Though I shouldn't be, considering how much sleep I got yesterday and last night. It must be a symptom of pregnancy."

"Well, you can use this to find out if it is," Granger said, and rattled his bag again. He handed her an oversized paperback book.

She examined the title. *What to Expect When You're Expecting.* Her lips curved into a smile. "Thank you," she said, looking up at him. "That was sweet of you."

"Yeah, well, you're going to love the other thing I got you."

"What is it?" She looked expectantly at his shopping bags.

"A bed."

"A bed?" she echoed. "Where is it?"

"It's going to be delivered any second now. I called that 800 Dial-a-Mattress number they're always advertising on the radio. I always wondered if it was that simple—one phone call, and a mattress shows up at your door. Apparently it is."

And apparently he had always wondered a lot of things that she had never given a moment's consideration. She stared at him, wondering how he could possibly be so enthusiastic about the mundane details of everyday life. Toilet brushes, and food served in paper wrappings, and box springs . . .

As far as Emmaline was concerned, she would just as soon snap her fingers and magically find herself back in Chimera at the palace, surrounded by luxury and a willing staff of servants whose only mission in life was to cater to her every whim.

Right now she would give anything for a massage, a cup of hot tea with honey and lemon, and a freshly fluffed pile of down pillows.

"When did you say that bed was coming?" she asked, rubbing her aching back.

"Any second now, so be prepared to duck into the bathroom and hide while the delivery men are here. I should warn you, though—it's not exactly a bed."

Uh-oh. "It's not? What is it?"

"Just a mattress and box spring," he said, to her immense relief. A mattress and box spring, she could handle.

"And it's a twin size," he went on. "I didn't want to pay extra for full-sized, considering my limited budget. I figured that would be a waste of space, anyway."

Her thoughts darted back to yesterday morning, when she had slept in his arms. Yes, all that king-sized bed had certainly been a waste of space. Was he picturing that, too? Was he insinuating that they would spend the night intimately intertwined in his newly purchased twin bed?

Somewhere inside her, at the core of her belly, something quivered.

It was too early for the baby to be moving. It must be something else. Some deep-seated, insatiable desire for Granger Lockwood.

She realized he had spoken.

"What was that?" she asked, feeling her cheeks grow warm, thankful that he couldn't read her thoughts.

"I said, you can have the bed, of course. I'll sleep on the floor."

"Oh . . . you don't have to do that." Disappointment coursed through her—yet that was a ludicrous reaction, of course.

How on earth could she be disappointed? What had she expected? Naturally they wouldn't be sharing a bed. He had made it more than clear that he wasn't interested in any kind of relationship with her.

"Don't be ridiculous," he said.

For a moment she was fearful that he had read her mind.

Then he said gallantly, "I wouldn't expect you to sleep on the floor in your condition."

Oh. Her condition. She had almost forgotten about that, so preoccupied was she with the very act that had *caused* the condition.

She glanced down again at the book in her hand.

What to Expect When You're Expecting.

It would undoubtedly address issues like exhaustion, morning sickness, and labor.

If only it could tell her what to expect from Granger Lockwood in the next seven months.

Seven

....

Late the next morning, Emmaline emerged from the bathroom, queasy and shaken.

"Sick again?" Granger asked sympathetically, looking up from the Business section of the morning *Times*.

She nodded and leaned against the kitchen counter to steady herself.

"You should eat something," Granger said, setting aside the paper and coming to stand beside her.

She groaned at the thought of food and wished he would just leave her alone.

"Here, this will help." He opened a cabinet door and took out a box of saltines.

He had stocked up on groceries last night, showing her each of his food purchases with a childlike delight he apparently didn't reserve for toilet brushes alone.

"No thank you," she said, as he offered her a cracker.

"It would settle your stomach," he insisted, waving the cracker under her nose. "Just take a bite."

She opened her mouth to demur and found it full of cracker. "I beg your pardon!"

"If you can't feed yourself, then I will," he said simply.

She chewed and swallowed. "I am quite capable of feeding myself, thank you very much."

"You're very welcome . . . and you may be quite capable, but you aren't doing it. That's my baby in there. I have to make sure he's well nourished."

"How do you know he's a he?" she asked.

He shrugged, offering the package again. "All right, he or *she*."

"*She*."

"Have another cracker."

She wanted to refuse, but found that he was right. The bland starch had instantly eased the nausea. Suddenly she was famished. She helped herself to another saltine. And another.

"Do you really have a sense that the baby is a girl?" Granger asked.

In truth, she had no idea. But still vaguely irritated at Granger's use of the male pronoun to describe the baby, she replied, "Yes. I'm fairly certain she's a girl."

"Huh." He fell silent.

She concentrated on her crackers.

"Emmaline, can I . . . ?"

"Hmm?" Crunching, she glanced up at him and found him staring at her midsection.

She stopped crunching and asked, around a soggy mouthful, "Can you what?"

"Can I . . ." He raised his eyes to hers. "Can I feel the baby?"

Flustered, she said, "I don't know what you . . ."

"I just want to . . ." He reached toward her and rested his large, warm hand over her lower belly.

She was wearing the long-sleeved cotton T-shirt she had slept in, along with a pair of low-riding sweat-pants Granger had bought for her from the discount store. They were two sizes too big, but he insisted that they would fit her in no time. For now, no matter how tightly she pulled the drawstring, the waistband settled in the vicinity of her thighs, well below her navel.

Which meant only a thin layer of cotton T-shirt separated Granger's hand from her bare flesh. She swallowed hard, and nearly choked on the mouthful of cracker.

"Are you all right?" Granger asked as she gasp-coughed. He didn't remove his hand.

And no. She wasn't all right. Not with his fingers sprawled across her belly and his clean, soapy scent enveloping her nostrils.

She nodded anyway. "I'm fine."

"It's amazing," he said quietly. "Isn't it?"

"That I didn't choke on that cracker? Quite," she quipped, desperately needing to lighten the moment.

"No, that a tiny human life is right in there," he said. "Can you feel anything? Can you feel him—I mean her—moving, or kicking?"

"Of course not. She's too small."

"How big does she have to be before she kicks?" He stroked her belly lightly.

"I suppose she has to have legs," she said.

"There are no legs yet?"

"I doubt it."

Emmaline cleared her throat and tried not to look into his eyes. But when she lowered her gaze, she only found herself staring at his lips, and that was even more disconcerting.

Something was fluttering deep within her, and she knew better than to blame it on the baby. What she felt was the stirring of arousal, brought on by Granger's deceptively gentle masculine touch. She wanted to pull away, to break the intimate connection between them.

No—she didn't *want* to. That was the last thing she wanted. But . . . she had to do it.

Somehow, she found the strength to step back. To reach for the box of crackers and shove another one into her mouth, chewing noisily, desperately nonchalant.

"Have you been around many babies?" she asked him, seizing the first conversational topic that entered her mind.

"Never. I've never even seen one close up."

"Don't you have any nieces or nephews?"

A shadow crossed his face. "I'm an only child."

"I see."

"I had a sister, once, but . . ."

"I'm sorry," she said softly when he trailed off, staring at his Gucci loafers.

For a moment, the only sound was the ceaseless dripping of the faucet, and, outside the window, traffic noise and the rhythmic throbbing of a jack-hammer.

Then Granger said, in a voice she had to strain to hear, "Her name was Charlotte. I never even got to see her, but . . . that was her name."

"You never saw her?"

He shook his head. "She died a few moments after she was born. In the boating accident that killed my parents and my uncle when I was five years old."

Emmaline was speechless. Her mind raced. She had a sudden, dim recollection of having read somewhere, long ago, that Granger Lockwood had been orphaned in childhood. Why hadn't the horrible reality of his plight sunk in until now?

Because you've been thinking only of yourself, she scolded. *You haven't been able to get past your own troubles.*

Now it was her turn to lay gentle fingertips on him. She touched his forearm. "How tragic. I'm so sorry for your loss, Granger."

He lifted his head. She half expected to see tears in his eyes, but instead she found a resolute acknowledgment of her sympathy.

"It's all right," he said. "It was a long time ago. And I never speak about it, so . . ." He inhaled deeply, exhaled heavily. "It's just that I sometimes wonder what would have happened if things had worked out differently. If Charlotte had survived."

Emmaline imagined life without her sisters, and it was all she could do not to shudder. Genevieve and Josephine were the only two people in the world who understood what it meant to be the royal offspring of the king and queen of Verdunia. There was a certain comfort in sharing the burden and the privilege.

But Granger had shouldered his burden alone.

"You're very lucky to have had a family who loves you," he told Emmaline. "To have parents and sisters who are there for you when you need them."

She nodded, compelled to point out, "And you've had your grandfather. Surely he cares deeply about you."

"My grandfather cares deeply about Lockwood Enterprises."

"And my father cares deeply about the future of his kingdom, but—"

"It's not the same thing," Granger cut in. "My grandfather merely sees me as an heir."

Emmaline's mouth clamped shut as she thought about her father. Papa loved her—she knew that. Yet he was willing to have her enter an arranged marriage for the sake of the kingdom.

What would happen to Verdunia now, if she didn't marry Remi and secure an alliance with Buiron?

Emmaline tried to summon a sense of royal duty—tried to tell herself that perhaps the best thing for her to do would be to return to Verdunia and go through with her marriage.

But that wouldn't make the baby go away.

And it wouldn't make Granger Lockwood go away.

Until a few moments ago, when he had touched her stomach and she had glimpsed the raw emotion in his eyes, she might have been able to convince herself that he would be relieved if she went back to Verdunia, baby and all.

Now she wasn't so sure.

"Do you know what would do us both some good?" Granger's voice interrupted her thoughts.

"What?"

"Soup."

"*Soup?*"

He nodded. "I'm hungry, too. I'll make us some soup. Homemade—not the canned kind. Homemade will be better for the baby."

"Do you have a recipe?" she asked dubiously.

"No, but how difficult can it be? Go ahead and relax and read the paper and I'll whip up a pot of something healthy."

"I'll help."

"You can rest."

"I'll help," she insisted.

"Have you ever cooked anything before?"

"Have *you*?"

"The omelets I made for breakfast the other day."

Precisely. "I'll help," she said for the third time, and rolled up her sleeves.

Soup.

Of course they could make soup.

As Granger put it, how difficult could it be?

Hearing Prince Remi's footsteps in the corridor outside his private sitting room, Princess Josephine checked her reflection in the window one last time.

Yes, she looked ravishing indeed. Her dark curls were caught in a sedate bun suitable for a concerned sister who presumably had no idea that Emmaline was shacking up in New York with an American bon vivant. She wore a rather somber navy suit but it was well cut enough to show off her curves, and she had recently ordered her seamstress to shorten the skirt several inches to reveal more of her long, toned legs.

"Dear Josephine," Remi said, stepping into the room. "This is a pleasant surprise."

"I thought perhaps you might need a confidante at a time like this," she told him, offering her cheek for his kiss. As his lips grazed a spot that was a good two inches from hers, she fought the urge to turn her head just enough to capture his mouth with her own. She couldn't. At least, not yet.

"Yes, I do need a confidante," he said, stepping back from her with what she sensed was reluctance— a very good sign indeed.

"Are you pining away for Emmaline, then?" she asked, crossing her fingers in the folds of her skirt.

"Of course."

It was a lie. How could she tell him that she knew it was a lie? He didn't want to marry Emmaline any more than Emmaline wanted to marry him.

"Papa told you that Emmaline left a note?" Josephine asked, just to be sure.

After all, she couldn't allow herself to fall for the kind of man who would be glad to be rid of his bride under any circumstances. If, for example, Remi believed that Emmaline might have been kidnapped by foreign nationals, she would expect him to at least show genuine distress.

"Yes, he told me that she left of her own accord."

Josephine breathed a silent sigh of relief. So the man had integrity, just as she'd suspected.

Yet he had the grace not to show a bit of anger—and he had every right to be royally peeved at what Emmaline had done.

Josephine's admiration for him blossomed into full-blown infatuation.

"Please don't take it personally, Remi," Josephine said, laying her French-manicured nails on his silk sleeve. "Any woman in her right mind would be eager to marry you."

"Do you really believe that?" Remi asked, gazing into her eyes.

"Of course. You're handsome, and cultured, and brilliant—you're one of the most eligible men in Europe, for goodness' sake. You will have no trouble finding a willing bride now that Emmaline has dumped—I mean left you."

He sighed. "It's not a willing bride I'm trying to find, Josephine. It's Emmaline. Your father has instructed me to do everything in my power to bring her home."

"Does Papa really expect the two of you to go through with the wedding?"

He averted his eyes. "For the good of both countries, we must."

Josephine considered that. What if she told Remi, right now, where Emmaline was?

You gave your word that you wouldn't tell, she reminded herself.

Yes, and Emmaline gave hers that she was coming home—well, not her word, exactly. But she said she'd be back, and she hadn't shown up. Apparently she couldn't seem to tear herself away from her divine American lover.

If you told Remi—

But you can't. You promised.

Josephine sighed. "It's noble of you, Remi. If you do find my sister, I only hope that the two of you will be very happy together."

He said nothing.

Josephine said, "Well, I suppose I should go."

"Don't go!"

Startled, she looked up to see Remi doing his best to conceal blatant longing. Hope fluttered.

"Perhaps you can help me," he said, composing himself instantly.

"Help you?"

"Help me search for your sister. Who would know

better where she might be than you would, as her sister?"

"I should think you would, as her fiancé," she couldn't resist saying slyly. "But I'll be glad to help you, Remi. Where shall we start?"

"I thought perhaps she could be in Ameri—"

"I was thinking New Zealand," Josephine cut in. "Emmaline has always been fascinated by . . . by sheep."

"Sheep?"

"Yes, she simply adores wool."

Prince Remi shrugged. "As I said, you know her best. Why don't we talk over dinner? Are you hungry?"

"Oh yes, I have a voracious appetite."

For you, my dear Remi. Only for you. And perhaps, someday, you'll be able to sate it.

And he had thought *he* was a slob.

Granger had never seen anything quite like Princess Emmaline in action in the kitchen. She had been hesitant to dirty her hands at first, but once she became caught up in the spirit of culinary creativity, she was a whirlwind of creative inefficiency. It was obvious that she had never before chopped, minced, diced, or even stirred.

Now, as he gazed from the olive oil slick on the stove to the scattered grains of rice on the countertop to the chunks of minced onion littering the floor, he shook his head.

For all her prim and proper persnickety attitude,

when push came to shove, the woman simply had no concept of how to clean up after herself.

Granger, too, had been raised with all the comforts of supreme wealth—and yes, he'd had a full-time housekeeper all his adult life—but even *he* wouldn't recklessly drip water from the tap to the soup pot, as she had repeatedly done, without grabbing a sponge to mop it up.

He watched Emmaline lift the lid from the bubbling concoction and reach for a spoon to stir it.

"Maybe I should add more water," she mused. "It seems a bit thick."

"No! I like it thick," he assured her, wiping up a puddle in front of the sink.

"It smells delicious, doesn't it?" she asked, inhaling the savory vapor, heedless of the spatters the boiling kettle was emitting.

He nodded, rubbing his shoulders. He was sore from hauling around luggage and shopping bags and groceries—not to mention from sleeping on the floor all night.

"It does smell good," he agreed. "I never would have thought to put whole tomatoes into it. That was an inspired idea."

"My chef makes tomato-based soup quite often," she said, replacing the lid with a clatter. She stretched up on her tiptoes, her T-shirt riding up to reveal a barely swollen midsection.

He watched, fascinated, his mind conjuring the image of what she would look like a few months from now, her belly protruding with his child. Never before had he found the idea of a pregnant woman the least bit erotic, but now, with Emmaline . . .

"Down, boy! Down!"

Startled, he assumed that she had read his thoughts, until he looked up and saw her shooing Kramer away from the stove.

"I think he's hungry," she told Granger, taking a wary step back from the panting dog.

"He's always hungry. He probably needs to go out for a walk. It's been a while. Come here, boy."

Kramer stayed put, looking up at Emmaline and wagging his tail hopefully.

"I think he likes you," Granger said, amused by the smitten expression on Kramer's face. "You should pet him. That's what he wants. That's the only way he'll leave you alone."

Emmaline reached out a tentative hand and gave the dog a perfunctory pat on the back of the neck. "Nice dog," she said guardedly.

Kramer stood on his back feet, rested his massive paws on Emmaline's shoulders, and licked her face.

She cried out in dismay, nearly falling in her haste to extract herself from the ardent canine embrace.

"Kramer! Come here, boy!" Granger hurried over to collar the dog, who barked in protest.

"I'm sorry," Emmaline said, "but I'm just not used to . . ."

"To being kissed by frisky dogs?" Granger grinned. "I guess frogs are more up your alley, huh?"

"Pardon?" She had seized a dish towel and was furiously wiping Kramer's saliva from her face.

"You know . . . princesses . . . kissing frogs . . . Forget it," he said, noting that she was hardly in the mood for lighthearted quips. She had turned on the hot water and was reaching for the soap.

"Listen," he said, "I'll take Kramer and Newman out for a nice long walk while you get everything cleaned up. I have a feeling it's going to take a while."

"You're right. I should probably just take a hot shower," she said, furiously scrubbing her cheek with soap.

"I meant the kitchen," he said, gesturing around them. "The mess."

She froze. "You want me to clean this up?"

From her tone, one would think he had asked her to lick the decade-old grease spatters from the range hood.

Granger bristled. "Well, since you can't take the dogs out for their walk, I figured you could—"

"But I wouldn't know where to start."

"The sink would be a good place," he said dryly, gazing at the heap of dirty dishes and utensils there. She had practically emptied the cabinets and drawers in her frenzy of creative cooking.

"You want me to do *dishes*?" she asked.

He nodded. "It'll be fun. You'll see."

"But I've never—"

"There's a first time for everything," Granger said

cheerfully, grabbing Kramer's leash. "You'll figure it out."

Whistling, he left the apartment.

As he took the dogs for a good, long walk around the neighborhood, he fought back twinges of guilt. But he told himself that this experience would be good for Emmaline. After all, she might have royal blood, but she had left the palace behind for good—willingly, he might add.

Then again, she must have assumed she would be joining him in the lap of luxury here in New York. She hadn't bargained on his sudden unemployment, much less on sharing household chores.

Oh well. She was stuck now. They both were. And the sooner they grew accustomed to the mundane reality of being "regular" folks, the better equipped they would be when their baby arrived.

Hmm. Try as he might, Granger couldn't imagine Emmaline cradling an infant, with a stained burp cloth over her shoulder.

In Verdunia, royal babies were undoubtedly kept in elaborate nurseries and tended by professional nannies around the clock. Parenting was virtually the same in the Lockwood social circle. Men like Granger wouldn't dream of spooning strained pears into a tiny mouth, or—God forbid—handling soiled diapers.

Naturally, he experienced a sufficient amount of distaste when he considered the notion—yet he also felt a quiver of anticipation.

Newman tugged his leash. Kramer followed suit.

Granger looked down at the dogs. "What's the matter, boys? You want to go back? You miss her already, huh?"

Kramer yapped.

"Yeah, me too," Granger said. "Come on. Let's go home."

When Emmaline heard him coming up the stairs, it was all she could do not to scurry back into the bathroom and bolt the door behind her.

But eventually she would have to come out. She might as well face Granger now, head-on.

She lifted her chin defiantly as his keys jangled in the lock.

She hoped that he wouldn't be able to see that she'd been crying. The last thing she wanted was for him to feel sorry for her—even if that was one way to avoid doing the wretched housework.

Whistling, he stepped over the threshold with the dogs.

Newman and Kramer spotted her and promptly trotted over, tails wagging, fat pink tongues hanging out.

"They missed you," Granger said.

She glanced down at the dogs. They clearly wanted her to pet them, but she wasn't feeling the least bit affectionate at the moment—not for the dogs, and most certainly not for their handsome master.

"How did you do with the . . ." Granger's voice faded.

She followed his gaze to the sink still heaped with dirty dishes and the cluttered countertops, to the spatters and spills and crumbs.

"Oh," he said flatly. "You didn't do the dishes."

"No, I certainly didn't do the dishes."

"Who's going to do them?"

"You are," she informed him.

He shot her a flinty glare.

She returned it.

"And why am I going to do the dishes?" he asked.

"Because I refuse to be told what to do like some barefoot, pregnant housewife."

He gazed pointedly at her midsection, and then at her bare feet.

She gasped. "You are a shameless chauvinist who seems to think women should do the dirty work!"

"And you are a spoiled, pampered princess who expects to be waited on hand and foot!"

"How dare you?" Her voice quavered.

Oh no. The last thing she wanted was to cry in front of him—especially now.

He peered into her face.

She turned away. Her lip was shaking. She bit down hard to hide the weakness from him, and tasted blood in her mouth.

"Hey, look, it's okay," Granger said, his tone softening. "I know that you're not feeling well—"

"I'm feeling *fine*," she said through clenched teeth.

"No, you aren't. And you've been through a lot these last few days," he said, leaning around as if to glimpse her expression.

She turned her back abruptly, unwilling to allow him to see the tears that had sprung to her eyes.

She didn't want his kindness or his pity. She didn't want anything from him.

After a moment he went to the kitchen and turned on the water at the sink, clattering pots and pans.

Emmaline went into the bathroom, locked the door, and cried her heart out.

Eight

·····················

 Nearly a week, several quarts of home-made soup, five Big Macs, many tears, and countless bouts of nausea later, Emmaline was lying on the twin bed listlessly watching the rain spatter against the windowpane. The dogs napped on the floor nearby.

There was, quite simply, nothing else to do. She had read her *What to Expect When You're Expecting* book cover to cover.

Twice.

Now that she knew what to expect—at least physically—she found herself torn between wishing the next seven months would fly by, and hoping to postpone labor and delivery indefinitely.

Try as she might, she couldn't imagine herself as an active participant in the childbirth experience.

And she certainly couldn't imagine Granger at

her side as her coach. A delivery room was probably the last place he'd ever want to be.

Not that she would want him there.

No, she would be much better off with Tabitha at her side when the time came. Better off, and less inhibited. She wouldn't want Granger to witness such an intimate, emotional, raw experience.

Then again, he had not only witnessed, but initiated, the intimate, emotional, raw experience that had gotten her here in the first place.   •

A rustling, scampering sound somewhere nearby startled her. Newman lifted his head and growled. She shuddered.

She had yet to actually see a mouse, but she was convinced that they were living in the walls. So were the dogs, judging by the way they sometimes paced and barked as though stalking invisible rodents.

Back in June, before Granger Lockwood turned her life upside down, Emmaline could never have imagined coming into contact with an actual mouse.

Now, every time she left the bed, she made her way gingerly across the floor, on the lookout for mice . . . or worse.

She sighed and glanced again at the rain-spattered windowpane.

Never in her entire life had she been so utterly lonely . . . or utterly bored.

Granger was out.

Again.

He had been gone yesterday from dawn until dusk. The day before that, too. And the—

Startled by a sudden knock on the door, Emmaline sat upright so quickly that she felt dizzy.

Newman and Kramer lifted their heads with a jingling of metal tags, then went back to dozing.

Granger must have forgotten his keys, she decided, padding over to the door in her bare feet. It had to be Granger—anybody else would have to be buzzed in.

Apparently, even the most decrepit buildings in Manhattan's most questionable neighborhoods had such security features. Though Emmaline, accustomed to elaborate palace surveillance and round-the-clock bodyguards, was hardly reassured by a couple of good-natured dogs, an antiquated buzzer system, and a dead bolt topped by a flimsy chain.

Not that she had spent much time, these last few days, worrying about unsavory characters who might be lurking in this less-than-desirable neighborhood, ready to pounce on women who were home alone. Nor did the prospect cross her mind now . . .

Not until she considered, as she unlocked the door, that it was awfully early for Granger to be home. He had told her not to expect him until this evening.

As she opened the door, it occurred to her that perhaps she shouldn't do so. But it was too late to stop.

She was already face-to-face with a stranger standing in the dingy hall.

"Excuse me . . . sir?"

Waiting on the corner for a traffic light to change,

Granger looked out from beneath his black umbrella to see a bedraggled, shabbily dressed woman standing nearby, huddled beneath the awning of an office building in the dismal drizzle, a baby in her arms.

"Yes?" he asked, wondering how old the child was. Two months old? Ten months old? A year? And was it a boy or a girl?

He had no idea. He had never even looked closely at a baby before. Now, gazing at the tiny, fuzz-covered head and gummy, drooling mouth, he found himself fascinated. Suddenly he understood why people made a huge fuss over babies . . . and he comprehended that he would most likely fall instantly in love with his own when he or she arrived.

"Can you spare some change?" the baby's mother asked.

He turned his attention to her, noting the forlorn, haunted expression in her gaunt face. He felt a pang of helplessness.

"Please," the woman said. "I need to buy milk for my baby."

And Granger needed to buy milk for *his* baby.

Okay, not right this minute.

But he would. He would need to buy milk, and food, and diapers, and tiny clothes, and blankets to keep it warm. He would need to buy a crib, and then preschool tuition, and braces, and a car, and a college education.

"Please, sir?"

"Of course." He fumbled in his pocket—which

A Thoroughly Modern Princess   207

currently held all the money he had in the world.

He handed the woman all the change he could find.

"Thank you," she said with a grateful, gap-toothed smile.

The baby gurgled.

Granger looked at the child, and was rewarded with a bright-eyed grin underscored by a trickle of drool.

His heart went liquid. He grinned back and reached into his pocket again.

"Here," he said, stuffing a couple of twenty-dollar bills—and then the polished wooden handle of his Brooks Brothers umbrella—into the woman's hand. "Take this, too."

Holding the umbrella aloft above her head and the baby's, she gazed down at the money, and then back at Granger with tears in her eyes.

"God bless you, sir," she said gratefully.

He already has, Granger thought as the light changed and he cast one last glance at the cooing infant before stepping off the curb and into a puddle.

Mindless of the gutter water soaking into his Gucci loafers, Granger Lockwood contemplated the fact that he had been blessed all his life with everything a man could want—and he had abandoned all of it, just when he needed it most.

No, he didn't need it.

But Emmaline did.

And his child would.

That was why he was doing this. *This* being an exhausting trek from one corporate office to another, day after day, calling on business connections from his former life. With his education and background, he could build a successful real estate development company of his own. All he needed was financial backing.

He hadn't thought it would be so elusive. Either his grandfather had gotten to his potential contacts before he had, or the falling stock market had scared everyone into holding on to his money.

You could go back to Grandfather, Granger reminded himself, gazing longingly at a shiny black stretch limousine heading down the avenue.

He *could* . . .

But he wouldn't.

Not yet.

That would be taking the easy way out. And it was time Granger stopped doing that. It was time he became the kind of man who was capable of taking care of himself—and somebody else.

The kind of man a child would be proud to have as a father.

The kind of man a woman like Emmaline would be proud to have as . . .

As what?

Surely not as a husband.

The princess had made it clear that she had no intention of staying with him any longer than was absolutely necessary. She wanted no part of his world, uptown or downtown, wealthy or destitute. Now that he had successfully rescued her and spirited her out of Verdunia, she wanted no part of him.

Well, that wasn't entirely true, he amended.

She seemed to want a certain—*ahem*—part of him, on occasion. But Granger was far too jaded to mistake lust—Emmaline's or his own—for anything more substantial.

No, they weren't destined to fall in love . . . not with anyone other than their baby.

The stranger was a woman, fully made-up and perfumed, clad from her shoulder-grazing elegant blond pageboy to her cherry red toenails in Prada, with platinum and diamond accessories.

Emmaline was instantly conscious of her own appearance.

She had showered and washed her hair that morning, but had been forced to use the generic brand shampoo/conditioner blend and plain white bar soap Granger had purchased at a nearby drugstore. She'd towel-dried her hair, which now fell past her shoulders in unkempt waves, untamed by pins or gel or spray.

She was wearing one of Granger's T-shirts, emblazoned with the word "FDNY," along with a pair of baggy sweat pants he had bought for her at Kmart after she'd complained that her own waistband felt snug. Besides, she'd brought only two changes of clothing with her when she'd fled Verdunia—and she'd already gone through both of them.

Her bare feet were desperately in need of a pedicure, and she had broken four fingernails trying to open the window the other day, before Granger got back from the hardware store with a crowbar.

"I'm sorry," the strange woman said. "I should have buzzed, but a Fed Ex guy was just coming out downstairs and he let me in. Anyway, I must have the wrong apartment. I was looking for . . ."

She trailed off, staring at Emmaline, who grew increasingly self-conscious. She wondered if she had streaks of dirt on her face. She had crawled under the kitchen sink a little while ago to see if she could tighten something and stop the incessant dripping. Having no idea what to look for, and no wrench to use even if she did find a relevant pipe or bolt or handle, she had crawled out and resigned herself once again to the steady *plop . . . plop . . . plop . . .*

"This might sound crazy," the woman said, still staring at Emmaline, "but are you . . . ? Nah. Never mind."

Emmaline forced a polite smile while frantically rubbing her cheeks, hopefully removing any smudges. What she wouldn't give to be in this woman's pricey leather sandals, looking as if she had just been lunching at Le Cirque and shopping on Fifth Avenue rather than . . . well, barefoot and pregnant.

"Anyway," the woman said, casting a discriminating glance around the dismal studio, "I was looking for Granger Lockwood, but this can't be—Newman?

Kramer? Oh my God!" The woman clasped a hand to her crimson lipstick, clearly startled that the canine companions of the esteemed Mr. Lockwood could possibly be found in such surroundings.

Newman and Kramer had at last roused themselves from their naps and trotted over to greet the visitor. Clearly, the three were already acquainted. The woman deftly blocked Newman's nose before it could make contact with her crotch, as though she was accustomed to his indecent overtures.

"I realize the place is quite a shambles," Emmaline said apologetically, "but we're working on clean . . ." She trailed off abruptly, struck by the expression of recognition on her visitor's face. This time it wasn't leveled at the dogs, but at Emmaline herself.

Oh no.

Please no.

How could she have forgotten?

Emmaline had been so certain she would find Granger on the other side of the door—and so subsequently distracted by the realization that she didn't measure up to this woman's polished appearance—that she had neglected to recall a key fact: she was supposed to be incognito.

Now here she was, sans wig, sunglasses, and feigned American accent, utterly helpless beneath her visitor's alarmingly discerning gaze.

"You're her," the woman announced in astonishment.

"I beg your pardon?" Emmaline made a feeble attempt at sounding like a New Yorker.

The woman's delicately sculpted face broke into a broad grin. "Leave it to Granger," she said, shaking her head.

She swept over the threshold, bringing with her a cloud of sultry perfume. She brushed past Emmaline and closed the door with a decided click. "The whole world is looking for you, and here you are, with him, in the last place anybody would ever expect to find either of you."

Deny it.

Deny everything.

"I . . . I'm afraid I don't know what you're talking about," Emmaline said in her best New York accent.

"Don't worry, Your Highness. I won't tell a soul."

Keep denying.

"I—I don't know what you're—"

"Of course you know what I'm talking about," the woman said, her blue eyes seeming to take in every detail of the apartment. "You're Princess Emmaline of Verdunia, and you're hiding out here on Eldridge Street, of all places, with good old Granger, of all people. Wait till I get my hands on him. Where did you say he is?"

"He's out," Emmaline said shortly. "And who did you say you were?"

"I didn't, but since we've already established who *you* are, allow me to introduce myself. I'm Brynn Halloway."

"Are you Granger's . . . ?" She wasn't quite sure how to phrase it. "Girlfriend" seemed too juvenile, "lover" too awkward, "paramour" too quaint.

"Don't worry, Your Highness, I'm just his good friend," Brynn said, clearly amused. "A good friend who assumed she knew everything about Mr. Granger Lockwood, but apparently he's been holding out on me. Maybe he's mentioned me?"

Emmaline shook her head, feeling as though she should apologize.

But Brynn shrugged, her self-esteem clearly intact. She said flippantly, "I'm sure he was getting around to it. Granger and I have always told our significant others about each other, lest there be the slightest bit of misplaced jealousy."

"But I'm not Granger's significant other," Emmaline protested. And she certainly wasn't jealous.

All right, she *was* jealous . . . but only of Brynn's appearance—and, yes, her access to the outside world with its salons, and restaurants, and stores . . .

"Granger and I grew up together," Brynn said. "We were like siblings. He only had his grandfather, and I only had my father—who is even older than Granger's grandfather, by the way."

Emmaline didn't know quite what to say to that.

"Daddy's senile now, poor thing. When I visit him in the home, he thinks I'm my mother. He tells me to get the hell out."

"That's terrible." Emmaline squirmed and wished that Brynn would stop sharing.

"Not really. She was a loser. A Vegas showgirl who slapped him with a paternity suit when she got pregnant with me. Daddy got a little girl to raise, lucky him, and she got a million bucks. We never heard from her again."

"I'm sorry . . ."

"Trust me, it's a blessing. From what I hear, she was a real piece of work."

Apparently the apple didn't fall far from the tree, Emmaline thought, watching Brynn walk to the window.

She looked out on the street, gasped, and made a face. "That's a man!"

"Pardon?"

"That pile of rags on the curb is a man. I didn't realize it when I stepped over him as I got out of the cab. Lovely neighborhood."

"Isn't it?" Despite herself, Emmaline almost welcomed this woman's breezy eccentricities.

It had been so long since she had spoken to anyone but Granger.

Brynn turned away from the window, shaking her head, and said, "First I drop by Granger's office, only to be told that he's no longer employed at Lockwood Enterprises. Then I pop up to the penthouse, only to discover that he's moved out and left this unlikely forwarding address with Antonia. *Now* I find that he's harboring a missing princess."

Emmaline was at a loss for words once again.

Which didn't matter, because Brynn had plenty to say.

"You know, Granger mentioned you a few times, but I had no idea that the two of you were involved."

"He mentioned me?" Emmaline felt like a schoolgirl with a crush. "What did he say?"

"He said that he felt sorry for you, because you were trapped in your golden coop—"

"I believe his phrase was 'gilded cage,'" Emmaline interrupted stiffly.

"That's right, trapped in your gilded cage, and saddled with an arranged marriage to that stuffy prince of Buiron. Personally, I thought the wedding plans had come together rather nicely. Porfirio is divine—he's doing a little something for me, for a Christmas ball—and the flowers were fabulous."

"How do you know that?"

"I've seen the television coverage," Brynn told her with a shrug, "and I have to say, I personally thought you might have been abducted by terrorists. I'm glad you're alive and well, but that was a hell of a way to break an engagement, Your Highness."

Emmaline swallowed hard over the sudden lump in her throat.

"Oh my goodness, don't cry!" Brynn said, looking dismayed. "I didn't mean to be so . . . Look, if Granger had told you a damn thing about me, you'd know that I have a tendency to say the first thing that pops into my head. Granger is always telling me that I should think before I speak. And I guess he's right. I didn't mean to make you cry. Please don't cry. Oh no. You're crying. Here—have a Kleenex."

Brynn snapped open her smart black Prada handbag and handed over a neatly folded tissue.

Emmaline wiped her eyes—then noticed that the

tissue was stained with several scarlet kiss marks.

"Oh no, I'm sorry—" Brynn reached into her handbag again and produced another tissue. "Take this one. You have lipstick . . . Here, let me help you." She put one hand on Emmaline's shoulder and dabbed gently at her face with the other. "There. The lipstick is gone, and so are the tears. I feel absolutely terrible."

So do I, Emmaline thought. She had never felt more miserable in her life.

But she managed a brave "It's all right," even as a fresh flood of tears burst forth.

"Oh, listen, it really is going to be okay," Brynn said, putting a comforting arm around her and patting her shoulder. The dogs huddled almost protectively at Emmaline's feet. "Granger is such a wonderful guy. You made the right decision. He'll take care of you . . . although I have to say, this isn't an impressive start. What are the two of you doing here? I mean, there must be other places you could hide. Like a suite at the Pierre. Or, say, Bora Bora. I know a wonderful resort in—"

"But this is all Granger could afford," Emmaline cut in, sniffling.

"Of course it isn't. He's filthy rich. Richer than I am. Richer than most people in New York. The Lockwoods are worth billions."

"Well, Granger isn't. Not anymore."

"What do you mean?"

Emmaline filled her in quickly—leaving out the

pregnancy, of course. When she finished, Brynn's mouth was hanging open.

"Let me get this straight," she said. "Granger has decided to live as a pauper?"

"Precisely."

"And he has inflicted this lifestyle on you?"

"I wouldn't say *inflicted*, exactly," Emmaline said with a twinge of guilt. After all, Granger hadn't exactly invited her into his newly shoddy world. She had more or less barged into it with little warning and an enormous bombshell.

"And where is Granger now?" Brynn asked. "Panhandling on some street corner? Plundering Dumpsters, searching for stray crusts of bread?"

"He's out. I presume he's looking for a job."

Brynn's professionally arched eyebrows disappeared beneath her fashionable fringe of frosted bangs. "A job? Where? At the sanitation department? Or a toxic waste dump?" Brynn shook her head in palpable dismay. "This can't be happening."

"I'm afraid it is. Granger is adamant about making a living on his own."

"But what is he trying to prove?"

"That he can survive without his grandfather and the family fortune, I suppose," Emmaline told Brynn.

And there was still some part of her that truly admired his noble goal and his tenacity. But the rest of Emmaline—the tired, uncomfortable, worried, pregnant part of her—wished he would hurry and come to his senses.

After all, she might have fantasized about giving up her royal lifestyle now and then. And yes, she had now done just that. But only because she'd had no choice.

At this point, she'd sampled quite enough of the commoner's environment to last her a lifetime, thank you very much.

Given the option, she would be back at the palace before you could snap your fingers and say "Dom Perignon."

Not that champagne—imported or otherwise— was any more an option, in her current state, than her being whisked back to her posh life in Verdunia.

"You know, I'm not certain Granger can survive on his own," Brynn said dubiously. "Much less support a princess. I can't help feeling less than confident about his prospects."

And she doesn't even know about the baby.

Nor does she know that Granger and I aren't a . . . a couple.

Emmaline protested, "But he doesn't have to support me. I'm only staying here temporarily. Just until things die down a bit and I can venture out on my own."

"In that case, I'm afraid you're in for quite an extended wait," Brynn told her. "It looks like you'll have to depend on Granger. And me."

And her?

"I don't think . . ." Emmaline began feebly.

"Don't worry about a thing, Your Highness,"

Brynn said breezily. "You're in good hands now that I've come along."

The phone rang shrilly, shattering the silent hotel room and Debi Hanson's dream, in which she was the new anchor of *The Today Show*.

She cursed and opened her eyes reluctantly, dissolving the enticing image of herself, flanked by Matt Lauer and Al Roker, greeting the cheering crowd in Rockefeller Plaza—most of whom were carrying posters that read "We love you, Debi."

Damn. It wasn't real. She wasn't in Rockefeller Plaza; she was in the Traviata Hotel in Verdunia. Damn, damn, damn.

Reaching for the phone, she saw the illuminated digital clock. It was three in the morning here—and early evening back in the States. Still, nobody at the network would bother her at this hour unless something important had come up.

Snatching up the receiver, she propped herself up in bed and croaked, "Hello?"

"Debi, it's Jack." Her boss didn't bother to apologize for waking her, and she didn't expect him to. Jack was all business, all the time, never the least bit prone to engaging in small talk—or anything else— with Debi.

Lord knew she had tried.

Not the small talk. The something else. After all, her boss possessed the rugged Harrison Ford good looks, and as an added bonus, he had the power to launch her into superstardom.

But apparently superstardom would only come to Debi Hanson the hard way. When Jack had failed to find her irresistible, she ultimately concluded that he was either secretly gay or the one high-powered news executive she had met who was actually faithful to his wife.

"Listen, something's come up," he said tersely.

A bawdy and utterly inappropriate comeback crossed her mind, but she pushed it away, leaning lazily against the pillows again and asking only, "Really? What's come up, Jack?"

"How quickly can you get from your hotel in Chimera to the palace in Buiron?"

Her heart skipped a beat and she sat up again, clutching the phone hard against her ear. "An hour or two. Why?"

As he told her, Debi Hanson realized that she would never again need to consider sleeping her way to success. She would never again have to worry about being eclipsed by Naomi Finkelmeyer.

She had just been handed an assignment that was guaranteed to launch her straight to the top.

Granger plodded up the fourth flight of steps, his stomach grumbling loudly. He hadn't eaten since the bagel he'd grabbed from a pushcart for breakfast, and that was—what? Fifteen hours ago?

Sixteen, he realized as he fumbled in his suit pocket for his keys. Make that *key*.

Now that he no longer had access to various Lock-

wood dwellings, offices, automobiles, and bank deposit boxes, he was no longer required to carry
enough keys to give a hotel chambermaid a run for
her money.

Yesterday he had felt exhilarated at having light-
ened his load.

Today, the thrill had worn off. Now he couldn't
help wishing that he had just stepped off an express elevator and was about to unlock the door to
his opulent penthouse. What he wouldn't give to
find a hot meal waiting in the oven, courtesy of Antonia.

Instead he clutched a pizza box under one arm,
certain the contents had grown lukewarm and the
congealed cheese melded to the cardboard during
the subway ride back downtown and the ten-block
walk from the station to Eldridge Street.

He couldn't help acknowledging that he'd have
been home an hour earlier if he'd had Jimmy and the
limo at his disposal. But then, if he had Jimmy and
the limo at his disposal, he wouldn't have spent the
entire day—and much of the evening—splashing
along the rain-soaked midtown pavement in his futile search for financial backing.

He couldn't help feeling guilty, as he unlocked the
battered, paint-chipped metal door leading to the
crummy studio apartment, where he would undoubtedly discover a moping, bored Emmaline. The
mother of his child—princess or not—deserved far
better than—

"What the hell?" Granger stopped short in the doorway, gaping in disbelief.

He backed up a step and checked the door.

5D.

This was the right place . . .

But somehow, the hovel he'd left this morning had been miraculously transformed in his absence.

It was still small, yes. But now it appeared charmingly cozy, bathed in soft light and smelling like roses.

It must be the potpourri, he thought, seeing a bowl of it on the table beside the door.

Table? Where had the table come from?

There was more.

Much, much more.

There were draperies. Lamps. Rugs.

The dingy walls were obscured behind framed artwork—and not reproductions, according to his practiced eye.

There was furniture, too. The twin bed had been replaced by a queen-sized one swathed in luxurious piles of pillows and a puffy down comforter whose duvet matched the curtains and the upholstery that covered a sofa and a couple of easy chairs.

There were tables, and mirrors, and an armoire.

There was a television set with a built-in DVD player and a computer and a stereo that played classical music at a low volume.

There were Newman and Kramer, napping side by side on dog beds he had seen in the latest Orvis catalogue.

And there was Emmaline . . .

Looking, once again, like the regal princess she was.

She was standing on the far end of the room, watching him.

Gone was the gloriously tousled hair he'd fought to keep from touching as he watched her finger-comb it that morning.

Gone were the sweatpants that had ridden too low on her narrow hips, revealing a tantalizing glimpse of barely swollen belly.

Gone was the vulnerable, uncertain, homesick girl he had left sixteen hours earlier.

She, like the shabby surroundings, had been replaced by something far more elegant.

Granger might not miss the scent of stale cigarette smoke and sour milk that had still pervaded the apartment that morning, but he found himself longing for the casual Emmaline as the new—or rather, the former—aristocratic Emmaline regarded him through a fringe of lashes that had been lavished with black mascara.

"Well? What do you think, Granger?"

Granger.

He would never tire of hearing her say that.

In fact, he was so struck, at first, by the sound of his name on her lips, that he didn't respond to her question. He found himself recalling the throaty, breathless way she had uttered his name in the throes of passion, that day in his bed uptown.

Oh, Granger . . .

What he wouldn't give to hear her say it again, in just that way.

But that wasn't going to happen.

He had promised himself that it wasn't going to happen again. He had to focus every ounce of energy on piecing together a new life for himself and securing a future for his child.

Their child.

"What do you think?" she repeated.

He looked around, shaking his head. "I don't know what to think. What happened? How did you do this?"

"I didn't."

"Who did? Your fairy godmother?"

"You could say that."

Emmaline nodded, a faint smile curving her lips—which were precisely the shade of a plump, luscious August tomato.

Granger noted, somewhere in the back of his mind, that she usually didn't wear such red lipstick even when she did have on makeup.

Hmm.

Red lipstick.

He knew somebody who considered red lipstick her trademark—that, and a certain spicy perfume that he could swear he smelled wafting in the air along with the rose-petal potpourri.

"You have a fairy godmother?" he asked Emmaline. "Would her name, by any chance, be Brynn Halloway?"

Emmaline's jaw dropped. "How did you . . . ?"

"Lucky guess," he said brusquely, plunking the pizza box down on the nearest table.

"Wait, is that hot?" Emmaline rushed toward it.

"It was an hour ago."

"Careful—the table is an antique. The heat will ruin the finish." She picked up the box and carried it over to the counter in the kitchenette.

He saw that nothing in that corner of the room had changed much.

"What is this? No Thermador six-burner range?" he asked sardonically, following Emmaline.

"Viking, only four burners. And it won't be delivered until next week," she said, opening the pizza box and peering inside. "Do you mind if I have a slice? I'm famished."

"Didn't your fairy godmother feed you?"

"She brought in sushi, but that was hours ago."

"Sushi? Should you be eating raw fish in your condition?" he asked, swept by sudden concern for the helpless child in her womb. He liked sushi himself, but wasn't it laden with potentially harmful parasites? That fact had never bothered him when he, personally, indulged, but it seemed like needlessly reckless behavior for an expectant mother.

"Don't worry. I checked that book you bought me first, and then I only had crab and shrimp and eel, all of it cooked."

"Good. Did you remember to drink three glasses of milk today?"

She made a face. "I don't think that's necessar—"

"Of course it's necessary. You need plenty of calcium so that—"

"I think I know what I need, thank you," she cut in primly.

"I don't think you do. In fact, you'll need to see a doctor. I was thinking that we could go to the clinic up in—"

"Brynn has taken care of that," Emmaline said.

"Oh, she has, has she?"

Emmaline nodded.

"So you told her that you're pregnant, just like that?"

"Of course I didn't tell her. She figured it out, just as she figured out who I am as soon as she laid eyes on me."

"Well, that's a no-brainer. You look just like yourself. But how did she figure out that you're pregnant? You aren't showing yet, despite the fact that you claim your waistbands are too—hey, is that a new outfit?" he broke off to ask.

"Yes. It's my first maternity dress. What do you think?"

He eyed the black knit jumper, which seemed to accentuate her breasts, which seemed to have grown since the last time he'd checked . . . and he checked often.

Doing his best to quell a surge of desire, he asked, "Don't you think it's a bit formal for knocking around the apartment?"

She shrugged. "I like it. I like everything she bought for me."

"There's more?"

"A whole new wardrobe. Brynn has a designer friend on the Upper East Side who runs a little boutique that specializes in maternity clothes."

"You went shopping with her?"

"Of course I didn't! Brynn called the shop and had them send over a selection. I hid in the bathroom while they were making the delivery."

He cast a glance around the fully furnished apartment. "You must have spent a good part of the day hiding in the bathroom."

"I did. But I'd have been in there anyway," she said ruefully, hugging her middle.

He felt a prickle of sympathy for her. "The nausea hasn't let up yet?"

"It comes and goes. But it doesn't go often enough. In fact, that's how Brynn figured out that I was pregnant."

"Couldn't she have assumed you'd eaten some bad clams or something?" he asked, scowling.

"I tried to convince her it was food poisoning when I had to rush into the bathroom for the third time," Emmaline told him. "And she might have believed me . . . if she hadn't stumbled across the book you bought for me."

"Didn't you hide it?"

"I did. Under the bed. But she found it while she was crawling around, measuring for the carpet."

Granger rolled his eyes.

"Anyway, we can trust her not to tell anybody," Emmaline went on.

"Is that the royal 'we'?" he asked. "Or am I included?" *For a change*, he added, feeling prickly.

"Of course you're included. I meant 'we,' as in you and I."

He felt better instantly. "We." What a terrific, cozy little word.

"And I'm almost relieved that she knows," Emmaline went on, "because thanks to her, we have an appointment a week from Wednesday."

"Where are we going?"

"You're not."

"Oh, this time it's the royal 'we'? As in, just you?"

"No, as in just me and Brynn."

Okay, so "we" wasn't terrific after all. Not unless it was limited to himself and Emmaline.

He disliked "we" intensely when he was left out of it.

"Where are you going?" he asked impatiently.

"To see Brynn's doctor, who normally doesn't take new patients."

"Not unless they happen to be pregnant princesses—is that it?" He sighed, and asked, "Is he an OB-GYN, at least?"

"He's a she, and of course she's an OB-GYN. And I just told you that we can trust Brynn. The doctor has no idea who I am."

Though she had shifted the "we" to once again encompass him, he couldn't help resenting her tone—that, and the fact that Brynn seemed to have suddenly stepped in and taken over.

He didn't waste time now wondering how his old friend had arrived on the scene in the first place, as Brynn had always had a way of popping up when— and where—you least expected her. She also had a way of taking over everything from his social life to his personal space.

He paced toward the window, suddenly needing air. "Do you mind if I ask what you're going to tell this physician?"

"I'm just going to tell her that I suspect I'm pregnant."

Granger stopped in mid-stride and turned toward her. "You *suspect* you're pregnant?"

A tide of some emotion that felt more like fear than relief washed over him.

"Well, I haven't taken a test yet. But I have all the symptoms, so I'm ninety-nine percent sure."

"Oh." He couldn't help wondering about that remaining one percent chance.

What if she was wrong?

What if there was no baby?

If there was no baby, he was off the hook. Her problem was solved. They could go their separate, merry, unencumbered ways.

But if there was no baby . . .

Then he wouldn't be a daddy.

And for some reason, he desperately wanted to be a daddy. He felt like one already; felt the weight of responsibility as acutely as the thrill of anticipation whenever he thought about March.

If she wasn't pregnant, March would be just another month.

His would be the only March birthday to celebrate, and he would be celebrating it solo. Forever.

Granger cleared his throat, conscious of Emmaline's green gaze resting on him.

He asked, "Don't you think it's going to be pretty difficult to maintain a disguise in a doctor's office? What if you knock your wig askew while you're disrobing?"

As he spoke, an image of Emmaline disrobing promptly skittered into his brain and lodged there. Acutely aware of a familiar stirring, Granger turned back toward the window, away from her, lest she glimpse the not-so-subtle evidence of his yearning.

"Oh, I won't need the wig after tomorrow," she was saying airily. "Brynn is going to dye my hair for me, and cut it."

"*Cut* it?" He spun back to face her, horrified. "She's going to cut your hair?"

"She thought a shorter style would be flattering."

"Well, she thought wrong," he said vehemently.

"But Granger—"

"What?" he barked.

She stared at him. "It's just . . . well, I'm surprised you have such strong feelings about my hair."

He had strong feelings about more than just her hair. And he didn't like it one bit. He didn't like caring this much about a woman.

About *this* woman, in particular.

She represented everything he was trying to escape. And yet there was no escape from her. Every time he turned around, every time he opened his eyes in the morning, every time he closed them at night . . . there she was. On his mind. Under his roof. In his dreams.

The only place she *wasn't* was in his bed.

These last few nights, lying on the unforgiving, dusty floor, listening to her hushed breathing in peaceful slumber, had been torturous for him.

Now his gaze fell on the inviting queen-sized bed that had materialized a few feet away. He pictured her there, naked beneath him, her long hair spilling over the pillow, just as it had that morning in his uptown apartment, and that night in his suite at the Traviata in Chimera.

"Go ahead," he said gruffly, turning away from her. "Cut your hair."

When she was silent, he assumed that she, too, had turned her back.

Then he felt her gentle touch on his arm.

He looked over his shoulder to see her standing beside him.

"I won't cut my hair," she said softly. "Not if you like it the way it is."

"I do. But not like that . . ."

He placed his hands on her shoulders and turned her to face him.

She looked up at him expectantly, as though she

were holding her breath, aware of what was coming, unable—or unwilling—to stop him.

And so he took the plunge.

"I like your hair like this," he said in a low voice, pulling out first one hairpin and then another, and another.

Her careful updo came tumbling down in a sweet-smelling, silken cascade.

Granger laced his fingers into it, then buried his face in it, filling his lungs with her intoxicating scent.

His mouth found its way to the nape of her neck, and she moaned as he nuzzled her there. Then he swept her into his arms and carried her over to the bed, careful not to jostle her as he set her on the comforter.

He stood looking down at her, thinking that he had never seen a more exquisite creature. Now there was nothing stately or proper about Emmaline as she settled her wavy hair against the heap of pillows and sent him a heated gaze in silent invitation.

He lay beside her, resting the hard length of his body against her soft curves. She squirmed, pulling him closer so that their bodies fit perfectly together.

For a long time, they lay kissing.

Just kissing.

Feathery light kisses; deep, hungry kisses.

And for a long time, the kissing was all either of them needed. It was enough just to lie in each other's arms, kissing, like a couple of high school kids who had all the time in the world.

Then, all at once, it wasn't enough. Their hands

began to wander, unfastening and then unzipping, helping each other out of their clothes until they were naked at last.

Granger rolled on top of her once again, and then into her. He savored her warm flesh against his, and her body's fragile quivers beneath him, and the hushed sound of her breathing as they moved.

With his molten release came her own shudder of movement beneath him. She clung to his shoulders and they rode it out together. When it was over, he pulled the quilt over them both and held her against his chest, stroking her head.

"Well? Did that convince you?" he asked after a while, when his heart rate had slowed.

"Convince me?" She lifted her head to look at him. "Convince me of what?"

"Not to cut your hair," he said.

A delighted grin lit her face.

"Not quite," she said slyly, a devilish gleam in her eye. "Maybe you should try to convince me again."

His heart rate quickened. "Gladly."

And he did.

A few hours later, lying in Granger's arms, Emmaline woke from a light, contented sleep.

She found Granger smiling at her.

"Didn't you sleep?" she asked.

"A little. But I'd rather watch you."

She should have felt self-conscious about that. But somehow she didn't.

"What time is it?" she asked, yawning.

"After midnight."

"That late?"

"Why so disappointed, Princess? You didn't turn into a pumpkin. Yet," he added playfully, his fingers grazing her barely swollen belly.

Before she could reply, her stomach did . . . with a loud growl.

"Oh my goodness, excuse me," she said, not the least bit embarrassed. It seemed that their incredible physical encounter had—at least for the time being—made Emmaline comfortable with Granger. More comfortable, somehow, than she had ever been with another human being.

"Either our child is part beast, or you're a little hungry," Granger said with a chuckle.

"I'm famished," she said. "What a pity that breakfast is hours away. How I would love a platter of eggs with bacon and fried potatoes, and toast with jam." Her mouth flooded with saliva at the thought. She swallowed hard.

"I bought eggs the other day," Granger said. "I can make some for—"

"But there's no bacon!" she protested sharply. "Or potatoes. I need potatoes. Fried potatoes. With lots of salt."

"Testy little thing, aren't you?"

"I just need bacon and potatoes," she said reasonably—or perhaps a bit frantically.

It was the oddest thing. She never ate fried anything, and she didn't even like bacon. But suddenly, she wanted—*needed*—to taste its fatty, smoky flavor more than she had ever wanted or needed anything.

Well . . . almost anything, she amended, allowing her fingertips to dance a trail down Granger's naked, muscular torso.

"In the morning, I'll go buy you some bacon and potatoes," he promised, stroking her hair. "I'll even fry the potatoes in the bacon grease for you. With lots of salt."

"That's sweet," she crooned. "But I need it now."

He stopped stroking. "Now?"

"Right now."

"You need bacon and potatoes right now? In the middle of the night? A rainy night, might I add?"

She shrugged. "I can't seem to help it, Granger. I'm quite ravenous."

"You've got to be kid—" He broke off, lifting his head and looking down at her face. "Wait a minute. Is this a pregnancy craving?"

"If you don't promise me bacon and eggs and fried potatoes and toast with jam—quince jam—I'm going to run stark naked into the street in the rain to find it myself," she said calmly.

"Yup, it's a craving all right." He sat up. "Come on. Let's get dressed."

"Both of us?"

"Yes, both of us. You don't think I'm going out in the rain alone at this hour, do you?"

"Surely you don't think I'm going to be able to protect you?"

Granger smirked. "No, but you're going to keep

me company. I know a place that serves terrific breakfasts twenty-four hours a day, and it's not far from here."

She licked her lips. "Do they have bacon?"

"Lots of bacon. And mountains of fried potatoes."

"Quince jam?"

"Don't push it, Princess. They have jam, but I'm not sure quince is as big around here as it is in Verdunia."

"I really need—"

"You really need to get dressed," Granger said. "And I promise you that if they don't have quince jam, I'll search every gourmet shop in town for it. Tomorrow."

She swung her legs over the edge of the bed, then froze. "Granger?"

"Now what?"

"I can't go out to a restaurant, that's what!"

"Oh, that." He waved a hand dismissively. "Trust me, nobody in this restaurant at this hour is going to be in any condition to recognize you. Especially not if you wear your wig and sunglasses."

"At night? Indoors?"

"I promise you won't be the only one. Oh, and wear comfortable shoes. We're walking."

"But it's raining!"

"Haven't you ever walked in the rain?"

"Yes, the other day with you," she remembered. "All right, as long as you bring your umbrella I suppose it won't—"

"I don't have my umbrella anymore."

"Where is it?"

"Long story. I'll tell you on the way. Let's go."

She hesitated, trying to quell her intense need for food. Specific food. "Granger, forget it. This isn't a good idea."

"Sure it is. I promised myself that I was going to spring you from your gilded cage, remember? And all I've done so far is swap one cage for another. You need to get out of here. You need to learn how to live a little."

"I know how to live," she said indignantly. "And I—"

"You need bacon and potatoes," he cut in. "Or am I wrong?"

No. He wasn't wrong. She needed bacon and potatoes.

And maybe she needed a wee-hour walk in the rain, too. "All right," she agreed. "I'll get my wig."

The sun was shining brightly this morning in Buiron, and Princess Josephine basked in its glow at the breakfast table on Prince Remi's private terrace.

She had spent the night at the palace again—in a guest suite, of course. It was just so much easier than traveling back and forth over the bumpy road home to Chimera.

Naturally, the press had followed her comings and goings with interest. There had even been a bit of innuendo about the youngest princess trying to take her missing sister's place in the prince's heart.

But for the most part, the media seemed to assume precisely what Josephine wanted them—and Remi—to assume: that she was comforting the prince in his time of need.

She had yet to hear from Emmaline again. There was no sign that her sister had any intention of materializing in Verdunia as promised. Presumably—and, all right, hopefully—she had been swept off her feet by one Granger Lockwood and was planning to stay right where she was. For a while, at least—if not forever.

And Josephine would be content to stay right where she was—forever. In a week's time, she had gone from admiration to infatuation to madly in love with her would-be brother-in-law. And unless she was mistaken, the feeling was mutual.

She had seen the appreciation—and longing—in Remi's eyes when he looked at her.

She had also seen the guilt.

If only she could tell him where Emmaline was—and what she was doing behind his back.

But familial loyalty wasn't easily jettisoned in royal circles. Josephine couldn't possibly break her vow to her sister—not even for love.

A shadow fell over her. She looked up from her mimosa to see Prince Remi standing beside her.

"Good morning." Her heart quickened at the sight of him, clean-shaven, hair still damp from his shower, crisp and clean in white trousers and a blue silk shirt. "Did you sleep well, Remi?"

"Unfortunately, I didn't." He sat across from her, and she noticed the deep circles beneath his eyes.

"There's something you should know, Josephine. I've come to an important realization."

"What is it?"

Her heart quickened. Was he going to tell her that he loved her?

"We aren't any closer to finding Emmaline than we were a week ago," he said. "The only place we haven't thoroughly investigated is America—and you're quite certain she wouldn't be there."

"Fairly certain," Josephine murmured, with a smidgen of contrition. Perhaps she shouldn't have tried quite so hard to keep Remi off Emmaline's trail.

Then again, he hadn't seemed all that eager to find Emmaline, either. In fact, the two of them had spent far more time flirting with each other and sharing candlelight meals and scintillating conversation than they had in earnest investigation of Emmaline's whereabouts.

"When I spoke to your father yesterday morning again, he seemed to believe that it was time to take a more drastic measure," Remi said, sitting across from her.

He stared glumly at the breakfast—which today included eggs with hollandaise sauce, thick French toast delicately dusted with powdered sugar, fresh raspberries, a fragrant pot of coffee, and the aforementioned mimosas.

"How drastic a measure?" Josephine asked, lifting her half-filled flute to her lips to stave off dread.

"He's urged me to use whatever means I must to

reach out to Emmaline and get her back here so that she and I can—"

"Here . . . have a berry. They're luscious." Josephine popped one into his open mouth, successfully cutting him off.

"Mmm . . . they *are* luscious," Remi said, swallowing. "As I was say—"

"Have another. You must be famished." As she swiftly placed another plump berry in his mouth, Josephine's fingers brushed against his lips. She longed to allow them to linger there.

"Mmm," he said again . . . with perhaps a hint of seduction.

"Would you like another?"

"Please."

She leaned closer and slowly fed him another berry.

He fairly moaned in ecstasy.

"I knew you were hungry," she crooned.

Their faces were inches apart, eyes locked together.

"Famished."

He leaned closer still.

"Remi . . ."

"Josephine . . ."

She felt his mouth brush hers, ever so lightly. She could smell spearmint toothpaste on his breath, mingling with the sweet taste of raspberry on his lips.

She trembled, her eyes closed, wanting more . . . so much more than this.

"I wish . . ."

Her eyes snapped open.

"What, Remi? What do you wish?"

"Never mind," he said, drawing away. "It doesn't matter what I wish. Wishes are for commoners."

I wish I had cab fare, Granger thought as he and Emmaline emerged from the diner two hours later. The rain had turned into a deluge.

To his astonishment, Emmaline—who had trudged gingerly there on the way over—splashed right out onto the sidewalk.

"Here, wait, you can put my jacket over your head," he offered, hurrying after her.

"No, it's fine," she said, tilting her face up to the overcast sky. There was nary a hint of light; dawn was still a few hours away. He had yet to sleep a wink but he wasn't the least bit weary.

"You're going to get soaked," he advised Emmaline, who didn't seem to mind.

"I got soaked on the way over," she said with a shrug. "It wasn't so bad."

He marveled at this bold turn. She seemed to have lost every ounce of restraint. She had ordered like a famished trucker, eaten every bite with gusto, laughed uproariously at all Granger's jokes . . . and now here she was, standing in the middle of the street in the rain.

It was as though she didn't care who saw her—or what anyone thought, including Granger.

Granted, the narrow block was off the beaten path

and all but deserted at this hour—though as he had predicted, the diner had been busy. He had also been right about nobody giving Emmaline and her wig and sunglasses a second glance.

Maybe the anonymity had reassured her.

Or maybe just the sweet taste of freedom. Of what life was like outside the cage.

Granger leaned against a street lamp and folded his arms across his chest, watching Emmaline.

Thunder rumbled overhead. Rain poured down on her as she stood, face tilted up and arms outstretched. She opened her mouth and caught raindrops on her tongue. He saw streaks of black makeup appear on her cheeks below the rims of the sunglasses.

"Shall we go?" he asked.

"Do we have to? This is glorious."

"We'll take the long way home," he promised.

She pouted. "I wish we never had to go back."

"We can go out again tomorrow night."

Her face lit up. "In the rain?"

"If it rains. If it doesn't . . ."

"We'll go out anyway. I'll probably need more bacon."

"After the pound you just ate?" He grinned at her. "What's gotten into you, Princess?"

"I don't know."

"I think I do." He lifted her sunglasses and looked into her eyes. "It's passion."

"Passion?" she echoed breathlessly.

"Passion for food, for life, for—"

"For you?" She stood on her tiptoes and kissed him. On the lips. With passion.

Granger kissed her back. With passion.

And they quickly concluded that it was best not to take the long way home after all.

Nine

....

Oozing contentment, Emmaline lounged on the couch, eating bonbons and waving her bare feet, toes separated by cotton balls, in the air as her cherry-colored polish dried.

"Look at that—Sultri has gained at least ten pounds," Brynn announced, transfixed by the television screen.

"Which one is Sultri?"

"The brunette. The other one is Jasmine, Eva's long-lost half sister."

"Who is Eva again?" Emmaline asked. They were watching *Dusk Till Dawn*, Brynn's favorite soap opera.

"Eva is the blind one. She lost her eyesight in the plane crash that killed her new husband, and then, just when she was getting the hang of her disability, her seeing-eye dog was hit by a steamroller driven by her ex-husband, Dirk."

"Isn't Dirk the one she was kissing in the last scene."

"They've reconciled," Brynn said solemnly, popping a bonbon into her mouth and offering the box to Emmaline, who helped herself to another.

The closest thing Emmaline had ever seen to an American soap were episodes of *Melrose Place* on Verdunian cable, a decade after the show had been popular in the States.

But Brynn was initiating her into the scandalous world of *Dusk Till Dawn,* explaining the characters and their relationships during the commercial breaks.

"The great thing about soaps," Brynn said, and paused to take a long sip of champagne from her half-filled flute, "is that you can miss two months' worth of episodes, watch for fifteen minutes, and pretty much pick up where you left off."

"That's good to know," Emmaline said, "because I can't imagine being able to actually sit down and watch a full hour of this every day."

"Why not? What else do you have to do?"

Emmaline thought about it. "Nothing," she said, marveling at the uncluttered days that stretched before her.

For the first time in her life, she was underscheduled. In fact, she wasn't scheduled at all. And she rather liked the feeling.

Granger had initiated her into life outside the cage. Now that she had been out and unrecognized

in her wig and sunglasses, she had let him talk her
into a variety of other escapades.

For someone who had lived his life in Manhattan's wealthy circles, Granger was full of ideas for
inexpensive ways to show her New York.

They had taken moonlit walks up and down Fifth
Avenue, daring midday strolls through Central Park
in broad daylight, and even a round-trip journey
through the harbor on the Staten Island ferry. She
had glimpsed the Statue of Liberty, Ellis Island, and
the dazzling city skyline from afar.

She had eaten hot dogs and pretzels from a pushcart; had seen a Yankee game from the bleachers and
second acts of several Broadway shows.

"Do you miss your old life, Emmie?" Brynn
asked, as another soap scene evaporated into a commercial for a feminine hygiene product.

"I don't miss it at the moment." And she certainly
didn't miss being called "Your Highness." She had
never had a nickname in her life, and she found herself reveling in having Brynn call her Emmie.
Fenella would have been horrified, she thought
gleefully.

"How about Prince Remi? Do you ever miss him?"

"Sometimes," Emmaline said, refilling her own
champagne flute with milk. "But not in a romantic
way," she found herself confiding.

"That's because you're in love with Granger."

Emmaline choked on her sip of milk. "I am not in
love with Granger. I told you—"

"Yes, I know what you told me," Brynn said with maddening aplomb. "You and Granger had a one-night stand, and that's how you became pregnant, and your staying here with him is only temporary and strictly platonic—"

"It *is!*" Emmaline protested, glad that Brynn couldn't read her mind, which was currently replaying an image of last night's heated encounter. She forced herself to keep her gaze on Brynn's face, rather than allowing it to drift across the room to the incriminating bed.

"I don't buy it," Brynn said. "I think that the two of you are madly in love."

"You haven't even seen us together!"

"Well, this is ridiculous. I've been here every day, and Granger hasn't been here at all."

Except at night, Emmaline thought. And the last few nights were something she didn't want to discuss with Brynn.

How could she possibly explain what was going on between her and Granger when she didn't understand it herself? She would tell herself, before he walked in the door, that she couldn't let it happen again. That she should sleep alone in the queen-sized bed and he should sleep on the pullout sofa.

Then Granger would appear, and their eyes would lock, and moments later she would find herself in his arms.

"Did you tell him about my offer?" Brynn was asking.

Emmaline forced her mind back to reality. Financial reality—which was dismal, indeed. "I told him," she said, "and he said to thank you, but to tell you that it won't be necessary."

"Did you tell him that the money would be a gift, and not a loan?"

"Of course. He said that he doesn't want a gift."

"Especially not from me. Is that it?" Brynn shook her head. "I know him so well. The man is as stubborn as his grandfather."

"He wants to find financing on his own."

"This is ridiculous," Brynn said impatiently, aiming the remote control at the television.

Emmaline glanced at the screen, where a box of juice with a human head and legs was dancing its way out of the refrigerator. "It is ridiculous," she said. "Nearly all American television commercials are ridiculous."

"I meant Granger's refusing to take a gift of money from me—not the commercial," Brynn said, flipping the channel.

Emmaline had noticed that she liked to do that—flip from station to station during commercials. Brynn called it channel surfing. Granger did it, too. Americans seemed to have incredibly short attention spans.

For some things, at least, she amended, blushing as she recalled certain things—pleasurable, erotic things—that seemed to hold Granger's attention. She felt a stirring in the pit of her stomach and wondered when, exactly, he would be home.

"What kind of man leaves a perfectly lucrative job

and one of the most desirable apartments in Manhattan?" Brynn asked. "Which reminds me . . . did you tell him that the two of you are welcome to move in with me? There's plenty of room. You can have an entire floor of the brownstone."

"I told him, and he said—"

"Let me guess. He said, 'Thanks, but no thanks.'"

What Granger had said was that Brynn should mind her own business and stop trying to thwart his efforts to support himself and Emmaline, and that it was obvious she didn't believe that he was capable of doing so.

Brynn sighed. "It's simply beyond me why—oh, Emmie, look!"

Emmaline looked.

There, on the television screen, was a close-up of Prince Remi. That, in and of itself, wasn't unusual. Though the news coverage of her disappearance had let up a bit, the royal wedding saga still made up a good part of the daily cable news coverage.

But this was fresh, recent footage of Remi—and he was, quite clearly, giving a sit-down interview.

That never happened. Remi didn't give interviews. Few royals did, particularly when they found themselves in potentially scandalous situations.

Suddenly the image of Remi gave way to one of a smiling blond reporter who looked vaguely familiar.

"I'm Debi Hanson, and you can see my exclusive interview with Prince Remi of Buiron this evening at eight o'clock right here on channel twelve."

Emmaline was speechless.

Brynn, as usual, was not.

"You know, Granger is good-looking and all, but there's something about that Prince Remi..." Brynn shook her head. "I just don't see how you could have jilted a man like that. And just think— you would've been Emmie and Remi."

Emmaline found her voice. "We would never have been Emmie and Remi, Brynn. We didn't have that kind of relationship."

"What kind of relationship did you have?"

Emmaline faltered. How could she possibly explain it to Brynn? To anyone? Nobody could ever understand what it was like to be engaged to a man you could never love.

Nor could anybody understand what it was like to be in love with a man you could never—

No.

No!

She was *not* in love with Granger Lockwood.

She simply refused to be in love with Granger Lockwood.

And that, she resolved firmly, was that.

Granger stepped into Klingerman's Kopies, carrying a manila folder containing his revised business plan. He'd been using the computer at a midtown library all day, trying to come up with something that would lure potential backers.

The place was quiet at this hour on a Friday afternoon. Only two of the two dozen or so photocopy machines were being operated, one by a befuddled-looking elderly woman, and the other by a college student with a goatee and several painful-looking piercings.

At the counter, a teenaged girl in a bright yellow Klingerman's smock was leaning against a desk and talking on the telephone.

He checked his watch. His meeting with one of his grandfather's most powerful rivals was scheduled for twenty minutes from now, forty blocks uptown and across the park.

He hadn't originally planned to approach Anderson Lowell. Personally, he couldn't stand the man. Professionally, he didn't trust him. But he was desperate.

He hurried to the nearest machine and began putting his papers in order, ready to make copies.

"Miss!" called the elderly woman.

"Yeah, so then I told him to get a life," the teenaged clerk said into the phone, as she twirled a strand of hair around her finger. "And do you know what he said to me?"

Granger pressed the Collate button and sent his first document through the machine.

"Miss!" the elderly woman called, more urgently.

"Yeah, totally! How did you guess?" the teenaged girl said, oblivious to everything but her conversation. "And do you know what I said to that?"

"Miss!"

Granger turned to find the elderly woman waving her arms in distress as the color copy machine she was operating spewed out sheet after sheet of paper.

"Help!" she called frantically. "Somebody, please. I can't stop this! I only wanted two copies!"

"That's exactly what *I* said," the teenaged girl told the phone. "And I'm soooo not into discussing it with him any further."

Granger glanced at the multipierced student. He was wearing headphones, absorbed in his music and his copies.

"Help!" The old lady jabbed button after button on the copy machine. "How do you turn it off?"

"Let me take a look." Granger hurried over to her and examined the machine quickly before pressing a button.

The copier abruptly went still.

"Oh my goodness! You are amazing, young man. How did you do that?"

"I just pushed this," Granger said modestly, pointing at a prominent red button labeled Off.

"Do you work here?"

No, but if I can't get my business plan off the ground, I might have to come back with a resumé, Granger thought. Then he shook his head.

The first Granger Lockwood had built an empire from scratch all those years ago. There was no reason he couldn't do the same. He was determined to succeed. Actually, *desperate* was more like it.

He had to do this. For himself. For his child. And . . . for Emmaline. Definitely for Emmaline.

She seemed to be losing patience with his daily trek around the city to try and find investors.

Spending so much time with Brynn was probably rubbing off on her, he decided as he helped the frazzled old woman gather the widely scattered papers. Then again, Emmaline hadn't exactly been enthusiastic about any of this before Brynn arrived on the scene, either.

Maybe she was right. Maybe he should stop slumming. Maybe he should do the responsible thing, apologize to Grandfather, and ask for his old job back.

But was that really the responsible thing?

Did he really want to spend the rest of his life as Grandfather's underling? For all the old man's talk of retiring and turning over the business to Granger, he wasn't going anywhere for a good, long time.

"Can I help you?" the girl behind the counter asked, hanging up the phone at last.

"I just want to pay for my copies," the old woman said.

"Fine." The girl glanced at a computer screen. "That'll be one hundred and twenty-four dollars and fifty cents," she said briskly.

"But . . . aren't the copies a nickel each?"

"The color copies are seventy-five cents."

"But . . . I didn't need color."

The girl shrugged. "That's what you made. And it's one-twenty-four-fifty."

"But I only wanted two regular black and white copies."

"Sorry, but I have to charge you for what you made, which is one hundred and sixty-six color copies. It says so right here," the girl said, pointing at the computer.

"But I couldn't figure out how to turn off the machine," the woman protested.

The girl shrugged again, as if to say, *That's not my problem.*

Steaming, Granger spoke up. "Look, why don't you give her a break?"

"If I give her a break, I have to give everybody a break. I don't have that authority. I have to charge her for one hundred and sixty-six copies. The system is computerized."

"Where's the manager?" Granger asked.

"Stuck in the Holland Tunnel. He won't be in until later. I'm the only one here. Look, I'm going to need one hundred and twenty-four dollars and fifty cents," the girl told the old woman in a bored voice.

"But I only have five dollars."

"What about a credit card?" Granger asked her.

"I don't have a credit card. And I'm on a fixed income. I can't afford a hundred and twenty-four dollars!"

"And fifty cents."

Granger shot the girl a withering look.

She ignored him, telling the woman, "Then I'll have to call the police."

"Listen, I'll pay for it," Granger said, reaching into his pocket.

"You can't do that," the woman protested.

"Of course I can." He pulled out his money and swiftly counted out six twenty-dollar bills and a five.

"How can I thank you?"

"You just did." He smiled at her.

"I can pay you back," the old woman said, "as soon as my Social Security check comes. If you'll give me your address I can—"

"Forget about it. It's a gift." Granger shoved his remaining cash back into his pocket.

It was all he had left in the world—at least, for the time being.

And a quick count had told him that it totaled thirty-seven dollars.

Emmaline was sitting in front of the television, sipping ginger ale—which wasn't helping to ease her nausea in the least—when Granger arrived home. Newman and Kramer greeted him with exultant yelps as always, then returned to their station by the floor at Emmaline's feet.

"How was your day?" she asked, her eyes focused on the television screen. Debi Hanson's exclusive interview with Remi was scheduled to begin in less than two minutes.

"I tried to call and tell you the news—the phone should have been turned on today, but all I got was a busy signal."

"I was using it," she said, watching the television.

"Who on earth were you—oh. Brynn, no doubt."

She nodded.

"Well anyway," he went on, "I found an investor."

"You did?" Startled, she looked up at him. "Who is it?"

"Anderson Lowell." He sat on a chair and bent over to take off one of his black dress shoes.

She tried to muster some enthusiasm. "Well, that's terrific. Congratulations."

"Thanks." He took off the other shoe and added, almost as an afterthought, "I turned him down."

"You turned him down? Why?"

"Because he's my grandfather's arch enemy, that's why. He gloated the whole time I was meeting with him. I knew what he was thinking. That it would kill my grandfather to know that I was begging him for money. If I agreed to let him back me, it would be selling out on my grandfather. Lowell is dying to get his hands on Lockwood Enterprises' secrets and he thought I'd be willing to tell him if he paid my price. I thought I might be, too. But it turns out I'm not." He sounded surprised by that turn of events.

"You did the right thing," Emmaline told him.

"I don't know about that. I can't support you and our baby on thirty-seven dollars—and that's what I have."

"You don't have to support me or our baby," she told him. "I just need some time to—"

"It's my baby, too," he cut in. "I want to support it. I want it to have the best of everything. The finest education, accommodations, travels, opportunities. After all, I always did," he pointed out. "And so did you."

And look where it's gotten both of us, she wanted to say, but didn't.

"Then . . . if you turned down Lowell, what are you going to do next, Granger? I thought you said he was a last resort."

"He was. I'm going to go back to work at Lockwood Enterprises."

Her mouth dropped open. "You are?"

He nodded glumly.

"But, Granger . . . you can't do that for . . ."

She trailed off, shaking her head.

She had been on the verge of saying, *For me.* But she reminded herself that he wasn't doing it for her. He was doing it for the baby.

Which meant a lot. In fact, it should mean everything to her. He cared about their child. He wanted to be a good father.

Gazing at his earnest expression, she felt a pang. If only things could be different. If only there could be a fairy-tale ending for them. If only they were in love, and getting married, and could be a real family— Emmaline, and Granger, and their baby.

But fairy tales didn't exist. Not in Verdunia, and not in New York. Not even for princesses.

He might be willing to support their child and to go back to Lockwood Enterprises, but he wasn't willing to give up his bachelor lifestyle for her.

Then again, she hadn't witnessed much carousing on his part in the past few weeks—not with anyone but her, she amended, feeling herself blush at the thought of their steamy nights together.

Yet when Emmaline had pressed her, Brynn confirmed Granger's status as a love-'em-and-leave-'em ladies' man.

"He'll never settle down," Brynn had told her. "So don't get your hopes up."

"My hopes aren't up!" Emmaline had protested vehemently. "I told you, my relationship with Granger is strictly platonic. I'm just curious about what kind of man he is."

"He's precisely the kind of man you think he is," Brynn said slyly.

But that didn't help. Because at this point, Emmaline wasn't sure what kind of man she thought Granger was. Every time she thought she had him pegged, he seemed to surprise her. She was beginning to wonder how well anyone knew him— including Brynn, perhaps even including Granger himself.

"Will your grandfather take you back?" she asked him now.

"He will if I beg."

She could see that it was the last thing he wanted to do. Again she opened her mouth to protest.

But from the corner of her eye, she glimpsed a familiar face filling the television screen.

The interview with Remi was beginning.

"Look, Emmaline, I'm prepared to do whatever—" Granger broke off, frowned, and followed her gaze. "Prince Remi is giving an interview?"

"Yes. Shh." She aimed the remote at the television, raising the volume.

"I'd be willing to guess that the topic isn't a guided tour of the palace of Buiron," Granger muttered, folding his arms and narrowing his gaze at the television.

"Your Royal Highness," Debi Hanson said, "let me begin by asking how you have been coping without any idea where your beloved bride is, if you'll ever see her again, or even whether she's alive at all?"

"Now there's an upbeat question," Granger said.

"Shh!"

"I haven't been coping well at all," Prince Remi was saying as the camera shifted to a close-up of his face. "Every moment she has been gone has been a nightmare. Rather, nearly every moment." He seemed to glance directly into the camera. "There have, of course, been times spent with dear friends who have no idea how much their support means."

"Do you have any idea where Princess Emmaline might be—or who might be responsible for her disappearance?"

"I have no idea what may have befallen my beloved," Prince Remi replied. "I can only hope for the best."

"And fear the worst, I suspect," Debi Hanson added.

"She's a regular ghoul," Granger declared.

"Shh!"

"Your Royal Highness, there is a possibility that Princess Emmaline might be watching this broadcast in some distant corner of the world," Debi Hanson stated theatrically, in her most eloquent Barbara Walters imitation. "What would you say to her if you knew she was listening?"

The camera zoomed in closer still on the prince's face.

"I would say . . ."

Emmaline watched in utter shock as Remi paused, appearing to be overcome by emotion. He bowed his head, as though attempting to compose himself. When he raised his face to the camera again, a tear glistened in his right eye.

"I would say, I miss you desperately, my beloved."

His *beloved*? But . . .

He had never called her that.

"I adore you. You are as desirable, and as rare as . . . as a perfectly ripe raspberry . . ."

"A *raspberry*?" Granger snickered. "Did he just call you a raspberry?"

" . . . and I would do anything to taste, once again, what we shared—and to hold you in my arms again."

To hold her in his arms *again*?

Baffled—yet undeniably moved—by his unabashed display of emotion, Emmaline thought back over their courtship. How often had she found herself in her fiancé's arms?

Not nearly as often, she concluded, as she had found herself in Granger Lockwood's these past few days.

Guilt surged through her.

"If you can hear me, darling, please know that there is nothing I wouldn't give to have you here with me now—and forever."

The camera darted to Debi Hanson, whose eyes glistened with tears. "Thank you for sharing that heartfelt message, Prince Remi," she said dramatically. "When we return, we'll explore the childhoods—and courtship—of His Royal Highness and Princess Emmaline of Verdunia."

The scene shifted to a commercial. Emmaline stared unseeingly at the ubiquitous dancing juice carton, her mind racing.

"Well, that certainly puts an interesting spin on things," Granger commented. "I had no inkling Prince Remi was so brokenhearted—or that he had such a fondness for fruit."

"Nor did I." Emmaline forced herself to look at him. "He seemed quite sincere, didn't he?"

"He did," Granger said with obvious reluctance. "Although I can't say the same for Debi Hanson's sob-o-rama. I'll bet she sliced into a big, juicy onion off camera to summon that display."

"Mmm hmm," she said absently, stroking Kramer's head as he rested it on the couch at her side.

"You know, this is the most idiotic commercial I've ever seen. If I see that idiot human carton doing the jitterbug one more time . . ."

Emmaline looked up at Granger.

He was glaring at the television, but she had the feeling his ire wasn't directed at the dancing juice box.

If she stayed with him, he would go back to work for his grandfather—providing the old man would even take him back.

What if he wouldn't?

Or what if he did, and Granger grew to resent her—and the baby? He would never forgive them for plunging him back into the world he had nearly escaped at last.

Meanwhile . . .

There was nothing Remi wouldn't forgive. At least, that was what he'd said.

Could it possibly be true?

And did she dare put him to the test?

Emmaline glanced at Granger.

He was brooding.

She swallowed hard over the sudden lump in her throat.

The feelings were mutual!

Elated, Josephine turned off the television, silencing Debi Hanson's narration of her sister's childhood.

Remi loves me!

There was no doubt in her mind. All that talk about longing, and raspberries . . . she knew that he wasn't referring to Emmaline.

Josephine strode across her bedroom, her first instinct to call Remi.

She stopped halfway to the telephone.

No.

For one thing, palace security probably had the

phones tapped, in the event that Emmaline called. For another—

Wouldn't it be better to go to Remi in person? To see his face when he admitted to her that he loved her?

Trembling, Josephine closed her eyes, recalling his yearning expression as he had looked directly into the camera. How easy it had been to imagine that he was looking directly at her.

Yet . . . what if she was mistaken?

What if Remi really did love Emmaline?

No.

No, he couldn't possibly. And Emmaline didn't love him. Emmaline had abandoned him. Humiliated him. Emmaline was in love with another man. If Remi knew the truth . . .

Josephine caught sight of herself in the mirror above her bureau. She gazed into her own eyes, searching for a sign—for her heart to send a go-ahead. Or perhaps for her conscience to put a halt to her impulse.

Her conscience was silent. Her heart was explicit.

Josephine was utterly consumed by her desire for Prince Remi. A desire so profound, so overwhelming, that it precluded all other emotion.

Perhaps the time had come to betray her sister's confidence at last.

Seated in his sun-splashed private dining room, Prince Remi was halfway through his third slice of French toast with fresh raspberries and whipped cream when a butler discreetly interrupted his breakfast.

"I do apologize, but there's a highly urgent telephone call for you, Your Royal Highness."

"Is it Princess Josephine?" Remi asked, his stomach fluttering. He had yet to speak to the princess after his interview had aired. She was back in Chimera—which was probably the best thing for both of them. Still . . .

"No, it isn't Princess Josephine."

Remi sighed, his fork poised in front of his lips, his gaze on the sports pages of the morning newspaper—not something he typically read, but the only section that didn't make mention of last night's televised interview.

The Debi Hanson piece had aired live around the globe at eight o'clock New York time—which meant the wee hours in Buiron—Remi hadn't slept a wink.

He growled at the nervously hovering butler, "I believe I asked you to hold all of my calls."

"I beg your forgiveness, Your Highness, but as I said, this particular call is most urgent and requires your immediate attention."

Remi sighed, wiped his lips with his ivory damask napkin, and pushed back his chair. "Very well, then. Who is it?"

He froze when he heard the butler's reply.

"It's Princess Emmaline."

Ten
....

"Good morning, Mr. Lockwood!"

Standing beneath the canopied entrance to Lockwood Tower, a uniformed Carlos was his usual cheerful, professional self, but his expression revealed his shock at seeing Granger there.

Frankly, Granger was just as startled to see Carlos at this hour. He usually didn't begin his Saturday shift before late afternoon.

"Good morning, Carlos," he said. "Or should I say good evening? Either the subway took a good eight hours longer than it seemed to get me uptown, or your usual Saturday schedule has been changed."

He knew that Carlos preferred to work Saturday evenings so that he could spend the days with his three young children—something Grandfather could never be expected to understand.

"Everything has changed since you left, Mr. Lockwood," Carlos said a bit wistfully.

"For the better?"

Carlos looked around, as though expecting to see Grandfather looming over his shoulder. "Actually, it's the opposite," he confided. "And might I add that your grandfather has been in a foul mood ever since you left. I'm hoping the weekend in Newport will revive his spirits a bit."

"Newport?" Granger's heart sank. "Grandfather is in Newport?"

"He hasn't been feeling well and he thought the sea air might do him good. He flew up last night."

"When will he be back?"

"First thing Monday morning."

Granger considered his options.

He could wait until Grandfather's return to speak to him.

He could call the Newport house and do it over the phone.

Or he could catch the next train to Rhode Island.

Make that a bus, he thought, mentally counting the money in his pocket. He probably couldn't afford the train. In fact, he wondered if he'd be able to afford the bus. He had never taken one before.

Of course, he could call Brynn and borrow money—or better yet, borrow her chauffeured limousine for the weekend. He was certain she'd be more than willing to help him accomplish this particular mission. Granger knew she thought he'd lost his mind and that she was more than willing to help him recover it.

But he wasn't in the mood to explain himself to Brynn and hear her say, *I told you so.*

Not that she *had* told him so.

But she would have, if he had mentioned to her that he was thinking of giving up his job and his home and his wealth to . . .

To what?

What had he expected?

To be free?

Yes, that was what he had expected. But that was before Emmaline and her womb descended on him, forcing him to do the noble thing.

A bus ride to Rhode Island being the noble thing, at this point.

With a heavy sigh, Granger headed across town toward the Port Authority Bus Terminal, too broke to spring for another subway fare.

But not for long.

Surely the thirty-seven dollars would buy him a one-way bus ticket—and that was all he'd need, of course. He could hire a limo or charter a plane to get home.

What if the old man tells you to get lost?

He scowled, trying to quell the annoying little inner voice, but it grew insistent.

What if you get all the way up there and Grandfather says he has no intention of ever welcoming you back?

What would Emmaline say if that happened?

He had left her asleep in the queen-sized bed, with Newman and Kramer snoring at her feet, when he stole out of the apartment that morning. Neither the princess nor his pets had stirred when he left.

He had slept on the pull-out couch, of course—like a rock, for a change. He was simply worn out from pounding the pavement these past few days—and from the soul-searching it had taken him to come to the realization that he needed the Lockwood fortune after all.

He and Emmaline could move right back into the penthouse. They could fix up one of the guest bedrooms as a nursery—and have it professionally decorated by someone with more pizzazz than Ann Smith.

He felt a twinge of excitement at the thought of it. They could buy a crib, and a high chair, and one of those tables you used to change babies—what was it called?

Oh yes. A changing table.

They could buy a changing table. And toys. And books. And lots of tiny clothes, in pink and blue and every other color he could think of. And a rocking chair so that when he got home from the office at night he could rock the baby to—

Wait a minute.

He was assuming that the baby—and Emmaline—would be living with him. Permanently.

That wasn't going to happen.

But he realized that he wanted it to. Desperately.

He wanted it more than he had ever wanted anything in his life.

Maybe . . .

If Grandfather welcomed him back . . .

Maybe he could convince Emmaline to stay with him.

After all . . . where else did she have to go?

Emmaline was staring out the window when the motorcade pulled up at the curb.

She gaped in dismay at the row of gleaming black sedans, flanked by a police escort.

Oh no.

"How could he?" she muttered to Newman and Kramer, who were beside her, front paws resting on the windowsill as they, too, looked out into the street.

She had requested discretion.

Her white, horse-drawn royal wedding coach would have been more discreet here than the motorcade, which might as well be accompanied by a pair of trumpet-bearing, costumed town criers bellowing the news that this dilapidated block of Eldridge Street was about to be graced with a royal presence.

Part of Emmaline was grateful Granger wasn't there—but the rest of her longed for his reassuring presence.

She had no idea where he had gone. The sofa bed where he had slept had been neatly folded by the time she woke up—far later than usual, given the fact that she hadn't dropped off to sleep until dawn.

Emmaline rose swiftly and brushed the toast crumbs from her white silk maternity blouse, with its discreetly sewn button flaps for future nursing sessions.

Maternity clothes really weren't a necessity yet, despite her slightly expanding belly. But they were all she had, courtesy of Brynn's shopping excursion, and anyway, in the past few days Emmaline had noticed that her waistbands weren't all that felt snug. Her bra size seemed to have increased as well, and her breasts were heavy and tender, even painful.

Emmaline made her way quickly and queasily to the door, with the dogs padding along beside her. The lightly buttered toast that had, only moments ago, helped to quell her daily nausea now felt ominously unsettled in her stomach.

Or maybe it wasn't morning sickness.

Maybe it was the knowledge that she was about to face the man who held her destiny in his hands.

Emmaline leaned her head against the door jamb, her hand on the knob, her heart racing.

She told herself that she couldn't get sick now.

She told herself that she couldn't back out now, either.

It was too late.

What was done was done.

Prince Remi was here.

And Granger wasn't.

Footsteps echoed up the stairs outside the apartment—several pairs of footsteps, belonging, no doubt, to the ever-present security detail.

A knock sounded on the door.

Newman growled.

"It's okay, boy," Emmaline said, giving him a reassuring pat.

Emmaline took a deep breath and opened the door, forgoing the usual peer through the peephole that Granger and Brynn had both advised was New York standard.

After all, she already knew whose face she would see on the other side.

But when she gazed across the threshold, she found herself looking into the stern eyes of a man she didn't recognize.

This wasn't Remi, after all.

But, given the motorcade out front, and the half-dozen official-looking clones who stood beside him, it was undoubtedly a member of Remi's security team.

"Good day, Your Highness," he said brusquely. "Are you ready?"

"Ready . . . ?"

She looked past the detectives, seeking the familiar face. Then she realized what was happening.

Remi wasn't there.

Remi had no intention of personally escorting her from the premises. He probably hadn't even come to New York.

Of course he did, she scolded herself. *He said that you were his beloved. You heard him with your own ears.*

He said that he would do anything to hold you in his arms again.

But . . .

Again? her inner voice scoffed.

And anyway, he hadn't said that to her personally. Only to Debi Hanson, on global television.

To Emmaline, when she had reached him last night, he had said only "Why on earth did you disappear?"

"Cold feet," had been her lame reply.

"Are you over it now?"

She had hesitated, unwilling to lie.

"I'm not sure," she finally told him, thinking that her feet really were cold at the moment, on the bare bathroom tile in the middle of the night, where she was huddled with the phone as Granger slept soundly on the sofa bed in the next room.

"Come back," he said simply. "We'll resolve this and get married."

But would he still want to get married when he learned of the baby?

She had no way of knowing until she spoke to him.

She reached down to grab Newman's and Kramer's collars as the dogs growled and barked at the visitors.

"It's okay, boys. Settle down. It's okay. Where is Prince Remi?" she asked the security team.

Perhaps he was waiting for her in a suite at the St. Regis, with roses and champagne.

"At the palace, Your Highness, awaiting word of your imminent safe return."

So.

He would do *anything*.

Anything except jump on the first Concorde to New York.

Instead he had sent his detectives to fetch her and

bring her home like a poodle that had strayed off the property.

"I thought . . . I thought he was coming for me. He said he was coming for me."

Was it her imagination, or did all the detectives suddenly avert their gazes, looking down and shuffling their feet.

"He was planning to come, Your Highness," one detective said. "But after he spoke to you, he received an unexpected visit from your—"

"Something urgent came up," another detective cut in sharply, with what appeared to Emmaline to be a warning glance at the other man. He quickly turned his attention back to her. "Shall we vacate the premises, Your Highness?"

Emmaline looked down at Newman and Kramer, and then over her shoulder. She couldn't just leave without gathering her things, could she?

And she couldn't leave without saying goodbye— and thank you—to Granger.

But when she pictured that—pictured actually bidding him farewell—she felt sick inside.

He might try to talk me out of it, she told herself.

He would probably tell her that she could stay— that she *should* stay. He would nobly try to pretend that he didn't mind the burden of a pregnant princess; that he was eager to go back to work at the Lockwood Enterprises for her sake.

But she couldn't let him do it.

She couldn't let him sacrifice his dream of being accountable only to himself.

Yes, but what about the baby?

There were times when Granger almost seemed to be looking forward to the baby.

Well, it most certainly was an act. Granger Lockwood IV wasn't cut out to be a father. He had said so himself.

"Your Highness . . . ?" prodded one of the security officers.

She spun abruptly toward him, turning her back on the apartment and lifting her chin to keep it from trembling.

"Are you ready to leave?"

"Yes," she said firmly, fighting back a wave of longing for Granger, and what could never possibly have been. "I am ready to leave."

At dusk, with an empty stomach and a throbbing head, Granger reached the foot of Newport's Bellevue Avenue at last. It would have been a four-hour trip, at most, by car from midtown Manhattan.

The bus was a different story. It was a local, which meant that it stopped in every rinky-dink suburban and New England town between the Port Authority and Pawtucket, located a good half hour past the Newport exit off the Interstate. In fact, it seemed to stop everyplace but Newport itself, meaning Granger had to catch a local bus and backtrack south to Aquidneck Island.

The bus had let him off downtown, where he had walked past the charming shops of tourist-clogged

Thames Street; past seafood restaurants with their tantalizing aromas; past luxury hotels, and rollicking bars, and extravagant yachts moored in the broad harbor.

Granger had never before walked from the heart of town to Bellevue Avenue. Now, as he headed toward Seaside Serenade, the Lockwoods' summer "cottage" located at the far end of the avenue, he found himself gazing at the opulent mansions. He had been inside most of them—all, in fact, but those that were now museums open to "regular" folks.

All his life, Granger had been a part of this world. He had been to parties, clambakes, and charity balls there; had sailed with the heirs and dated the heiresses who inhabited these lavish homes.

Now he was an outsider, who didn't belong here any more than the nearby pair of sweatsuit-clad Midwesterners who stood gawking and taking pictures of the Vanderbilts' Marble House through the massive gates.

But that would change if Grandfather agreed to take him back. He could spend the night in his luxurious bedroom at the top of the sweeping marble staircase, and he could breakfast tomorrow on the terrace overlooking the Atlantic before departing for New York in a chauffeured limousine.

Never, until these last few days, had he appreciated the trappings of his wealth. He would no longer take for granted the comforts and perks that accompanied the Lockwood name and fortune.

Money couldn't buy everything—but Granger had now come to realize that it could buy most of the things that mattered. And if you also possessed the other meaningful things—the things money couldn't buy, like health, and family, and love—then you did, indeed, have everything.

Brimming with renewed determination, Granger arrived at the tall iron gates of Seaside Serenade. The curving drive was lit by century-old lampposts, and strategically placed spotlights illuminated the mansion's three-story granite face. Even now, at summer's end, lush gardens gave off a tantalizing floral scent that carried Granger back to that day in the palace rose garden at summer's beginning.

He was filled with a fierce, aching need to hold Emmaline in his arms once again. Mere hours had passed since he had tiptoed out of the studio apartment, giving her one long, last look as she lay sleeping.

Yet already he missed her desperately.

He had so much to tell her. So much to ask her.

If he dared . . .

And he would dare, he decided—as long as he had more to offer her and their child than a cramped studio apartment in a lousy neighborhood.

He wouldn't spend the night here, Granger decided restlessly.

He would do what he should have done upon discovering that Emmaline was pregnant. He would swallow his pride and have his conversation with Grandfather.

Then he would rush directly back to New York,

and Princess Emmaline, and say what he should have said all along.

Thanks to supersonic trans-Atlantic flight, Princess Emmaline found herself back in Verdunia less than eight hours after leaving Granger's studio apartment. While Prince Remi's security escorts had tried to insist that she go directly to Buiron, all it had taken was a simple heartfelt phone call placed to Papa to get her own way.

Remi had apparently kept the king apprised, so he knew already that she was en route to Europe. But Papa was elated when he heard her voice—so elated that he had quickly agreed that her reunion with Prince Remi should take place in Verdunia and not Buiron.

Midnight had long since come and gone there, but the palace in Chimera was ablaze with light when Emmaline's motorcade pulled through the tall gates. There was a crowd of press gathered in the street, but nowhere near the size of the throng that had been there on her wedding day only a few weeks earlier.

A lifetime seemed to have passed since then, Emmaline thought wearily, resting her head against the leather upholstery as the car pulled around to the side entrance of the palace, out of view of the media.

Her family was waiting inside, she knew, along with Prince Remi, who had been spirited into Chimera a short time ago without the knowledge of the press.

As the car pulled to a stop, Emmaline brushed

dog fur from her lap, trying not to think about the reproachful gazes Newman and Kramer had given her when she hugged them goodbye earlier.

• She closed her eyes, and Granger's face appeared before her.

"Your Highness, we've arrived," a security guard said from the front seat beside the driver.

Emmaline sighed and opened her eyes. "Yes, I see that, thank you."

Another guard was already opening the car door for her.

She stepped out into the chilly night air and wrapped her bare arms around her stomach, subconsciously cradling the child within.

The palace door was opened by a familiar uniformed butler.

She looked past his shoulder, half expecting to see her parents, or her sisters, or Remi himself waiting there.

But the great hall was empty.

"Where is everyone?" she asked the guard.

"Asleep, I would guess, at this ungodly hour."

Asleep. They were asleep. All of them. Even Remi.

I adore you, and I would do anything to hold you in my arms again.

Anything except fly to New York.

Anything except lose sleep.

Granger would have been waiting for me.

The thought flitted into her mind out of nowhere, along with another image of the face she never again expected to see outside her wistful daydreams.

She retreated to her private quarters, where she took the long, hot bath she had craved for days. Afterward she slipped into silk loungewear with a convenient drawstring waist. As she was combing her damp hair, there was a knock on the door.

"Who is it?" she asked, braced to hear Remi's voice.

"Tabitha," came the reply.

Emmaline dropped the brush and hurried to embrace her lady-in-waiting, who had brought her a mug of hot tea and some buttered toast.

"You look well," her loyal friend told her.

Emmaline glanced at her reflection in a gilt-framed mirror. She didn't look well. She looked exhausted and ill, and there was a haunted expression in her eyes.

Brynn would have told her the truth, she realized. But Tabitha wasn't Brynn, and Emmaline wasn't in America any longer. She was home in Verdunia, where she was royalty, and treated with the customary reverent respect.

"Thank you, Tabitha. I feel well," she lied.

Tabitha lowered her voice to a whisper. "Did Mr. Lockwood take good care of you in your absence?"

Mr. Lockwood. Granger. Emmaline was struck by a fierce wave of longing. She hadn't even said goodbye.

She looked at her loyal friend, and this time, she dared to speak the truth, heedless of the wistfulness her tone or expression might betray.

"Yes, Tabitha," she said softly. "He did take good care of me. Very good care, indeed."

* * *

This time Debi Hanson wasn't alone *or* asleep when the phone rang in her hotel suite in Buiron at three-thirty in the morning. She groaned and extricated herself from her companion's bare, muscular limbs and reached past several cellophane-wrapped congratulatory gift baskets on the bedside table.

"Yes?" she said curtly, trying not to pant into the receiver.

"How quickly can you get back to Chimera?" Jack asked from across the Atlantic.

Déjà vu, she thought, running a hand through her sweaty, passion-snarled hair.

"At least two hours—why?" She wondered if the hotel conditioner would untangle her tresses. She had left her own back in Verdunia in her haste to get out of that last hotel in the wee hours.

Jack said, "Because there's a rumor—"

She stifled a moan as a warm, wet mouth nuzzled the back of her neck.

"—that Princess Emmaline is back at the palace."

Debi froze. "She's back?"

So Prince Remi's ploy had actually worked?

This was even better than she had imagined. Not only had she landed the interview of the century, but she had played a role in getting the star-crossed couple back together. Yes, it certainly appeared as though she, Debi Hanson, had singlehandedly— well, with a little help from Jack and of course Prince Remi—saved both kingdoms.

"Where has she been all this time?" she asked

Jack, brushing her lover's groping hand from her breast as though it were a buzzing insect.

"Nobody knows where she's been. Possibly in New York, holed up in a grungy downtown apartment."

"In New York? In a grungy apartment?" Debi tried, and failed, to picture the elegant princess slumming it in lower Manhattan.

It was easier to imagine Princess Emmaline anywhere else—here, for instance.

Debi gazed appreciatively around the lavish hotel suite, which had been upgraded as a courtesy after her triumphant interview aired. Management had also sent her a complimentary bottle of champagne— now empty, having rolled somewhere under the king-sized bed, she assumed, thinking back over the last few decadent hours.

If Naomi Finkelmeyer could see me now, she thought gleefully, before turning her attention back to the conversation at hand.

"Was she abducted?" Debi asked Jack, imagining a blindfolded, handcuffed princess with a duct-taped mouth being held in some downtown rathole.

"It doesn't sound like it. I've heard that an accomplice must have helped her escape Verdunia and that she willingly went to New York, but it's unsubstantiated," Jack was saying.

"Was she actually seen there?"

"A couple of homeless drunks claimed they saw a royal motorcade whisk her away this morning. So far nobody's given them much credibility, but you never know. I've got a news team interviewing them now, and another one out at JFK trying to confirm that Princess Emmaline boarded a Concorde earlier. In the meantime, you have to get yourself over to the palace right away, Debi."

"Are they giving me another exclusive?"

Jack hesitated.

Debi scowled, knowing what that meant.

"There's been no official comment from the palace," he said, "and no indication that the princess is willing to do any press with anyone."

"What about Prince Remi?" She certainly had an in with him.

"Nobody's saying a thing in Buiron, either. But you have to get to Chimera and see what you can uncover."

"I'm on my way," she said, and hung up the phone.

"Come on, baby," Dolph Schumer said in his thick German accent, trailing moist kisses up her throat to her mouth, his breath hot in her face.

"I have to get out of here," she said, pushing him away. She wrinkled her nose as she bolted from the bed.

He might be the most sought-after rock star in Europe, and a phenomenal lover as well, but he had the worst breath she had ever encountered.

"Aww, don't go, baby!"

"I have to go. And stop calling me baby!"

"Mind if I have some of these?" He was nothing if not resilient, reaching for a box of Frango Mints that had been sent from Marshall Field's by one of her colleagues at the Chicago affiliate.

"Have them all," she called over her shoulder, and muttered, "But it'll take a lot more than that to sweeten your breath."

"Where are you going?" he asked, munching.

"To Verdunia. To the palace." She jerked open the closet door and began yanking hangers along the pole, looking for something suitable to wear. "The princess has come back, and I suspect she and Prince Remi are going to go ahead with the wedding."

"Don't hold your breath," he said. "I hear she's about as in love with Prince Remi as I am with a visit to the dentist."

Which might go a long way toward explaining his halitosis problem, Debi thought, stooping by the bed to retrieve her black pumps.

Aloud, she asked Dolph, "Oh, really? How do you hear that?"

"I dated her sister. Not the fat one. The other one."

"Princess Josephine?"

He nodded, popping another mint into his mouth.

"What did she tell you about Princess Emmaline and Prince Remi?"

"Wouldn't you like to know," he said, closing his beefy hand around her wrist and pulling her toward the bed.

"I'm not *that* curious." Debi extricated herself from his grasp and rushed for the shower, her mind racing.

She had been anticipating a tragic end to this fairy tale—not the news that Princess Emmaline was alive and well and back in Verdunia.

She could have gotten considerable mileage out of a royal funeral, and she had nearly perfected her on-camera tears. Then again, people cried at weddings, too. Especially when the bride had vanished for a couple of weeks before returning home to live happily ever after with her royal groom.

Happily ever after.

Yeah, right.

Debi Hanson was no expert on men, but she would bet her surgically lifted ass that Prince Remi's on-camera plea to his missing bride hadn't been any more heartfelt than Debi's own emotional reaction.

Could the sophisticated princess possibly have been naive enough to have fallen for his act?

Why else would she be back in Verdunia?

And what on earth had brought her to New York in the first place?

What . . . or *who*?

As she shed her clothes and stepped into the shower, Debi narrowed her eyes shrewdly.

She needed a source. Somebody with the inside scoop on the royal courtship—and anything else that might have been going on in the would-be bride's life.

Hmm.

Debi stopped soaping her nude body, poked her head from beneath the steaming spray, and called seductively. "Dolph . . . oh, Dolph? Could you come here for a moment?"

Eleven

....

Grandfather kept Granger waiting more than an hour.

He supposed he deserved it, really. The old man must know why he was there, and obviously had no intention of making this easy for him.

As he waited, Granger paced the length of the study, stopping every so often to gaze absently at a title on one of the floor-to-ceiling bookshelves or at his own reflection in the French doors that faced the back of the house and the sea.

Through the open window, he could hear the sea crashing in the distance. It was a sound that had lulled him to sleep on childhood summer nights. Now, however, the rhythmic surf seemed only to underscore the intensity of his inner turmoil. So did the ticking of the mantel clock, which seemed to grow more insistent with every minute.

A rare, endangered Hyacinth macaw occasionally

squawked from its perch in a nearby cage. Its round, deep brown eyes seemed to bore reproachfully into Granger, as though the bird sensed the woe this interloper had caused its master.

At last Granger heard a welcome sound from somewhere above: the old elevator beginning its creaking descent to the first floor. It had been installed by the first Granger Lockwood, who had built the house back when the Astors and the Vanderbilts were trying to outdo each other's Newport cottages.

Seaside Serenade—with its own ballroom, gym, indoor and outdoor swimming pools, Japanese water gardens, aviary, and yes, elevator—had taken its place alongside Marble House, Belcourt Castle, the Breakers, and other famed summer residences.

Granger shoved his hands into the pockets of his linen trousers and rocked nervously back on his heels, listening to the elevator grind to a halt in the adjacent hallway.

His broken hip long since healed, Grandfather was perfectly capable of using the stairs to descend from his second floor suite, but he insisted on the elevator whenever he was trying to prove a point to Granger.

The point being, *I'm old and frail and you are making my life even more difficult than it already is.*

Granger steeled himself against a tide of guilt as his grandfather hobbled into the room.

"Is your hip bothering you, Grandfather?" Granger asked, mustering concern.

The old man ignored his question and gruffly

posed one of his own. "How did you get here?"

"The bus."

Granger Lockwood II recoiled as though Granger had told him that he had hitched a ride with a serial killer.

The macaw ruffled its brilliant blue feathers indignantly.

"I see. And how are you planning to get back to New York?" Grandfather asked, sitting heavily in a leather wingback beside the marble fireplace.

It was Granger's turn to ignore the question.

He took a deep breath. "Grandfather," he began.

"Sit."

Granger sat.

"Grandfather, I said some things last time that were a bit rash. Please accept my apology . . . and my request."

"Request?"

"I'd like to return to Lockwood Enterprises," Granger said in a rush. "And to my apartment in Lockwood Tower."

There was a long pause.

Granger stared at the floor, and then glanced up to see his grandfather looking pleased, if not smug.

"Then you have come to your senses and realized that you want to go back to the way things were," the old man said. "Is that it?"

No! No, that wasn't it.

Granger didn't want to go back to the way things were. He didn't want to be his grandfather's flunky again.

How could he have any self-respect when the old man, for all his talk about Granger being the future CEO of Lockwood Enterprises, refused to relinquish the slightest bit of power?

"I thought we could compromise," he heard himself tell his grandfather.

"Compromise?"

Granger nodded. "You always talk about my future. How I'll take over the company one day. But that isn't going to happen as long as you're around, is it?"

"Are you saying that you wish me dead and buried?" Grandfather asked in horror.

"No! I'm saying that I wish you would retire. Or at least semi-retire. Or at the very least, that you would allow me some dignity and the chance to have a real say in what goes on with the company."

"Retirement would kill me," Grandfather said staunchly.

"I doubt that. You would have time to enjoy yourself for a change."

"I do enjoy myself. I golf, I travel, I dine out . . ."

"But you only do those things when they're tied into business," Granger pointed out. "You never do anything for pleasure."

"My pleasure *is* business."

Okay. That much was true.

"And I have my birds."

Also true.

So Grandfather had his birds, his business, his billions. Everything an old man's stilted heart could possibly desire.

Granger sighed. "As long as you're in charge, Grandfather, there is nothing fulfilling for me in Lockwood Enterprises."

"Oh really? So you don't find fulfillment in your salary, and job stability, and having a roof over your head, and knowing that you're carrying on the Lockwood tradition?"

"I do. But I need more."

"So you said. And you expected to find it in a dilapidated fifth-floor walk-up? And by selling out to Anderson Lowell?"

"How did you—?"

"I know more than you think," the old man said cryptically.

Which undoubtedly implied that he had used his money and connections to keep tabs on Granger.

Did that mean he knew about Emmaline, too?

Granger gazed at his grandfather's face, trying to read his mind.

No. Grandfather couldn't possibly have found out about Emmaline, Granger decided. He had kept her well disguised, and he knew that Brynn, for all her social gallivanting, wouldn't have told a soul.

But what about the parade of deliverymen who had been in and out of the apartment? Emmaline had sworn she hid in the bathroom every time, but . . .

"If you know so much about me," Granger said, shoving aside his uncertainty, "then you know that I'm trying to do the right thing here. The honorable thing. And that I would hope—no, *expect*—you to do the same."

"If taking you back is the honorable thing, then you will find your expectations met," Grandfather replied.

Granger exhaled. So that was it. He could have his job, his apartment, his life back.

But . . .

"Back on whose terms?" he found himself asking. "Mine, or yours?"

"On my terms, of course," Grandfather said, all but brushing his wrinkled palms together briskly, as though there was no room for debate.

Granger nodded bleakly. "Yes. That's what I thought."

Morning sickness and sheer exhaustion got the best of Emmaline after she had been welcomed by Tabitha, followed by her sleepy, relieved parents.

"Where are Genevieve and Josephine?" Emmaline had asked the king and queen, both of whom had hugged her profusely.

"Genevieve had to fly to London for a breakfast meeting with the prime minister's wife," the queen said. "And Josephine must be sound asleep—she didn't answer the knock on her door."

No surprise there. Emmaline's younger sister enjoyed her beauty rest immensely.

"And Remi?" she had asked tentatively.

"He, too, is still presumably in bed in the guest quarters," Papa had said.

Now, at last, Emmaline had received word that Prince Remi was ready to confront her. The sun was coming up, streaking the Verdunian sky pink and gold. It was a breathtaking sight. But all she wanted to do was draw the heavy draperies, crawl into her old bed, and sleep for the next week.

Instead, she found herself in a small parlor located in a quiet, private corner of the palace, coming face-to-face with the man she had betrayed and jilted.

She rose when he entered the room.

He looked the same as always: handsome, impeccably dressed, and fresh from an invigorating shower. She found herself wondering whether Granger would have stopped to shower, shave, and don neatly pressed street attire if he had spent so many days apart from the woman he professed to love.

She doubted that. And she found herself irrationally jealous of the woman who eventually captured Granger's elusive heart.

Emmaline had no doubt that some enchanting female eventually would do just that. For all his faults, Granger had proven that he wasn't necessarily destined to spend the rest of his life as the footloose, spoiled playboy she had assumed he would always be.

Already she was able to glimpse someone other than that man.

She suspected that it was a facade; that somewhere deep down inside, Granger longed for stability. For the family he had never had. For love.

But Emmaline couldn't help thinking that simply

longing for those things didn't mean that a person could actually find—much less sustain—them.

She recalled one of the few occasions they had talked about their childhoods. Granger had wistfully commented that she was lucky to have had loving parents and sisters, while he had grown up an only child, an orphan. For all his millions—indeed, billions—he had lacked fulfillment of a child's most basic needs.

He was never nurtured—only groomed, she realized in wondrous dismay, overcome by the notion of Granger as a lost little boy.

In their time together, she had never allowed herself to fully contemplate his past—or his vulnerability. She was too busy feeling sorry for herself, too preoccupied with her own discomfort—and his shortcomings.

Well, there certainly are enough of them, she reminded herself defensively, as Prince Remi strode toward her now.

Would he take her back once he knew the whole story?

For a moment she thought he was going to sweep her into his arms. But he didn't, despite the fact that they were alone, behind closed doors.

"Welcome home, Emmaline," Remi said tersely, stopping a few feet away from where she stood beside the sofa.

"Thank you, Remi."

There was so much more to say . . .

Yet there was nothing more to say.

This was not the emotional reunion she had convinced herself was possible. Try as she might, she couldn't muster anything other than mild affection at the sight of her fiancé after being apart for so long.

"What were you doing in New York?" he finally asked, providing a reprieve of sorts as she searched for the right words—or any words.

"I was . . ." She trailed off, riddled with uncertainty.

"Hiding?"

She was caught off guard by a flicker of amusement in his otherwise somber gaze.

"I suppose I was hiding, yes," she admitted.

"From me? Or from your royal duty?"

"A bit of both, I would say." She raised her chin and looked him in the eye. "I am truly sorry, Remi. If there had been any other way . . . well, I never meant for it to happen."

He seemed to ponder that.

She waited, holding her breath.

"How on earth did you pull it off?" he finally asked.

"Hiding?"

"The escape itself. You vanished from the wedding coach, which would seem an impossible feat."

"Yes, it would seem that way, wouldn't it?"

He was waiting.

She hesitated.

Explaining the mechanics of her disappearance

would mean bringing Granger into the plot, and she wasn't sure that she was prepared to open that door yet.

Then again, she couldn't keep it closed indefinitely. Now was as good a time as any to have that conversation. They were alone, and they had a decision to make—rather, Remi had a decision to make. Emmaline was fully aware that her fate was now quite out of her own hands.

She looked at Remi.

He pressed the issue. "Surely you didn't manage to flee the country entirely on your own. That would seem quite unlikely, unless you suddenly sprouted wings and flew away."

Wings.

She was thrust back to that June day in the rose garden, with Granger. She had teasingly told him that she had wings, and he had called her a fairy princess.

If only.

If only she had wings. She would fly right back to New York, and Granger . . .

Oh, what on earth was she thinking? She didn't belong there, in dirty, noisy, crowded New York City, in that cramped apartment ridden with mouse droppings.

This was home.

Yes. This opulent European palace—filled with the trappings of wealth and a staff of servants trained to cater to her every whim—was home.

And Remi . . .

Well, Remi was royalty. He understood what Granger Lockwood did not. He might not be in love with Emmaline—nor she with him—but his heart-felt televised plea rang in her ears.

Perhaps, in time, they would grow to love each other. Just as their parents had. Just as countless royals had before them.

There were, after all, viable reasons for arranged marriages.

Yes—and one of them is to keep the bloodline pure. In which case Remi and I already have one strike against us.

But nobody had to know that her firstborn wasn't Remi's child.

Nobody other than the two of them.

And Brynn Halloway.

And of course Granger.

But Granger would be relieved to have the burden of fatherhood lifted . . .

Wouldn't he?

Turmoil bubbled within her. She simply wasn't sure. About Granger. About Remi. About anything—including what she wanted.

"Gee, what took you so long?" Granger asked, his voice laced with irony. He certainly hadn't expected her for another hour—maybe two, depending on whether he'd interrupted the REM stage when he'd roused her earlier.

"Wonderful to see you, too, darling." Brynn bent

over the booth and kissed him on the cheek. "Though you have looked better."

"You never have, of course." He wiped the inevitable red lipstick stain from his cheek with a Dunkin' Donuts napkin.

"Thank you. You're sweet." Brynn smiled smugly, glancing at her reflection in the plate glass window before settling across the table from him. "We need to talk, but first . . . are you going to buy me a cup of coffee for my trouble?"

"I thought you didn't drink coffee anymore."

"I don't. Unless it's"—she examined her Rolex—"ten to three in the morning and I've spent the last hour and a half unexpectedly flying to Rhode Island."

"What happened—did somebody remove the sleeping quarters from your private jet?" he asked, rising as she yawned into her scarlet fingernails.

"No, but I couldn't fall asleep. I was too worried about you."

He shrugged and reached into his pocket, counting change. It was mostly pennies and nickels.

"Here." Brynn produced a twenty dollar bill from her bottomless brown leather Dooney and Bourke wallet. "Buy yourself a couple of crullers with the change. You haven't eaten all day."

"How do you know?"

"I just know."

He had to admit, she was right. His stomach was painfully hollow, but he hadn't realized he was hungry until she said it.

That was the thing he loved about Brynn. She knew him better than he knew himself.

He accepted the money from her and asked, "Cream and sugar, darling?"

"A splash of skim milk and half a packet of artificial sweetener. The kind in the blue packet, not the pink."

"Has anybody ever told you that you're impossibly high maintenance?"

"And you aren't?" She raised a brow at him.

Smiling at the realization that he'd missed her desperately, he walked up to the counter to get the coffee for Brynn and another for himself, along with a couple of mouthwatering frosted donuts. In the few hours he'd spent there since calling Brynn collect, he could only scrape together enough money for three cups of surprisingly tasty coffee.

He'd never realized Dunkin' Donuts had such good brew for such a reasonable price. He was used to the pricey chain cafés of Manhattan.

Well, from here on in, it would be Dunkin' Donuts all the way.

After all, he had—for the second time in as many weeks—told his grandfather to keep his job, and his money.

He wondered if Anderson Lowell's offer was still open.

He wondered what he would do if it wasn't.

But most of all, he wondered if he could possibly convince Emmaline to give him—to give *them*—a chance now that all he had to offer was himself.

* * *

Emmaline faced Remi, looking him in the eye. She owed him honesty. Much more than that, really, considering what she had put him through—but honesty was a start.

"A friend helped me to escape Chimera that day," she confessed.

"Tabitha?"

She hesitated.

Yes, Tabitha had played a role. But she couldn't implicate her loyal lady-in-waiting. Now that she was home to stay, she must do everything to secure Tabitha's future in the royal household. Certain details about her wedding day escape would be better kept to herself.

"An American friend," she confessed. "His name . . . his name is . . ."

"Granger Lockwood?"

She gasped. "How did you—?"

"It doesn't matter how I knew, Emmaline. What matters is—"

"You don't understand," Emmaline cut in hurriedly. "I didn't run off to New York because I'm in love with Granger Lockwood."

That had come out all wrong.

She tried again, her cheeks flaming. "That is to say, I wasn't in love with Granger Lockwood when—I mean, I'm not in love with him now, and I—I never was in love with him, and I never could be."

"The lady doth protest too much," Remi observed quietly, watching her thoughtfully.

"No, Remi, truly, I don't love him." Guilt and shame filtered into her. She forced her gaze to remain steadily focused on Remi's.

"Why else would you have run off with another man on our wedding day, Emmaline?"

"Because . . . I did it for you, Remi."

"Forgive me if I'm not entirely appreciative. It does seem to be an odd sort of wedding gift, Emmaline."

He smiled faintly.

She did not.

"Oh, Remi . . . you know we weren't in love, and—"

"You've mentioned that, yes. You weren't—and aren't—in love with him."

"No, I meant with you—nor you with me. We weren't in love. I care about you deeply, and—"

"As I care about you," he said, his honesty so raw that she felt a rush of affection toward him.

"I only wanted to spare you," she murmured.

"To spare me a loveless marriage?"

"Not only that . . ."

"Then . . . what?"

She took a deep, shaky breath. "I'm pregnant, Remi."

Granger had just allowed himself to doze off in the backseat of the limousine when Brynn jabbed him fiercely in the ribs.

"Ouch!"

"Did you hear that?"

"The sound of my bones cracking? Yes." He glowered at her in the dim post-dawn light, made brighter by the gleam of passing headlights. They were headed back to Manhattan, and Emmaline, from the airport.

"Shh! Listen!" Brynn cocked her head.

Frowning, he listened.

He heard nothing but rain falling on the roof of the car, and the radio droning from the front seat.

Then he heard it.

". . . Princess Emmaline . . ."

The radio announcer was talking about her.

He leaned forward in his seat, straining to hear.

"Can you please turn it up?" he barked at the driver, who obliged.

But it was too late.

The announcer's voice gave way to a commercial jingle.

"What was that about?" he asked, turning to Brynn.

Brynn yawned. "The usual, no doubt. She's been the main global news topic from the moment she was engaged. With any luck some epic natural disaster will come along and knock her out of the headlines. A catastrophic earthquake in some third world country would probably do it."

"How noble of you," Granger said dryly. "Wishing death and destruction on the masses."

He shook his head and leaned back to doze again, utterly exhausted.

Too soon—yet not soon enough—they reached Eldridge Street.

"I'd come up with you, but I'm incapable of negotiating stacks of stairs at this ungodly hour," Brynn said as the driver opened the door for Granger. "Please give Emmie my regards."

"I will. And thank you for everything." Granger kissed her on the cheek and stepped out into the urine-scented street, grateful that he would be unaccompanied for his reunion with the princess.

He desperately needed to be alone with Emmaline now.

He had no idea what he wanted to say to her—only that he needed to make her understand that everything was going to be all right. That he would be there for her, and for the baby. He trusted that the words would flow when he saw her.

His pulse quickened, and it wasn't just from the exertion of taking the creaky steps two at a time. How he longed to take Emmaline into his arms, to kiss her, to—

Good God.

He stood abruptly still, one foot on the fifth floor landing, his hand clutching the splintered wooden rail.

Was he in *love* with Emmaline?

When he envisioned the two of them together—and the two of them becoming three—was he envisioning a real family?

Was he planning to propose to her?

Marriage.

Marriage was commitment.

Permanent commitment.

As in forever.

He had never thought of himself as a forever kind of guy.

But if he didn't plan to stay with Emmaline—and the baby—forever, then what, exactly, was he planning? To merely stick around for a while? To be there for the birth, perhaps even for the baby's first tooth and first steps ... but not for the first day of kindergarten, or the sweet sixteen party, or high school graduation?

Was he capable of starting this adventure and not finishing it?

Then again, was he capable of seeing it through?

He had no idea. He *wanted* to be the kind of man who could get down on one knee and sincerely pledge his heart to one woman. All at once, he wanted that more desperately than he had ever wanted anything before.

But the concept of marriage—of marriage *and* love—was so earth-shatteringly new that it was all he could do not to give in to his flimsy knees and sink to the dusty landing.

Instead he mustered every ounce of strength, lifted his stubbly chin, and forced himself to walk toward the apartment door.

I'll know when I see her, he told himself. *I'll know what to do. I'll know what to say. Everything will fall into place when I see her.*

As he pulled his keys from his pocket, he heard scampering paws on the other side of the door. Newman and Kramer launched into a high-pitched frenzy. Their barking was infused with a desperate quality that sent a chill through him . . .

And he knew.

He knew, even before he unlocked the door.

She was gone.

But . . . gone where?

Anger—and fear—surged within Granger as he strode into the empty apartment. He took in the soiled floor, the spilled bag of dry dog food his pets had ripped into. Clearly, Newman and Kramer hadn't been walked, or fed, in . . .

In how long?

When did she leave?

Judging by the mess, she must have been gone since yesterday morning, not long after he snuck out the door. Guilt seeped in to complicate his inner turmoil. It wasn't as if he had told Emmaline where he was going. She must have assumed, when she awakened to find him gone, that he was out buying a newspaper or a bagel. It wouldn't have crossed her mind that he might be traveling on a bus to Rhode Island.

His anger subsided. No, Emmaline would never have deliberately left the dogs alone for any length of time. She must have assumed Granger would be back to take care of them. But . . .

Newman nudged his leg and yapped.

"All right, boy. I know you're hungry." Granger absently reached into a cupboard for a couple of cans of dog food. Kramer trotted over swiftly.

"Where the heck did she go, fellas?" Granger

asked as he dumped the food into their bowls. "Did she leave a note?"

He began searching the apartment, but came up empty-handed. His frustration was rapidly turning to fear. What if something had happened to Emmaline? What if somebody had broken in and—

The ringing telephone interrupted his dire imagination.

He leaped for it, knowing without a doubt that it was Emmaline.

"Granger?"

His heart sank. So much for his psychic abilities. "Brynn?"

"I'm in . . . car . . . on . . . cell phone."

"This is a bad connection, Brynn," he said as the line crackled.

". . . just heard the . . . news . . . radio . . . Emmaline . . ." Her voice crackled.

"Emmaline?" His heart sank. "What news? What did you hear?"

The phone went dead.

"Dammit!"

Brynn was trying to tell him something about Emmaline. Something she'd heard on the car radio.

Granger hurriedly turned on the television set and, with shaking fingers, flipped past a baseball game and a cooking show to the cable news channel.

Bingo.

A reporter stood before a familiar backdrop, above the caption *Live from Chimera.*

Granger's heart attempted to pulverize his rib cage.

What had happened?

Oh Lord, had something happened to Emmaline now, just when you finally figured out that you—

Shut up! he ordered himself. *Calm down and pay attention to the news.*

"—say the princess returned to the palace sometime during the last twenty-four hours," the reporter was saying, "escorted by a security team furnished by her fiancé. Prince Remi is believed to be here at the palace, and we have an unconfirmed report that the prince and princess are eager to reschedule their wedding as soon as—"

Granger turned off the television.

So.

That was it.

Emmaline might not have abandoned his dogs, but she had most certainly—and willingly—abandoned Granger himself.

The phone rang again.

If he hadn't still been holding the cordless receiver, he might not have bothered to answer it. He felt limp, weary, exhausted . . .

But the phone was ringing, and he was holding it, and he answered it. He knew that it was Brynn again, and that she wouldn't leave him alone until he spoke to her.

"Hello?"

"Granger?"

"*Emmaline?*"

"Granger, I just wanted to say that I'm sorry."

"You're sorry?" He was incredulous. "You abandoned the dogs."

You abandoned me, dammit.

"I didn't mean to leave so suddenly. But you weren't there, and I . . . I had to go."

"Why? Because he sent his security guards for you? How did they even find you?"

There was a moment of silence.

And he knew the answer before she told him.

"They found me because I called Remi and told him where I was. I thought it was the right thing to do, Granger."

He nodded, misery twisting in his throat, strangling any words he might possibly have uttered.

"And now that I'm back here," she went on, "I'm just not sure of anything."

Hope soared within him.

She wasn't sure?

That meant there was a chance. A chance for him. A chance for them.

"Emmaline, we need to talk," he said.

"We will. Someday, when . . ."

He frowned at the sound of somebody knocking on the apartment door.

"Not someday," he told Emmaline, ignoring the knock. "Now."

"Not over the phone," she protested. "We have to talk in person. But not—"

The knocking grew more urgent.

The dogs barked anxiously.

"Emmaline—"

"Granger, I have to hang up. I'll call you again."

"When?"

"I don't know. I don't know what's going to happen, or what I—"

"Granger?" Brynn's voice called from the hallway, above the yapping dogs. "Granger, open up!"

"Emmaline—"

"Granger, I have to go," she said softly. She sounded as though she was crying.

"Don't go, Emmaline!"

"I . . . I'm sorry."

Click. Dial tone.

And she was gone.

He cursed softly. She was gone . . .

But she had called.

That meant something.

Right now, that meant everything.

"Granger, open this door, dammit!"

"All right, all right, I'm coming."

A moment later, he was face-to-face with Brynn.

"My cell phone battery died," she said, brushing past him and into the apartment, "so I rushed back over here to tell you that Emmaline—"

"Is back in Verdunia. I know." He took a deep breath. "Brynn, I need another favor. A huge favor . . ."

Josephine hesitated in the corridor outside her sister's suite.

She didn't want to do this.

She didn't want to do this.

She *so* didn't want to do this.

She was afraid Emmaline would know, just by glancing at her, what she had done.

But that was nonsense. Emmaline couldn't possibly read her mind—and Remi had sworn never to tell a soul.

Dear, sweet Remi.

She had lingered in the bath for nearly an hour just now—as much to postpone the reunion with her sister as to rid herself of every physical remnant of her morning encounter with Remi in the guest room. But she could swear she could still smell his cologne in her hair, on her skin. She could still taste his mouth inside her own, could feel his hands on her bare flesh . . .

No. Stop thinking about it. It should never have happened.

What if Remi had only made love to her out of spite? What if he had simply been so angry at what she had told him about Emmaline being in New York City with Granger Lockwood that he had used Josephine to get revenge?

No. She couldn't believe that. And Remi hadn't seemed angry at all when she had told him Emmaline's secret. On the contrary, he had seemed almost . . . relieved.

But if that was the case . . . why had he left the palace immediately after speaking with Emmaline that morning? When he left Josephine lying sated in his tangled sheets, he promised her that he was going to break his engagement with Emmaline.

But something had happened when he spoke to her sister. He hadn't even stuck around long enough to bid Josephine farewell. Granted, she was soaking in the tub when he left. Still . . .

Stop procrastinating. You must face Emmaline.

Josephine shook away her muddled thoughts and rapped gently on the door.

It opened almost instantly.

"Hello, Tabitha. Is Emmaline—"

"She's resting in bed," the lady-in-waiting said in a hushed tone. "She doesn't wish to—"

"Who's there, Tabitha?" Emmaline's voice called from the next room.

"It's Her Royal Highness Princess Josephine."

"Josephine? Where on earth have you been?"

Josephine brushed past Tabitha and entered her sister's bedroom, but stopped short just inside the doorway.

Oh my.

Emmaline looked pale and exhausted, propped against a pile of pillows in her bed. Her eyes were swollen, as though she had been crying.

"I'm sorry, Emmaline. I'd have greeted you sooner, but I was . . ." *I was having a merry romp between the guest room sheets with your fiancé.*

"It's all right," Emmaline said. "Tabitha, would you mind leaving me alone with my sister?"

The lady-in-waiting quickly obliged.

"Are you all right, Emmaline?" Josephine asked cautiously, approaching the bed.

Her sister sighed and shook her head.

"What is it? Is it . . . is it because of Granger?" *Please let it be because of Granger. Please don't let it be because you know I've betrayed your trust.*

"Yes . . . in a way."

"Did you tell Remi about him?"

"I did . . . But he already seemed to know."

Josephine's breath caught in her throat. "Emmaline, I—"

"Of course you didn't tell him."

Caught on the brink of her confession, Josephine clamped her mouth shut.

"I'm not surprised he found out somehow, Josephine," her sister went on. "You and I both know what it's like to live in a fishbowl. Every move we make is public knowledge, and always will be." Her eyes filled with tears. "How I wish there were a way out."

"Maybe there is. What about Granger? If you're in love with him, can't you marry him and go off to live in America?"

"If only it were that simple."

"It is, Emmaline! You and Remi don't love each other. You and Granger do—"

"Why on earth would you say that?"

"No reason," Josephine said hastily. *Oops.* "It was just that neither of you seemed very happy about marrying each other, so I simply assumed—"

"I meant about Granger and me. Why would you think *we* love each other?"

"I can see it in your eyes," Josephine said truthfully, hoping that her sister couldn't see in *her* eyes the feelings she was trying so desperately to mask.

"Well, that doesn't matter now," Emmaline said, sounding as desolate as she looked, lying there in the big, empty bed. "Neither Granger nor Remi will have me."

"Remi won't have you?" Josephine asked, as a guilt-laced thrill shot through her. "Why not?"

Her sister looked down, toying with the folds of the quilt. "He says he's gone off to think about our future, but I can't imagine that he'll take me back now. Not after . . ."

"After what?"

"After everything I've done." Emmaline closed her eyes and leaned back. "I'd like to be alone now, Josephine. I need to rest. It's been a difficult day."

"I'm sorry, Emmaline."

Sorry for so many things . . .

Josephine crossed to the bed and pressed a kiss against her sister's cheek before tiptoeing out of the room.

Twelve

....

"You really should eat a bit of something," Tabitha said gently two days later. "At least try to sip some soup."

Emmaline lifted her aching head from the pillow to glance at the bedside table. On it was a wooden tray of food that had undoubtedly grown cold since a maid had brought it up from the kitchen at lunchtime. Untouched, the bowl of consomme, toasted cheese sandwich, and tea were elegantly accompanied by two pink linen napkins and a pink rose in a bud vase. Beside the tray was a nearly empty box of tissues.

"I'm not hungry, thank you," Emmaline said glumly, rubbing her tear-swollen eyes as Tabitha bent to retrieve a litter of soggy, crumpled tissues that had bounced out of the overflowing wastebasket a few feet from the bed.

"Perhaps not. But you must eat, if not for your own sake, then . . ." Tabitha trailed off.

Emmaline darted a sharp gaze at the lady-in-waiting.

"If not for my own sake," she said warily, "then for whose?"

Tabitha shrugged, eyes downcast.

She knows, Emmaline realized. *How on earth does she know?*

"Tabitha, were you eavesdropping when I spoke to Prince Remi the other day?"

"Of course not!" Tabitha met her gaze staunchly, shaking her head. "I would never eavesdrop, Your Highness."

"Not intentionally, but perhaps you happened to overhear . . . ?"

"I didn't overhear your conversation with Prince Remi," Tabitha protested.

"Then what *did* you overhear?" Emmaline sat up in bed, her abrupt movement jarring the tray of food at her side. A tide of soup sloshed over the rim of the bowl.

Emmaline automatically reached for one of the pink linen napkins to sop it up.

"Your Highness . . . ?"

She saw Tabitha's hand poised to take the napkin from her.

Of course.

Emmaline froze, clutching the soggy cloth.

Had she been away this long? Had she actually managed to get used to cleaning up after herself?

All her life, others had been hovering in her shadow, quite capable of—and quite willing to do—the dirty work. After all, a princess was expected, indeed, encouraged, to keep her hands unsullied.

Emmaline was still a princess.

And now that she was back in her palace . . .

Emmaline slowly handed the napkin to Tabitha, who took it and finished wiping up the soup.

When the lady-in-waiting had set the wet napkin aside, Emmaline asked again, "What was it that you overheard, Tabitha?"

"I heard you vomiting in the lavatory earlier. Yesterday, too. We all did."

"You all heard? The entire household staff?"

"All of us who were within earshot. But the others assume you've caught a distressing gastrointestinal virus."

"I see. And what do you assume, Tabitha?"

"That you are enceinte," came a reply that was anything but tentative.

Emmaline sighed.

Tabitha added hurriedly, "If I'm mistaken, Your Highness, then please—"

"You're not mistaken, Tabitha. I am pregnant."

Empathy flickered in Tabitha's familiar face. "Does Mr. Lockwood know?"

"Mr. Lockwood?" Her heart pounding, Emmaline feigned shock. "Why on earth would I tell Mr. Lockwood?"

Tabitha merely gazed at her.

"Oh, all right," Emmaline said after a long, uncomfortable moment. "Yes, Mr. Lockwood knows. And so does Prince Remi."

Tabitha's breath caught in her throat. "Was . . . was His Royal Highness disturbed by the news?"

Disturbed?

Disturbed.

That was one way to put it.

"Yes, Tabitha, he was certainly quite disturbed." Emmaline looked out the window adjacent to the bed. All she could see was a patch of dismal gray sky. When had the clouds rolled in? It had started off as a beautiful day.

"Prince Remi is back in Buiron, pondering the situation," Emmaline told Tabitha.

She winced at the memory of how he had stormed out after she broke the news about the baby. She had no reason to believe that she would ever hear from him again. She couldn't blame him for being hurt and angry.

But if Remi wouldn't marry her, she was destined to be a single mother. Her baby would never have a father. Not unless . . .

No.

No, you mustn't even consider going back to Granger, she scolded herself. He had his own life to lead.

It had been a mistake to call him on Sunday. But after Remi left, she had found herself missing Granger desperately, needing to hear his voice, if only one more time. She had known as soon as she spoke to him that it would never be enough just to talk to him. She wanted to see him. Just one more time . . .

But one more time wouldn't be enough, either.

She wanted more than that.

She wanted the impossible.

Tabitha's voice interrupted her melancholy deliberation. "Prince Remi may forgive you when he's had time to think things through, Your Highness."

"I doubt that." Emmaline stared into space, thinking about poor Remi. And about her poor, fatherless future child.

What had she done?

"Please, Tabitha," she said dully. "You must not breathe a word of this to anyone."

"Of course not, Your Highness."

"If the press ever found out, there would be a tremendous scandal. It would only bring more pain to Prince Remi."

"I understand."

To her surprise, Emmaline felt a soft touch on her arm. She looked up to see Tabitha standing beside her, wearing an expression of concern.

"Is there anything I can do, Your Highness?"

Emmaline swallowed against the ever-present lump in her throat.

"No, Tabitha," she said quietly. "There's nothing you can do."

"Are you in love with him?"

The question stunned her. Never before, in all their years of friendship, had Tabitha posed so intimate a question.

Emmaline gave careful thought to her reply before saying, "Prince Remi is a good, kind, decent man."

"Yes, he is . . . but I was referring to Mr. Lockwood, Your Highness."

"You were asking if I am in love with Mr. Lockwood?" Emmaline felt a telltale flush warming her cheeks. "Why on earth would you think—?"

"I apologize, Your Highness," Tabitha said quickly.

"It's all right. I can understand why you might assume—but I can assure you that this particular assumption is entirely erroneous. I am certainly not in love with Mr. Lockwood . . ."

Oh, aren't you?

Why does the mere thought of him make you quiver?

She closed her eyes, trying desperately to forget him—but instead remembering. Remembering everything, from that first moment . . .

She took a deep breath, and smelled roses.

Her eyes snapped open. Her gaze fell on the bedside table. On the bud vase.

Why on earth did the kitchen staff find it necessary to adorn every meal tray with flowers? And a rose, of all things . . .

Emmaline made a mental note to speak to someone about it as soon as possible. She couldn't possibly forget Granger Lockwood or that fateful day in the garden when the very air she breathed was continually scented with roses.

"I am certainly not in love with Mr. Lockwood," Emmaline repeated.

She squirmed, cleared her throat, and continued firmly, ". . . and Mr. Lockwood is certainly not in love with me."

At least that part was entirely true.

But saying it aloud was more distressing than she had anticipated. She was left feeling bleak and wistful.

Granger Lockwood didn't love her.

Of course, if Granger Lockwood *did* love her—and if she loved him—matters would only be more complicated.

If they were in love, she would still be in New York, and he would be begging his grandfather to take him back.

And if they were in love, it would only be a matter of time before Granger broke her heart.

Then where would she be? Miles from home, penniless and alone with a baby to raise.

It was far better this way, with her heart intact and her feet planted firmly on the ground right here in Verdunia, where she belonged.

Night had fallen over Chimera when Granger and Brynn emerged from the airport terminal and stepped into the waiting limo.

"The Traviata Hotel, please," Granger told the uniformed driver, still feeling groggy, having slept through most of the overseas journey.

"What? Why aren't you going straight to the palace?" Brynn asked, reapplying her red lipstick in the glow of a miniature lighted mirror she had pulled from her purse.

"I am," Granger said. "I'm dropping you off at the hotel first."

"No, you aren't."

"I'm not?"

Brynn shook her head decisively, snapped her mirror closed, and put it away with her lipstick. "You're going to need me."

Granger rolled his eyes. "Look, Cyrano, regardless of your way with words, I think I'm perfectly capable of speaking to Emmaline on my own."

"She wouldn't take your call."

That, unfortunately, was true. He had made several attempts, over the past few days, to reach Emmaline at the palace. He couldn't get past the switchboard.

"She wouldn't take your call, either," he pointed out to Brynn.

"My guess is that she didn't know either of us was trying to reach her. She probably told the palace operator to hold all calls for her. And who can blame her? The press is camped out at her doorstep and the entire world is hounding her."

He nodded. According to the news, the princess had been holed up in her castle ever since her return to Verdunia. The royal family had yet to issue a statement, and the media—not to mention the general public—were rife with rumor and wild with curiosity.

"So what's your plan, loverboy?" Brynn asked him.

"I'm going to talk to Emmaline. I'm going to tell her that . . ."

That what?

That she had to come back to the States with him, so that they could raise their child together as paupers?

Together.

The word sent shivers through him. He simply wanted to be with her. Every minute, every day. But . . . *why?*

He told himself it was just that he had grown accustomed to having her around.

But he had never felt this way before. Women had come and gone from his life, and he had never missed any of them more than momentarily. When the others left, he didn't feel as if . . .

As if he had lost Charlotte all over again.

But Charlotte never really existed, Granger reminded himself. His poor infant sister had lived only in his imagination.

Perhaps it was the same with Emmaline—at least, with the Emmaline he remembered. The sweet, vulnerable, witty, human Emmaline a man like Granger Lockwood could love.

"You're going to tell her . . ." Brynn prompted, beside him in the limo.

"I can't possibly tell her . . ."

"Tell her what?"

"That I love her."

Too late, he caught up with the conversation and realized what he had said.

"Be-because I don't love her, of course," he stammered, glad Brynn had put away that ridiculous lighted mirror and couldn't use it to glimpse his face in the shadowy backseat. "I'll simply tell her that she belongs in New York."

"With you."

"With me," he agreed.

"Not here, with Prince Remi."

"Of course not."

"But you don't love her any more than he does," Brynn said in what might have been an accusing tone—or perhaps she was baiting him. Perhaps she suspected that he was lying about his feelings.

That was one thing he couldn't stand about Brynn—the way she thought she knew him better than he knew himself.

"I care about her, and she's carrying my child," Granger said stubbornly. "That's reason enough for her to come back with me."

"How will you take care of her and the baby?"

He sighed. They had been over this, repeatedly, ever since he had told Brynn that he had walked away from Lockwood Enterprises for the second time.

"Brynn, you know as well as I do that I'm going to go back to New York and earn a living, like any regular father-to-be would do."

"But you're not going to marry Emmaline."

His breath caught in his throat.

Marry Emmaline?

Marry Emmaline.

There it was.

The notion that had been on his mind for two days

now, the terrifying, wonderful, *terrifying* notion.

"I'll marry Emmaline," he told Brynn, careful to keep his emotions in check, "if that's what she wants."

"Then it would be a loveless marriage," Brynn replied, watching him intently.

He refused to argue.

Brynn went on, "So you happen to think that a loveless marriage to the disinherited scion of the Lockwood family would be infinitely more appealing to Princess Emmaline than a loveless marriage to the heir of the Buironese throne."

"I happen to think that I'm infinitely more appealing and a hell of a lot more fun than Prince Remi," Granger retorted.

"I hope the princess shares your opinion." Brynn cleared her throat. "And since there's no way you're going to be able to get into the gilded cage—"

"What do you mean there's no way?"

"Well, what are you going to do? Just show up at the palace?"

"That's exactly what I'm going to do. I'm going to show up at the palace . . ."

"Along with throngs of other people," Brynn put in.

"They're strangers. Emmaline knows me."

"And you think she'll want to see you? If she wanted to see you she'd have gotten in touch by now."

"I wasn't home," he pointed out. "I've been staying at your place. And traveling."

Yes, and checking his voice mail at the apartment every other moment since he'd left, to no avail—a fact Brynn knew as well as he did.

"Go on," Brynn said with exaggerated patience. "I'm listening. What are you going to do when they won't let you simply stroll into the palace and sweep the princess off her feet?"

"I'm going to insist. I'm not going to leave until Emmaline agrees to see me."

Brynn sighed. "This is what I mean. You need a plan, Granger."

"I have a plan."

"A plan that will work. You don't have one. That's where I come in."

It was Granger's turn to sigh.

He supposed he had no choice but to listen to Brynn at this point.

After all, if it weren't for her—and her money—he wouldn't be here in the first place. He would be back on Eldridge Street, helpless, alone, wallowing in despair.

"Okay," he told Brynn reluctantly. "I'll listen. Tell me how we're going to break into the gilded cage."

Seated on the sofa in her private sitting room, Emmaline stared at the glass of milk and plate of buttered whole grain toast she had reluctantly ordered from the kitchen as a pre-bed snack.

Tabitha was right. She had to start eating again, regardless of her nausea and lack of appetite.

She picked up a slice, forced herself to take a bite,

chew, and swallow. The toast plunked leadenly to the depths of her stomach.

Ick.

Think of the baby. The baby needs nourishment.

She was about to take another bite when she heard a knock at the door.

"Who is it?" she called, grateful for the distraction, yet unwilling to see anybody.

"It's Josephine."

Emmaline sighed. "Come in."

Her sister sailed into the room, carrying a small gift package.

"This is for you," Josephine announced, handing the elaborately wrapped present to Emmaline.

"Thank you."

"Don't thank me," Josephine said. "Thank Pierre."

"Who on earth is Pierre?"

"My personal trainer. He asked me to give you this. He said that you've obviously been under a tremendous amount of stress and thought you could use this."

Emmaline unwrapped an unusual pendant hanging from a silver chain. "What is it?"

"He said to tell you it was a crystal that would bring you positive energy. You're supposed to wear it for luck."

"That's sweet of him," Emmaline said, wondering absently whether she had ever met Pierre.

"Yes, it was sweet of him," Josephine agreed. "Although frankly, I was a bit surprised that he was so concerned about your well-being. He didn't even ask how *I* was coping the whole time you were missing."

Emmaline bit back a smile. How like Josephine. She had missed her sister, she realized. Self-centeredness and all.

"Anyway, I told Pierre I didn't think you'd wear anything so New Age," Josephine went on, "but he insisted."

"It's pretty." Emmaline placed it around her neck. "And heaven knows I can use some positive energy these days."

"Have you heard from Remi?" Josephine asked, her gaze falling on a framed photograph on the mantel. It showed Emmaline and Remi, arm-in-arm, in happier times.

"Not yet," Emmaline said, all traces of the smile fading from her lips.

She longed to tell her sister the real reason she had fled her wedding—and Remi had subsequently abandoned her. The truth would become evident soon enough, she thought, glancing down at the barely visible swelling in her belly.

"Do you still want to marry him, if he'll have you?" Josephine asked.

Emmaline hesitated. "Of course," she said with a conviction she didn't feel.

An image of Granger Lockwood invaded her thoughts. She pushed it firmly away. He was history.

"Emmaline, it isn't healthy for you to stay alone here, day after day, brooding."

"What else can I do?" Emmaline walked to the window and gazed out at the night sky. "The palace is surrounded by the press. They're even more bloodthirsty now than they were before the wedding. It was so wonderful to have a reprieve from all that for a few days, in New York . . ."

She trailed off. Granger Lockwood again.

"A reprieve? How can you call being a virtual prisoner in that dreadful little hovel a reprieve?" Josephine shuddered. "I suppose when you're in love—"

"I wasn't in love! And the apartment was quite comfortable," Emmaline protested. "You didn't even see it."

"I didn't have to. You said that it was a one-room apartment. On the fifth floor. Without an elevator. Without a single servant. How on earth did you manage?"

"It wasn't that awful," Emmaline said. "And I wasn't a prisoner. We went out. He showed me the sights."

"Did you cook and clean?"

"A bit."

"Good Lord, Emmaline, what were you thinking?"

Emmaline scowled. "Josephine, if you wouldn't mind, I would like to be left alone."

Her sister hesitated, her expression having grown serious. "Emmaline, before I go, there's something I have to tell you."

"What is it?"

"I'm afraid it's a confession. Two confessions, really."

"Whatever have you done now, Josephine?" Emmaline asked, suppressing a smile. She recalled their younger days, when her sister used to sneak into her bedroom to douse herself in Emmaline's French perfume and try on her formal gowns. "Let me guess. Did you help yourself to something of mine while I was gone?"

Josephine looked even more distressed at her words. "Oh, Emmaline, I'm terribly sorry. I never meant to—"

She was interrupted by a sharp knock on the door.

Emmaline sighed. "Just a moment, Josephine." She called, "Come in."

A maid materialized in the doorway. "Your Highness, a Ms. Brynn Halloway has requested that you contact her at the Traviata Hotel."

"Brynn Halloway?" Emmaline's heart leaped. "She's here in Chimera?"

"Who is Brynn Halloway?" Josephine asked.

"She's a friend," Emmaline said, already reaching for the telephone. "A very good friend. You must excuse me, Josephine." Noting her sister's dismayed expression, she added, "We'll talk later. You have my word."

"But Emmaline—"

"Please, Josephine. This is important."

Her sister hesitated. "All right. But we really will talk later."

* * *

Seated in the back of his chauffeured limousine, Prince Remi gazed out the window at the passing farmland. Soon this bumpy two-lane road to Verdunia would become a six-lane superhighway—provided he married Emmaline.

If he went ahead with the royal wedding, the coastal access and development plan created by Lockwood Enterprises would proceed as planned.

If he didn't marry Emmaline, there would once again be bad blood between his family and the Verdunian royals. Buiron would lose its access to the shipping port. Verdunia would lose Buiron's financial backing. The people of both kingdoms would suffer.

Remi shook his head sadly.

Unless . . .

Unless, of course, he married Josephine instead of Emmaline.

But how on earth could he expect either kingdom to take him seriously if he merely swapped one princess for another, as though they were interchangeable?

They weren't, of course.

Josephine . . . ah, Josephine had captured his fickle heart.

And Emmaline . . .

Emmaline had betrayed him. She was going to give birth to another man's child.

Nobody will ever have to know, Remi reminded himself. If they were married immediately, the world would assume the baby was his.

But you would know. Emmaline would know.

And Granger Lockwood would know.

Remi tried to summon hatred for the dashing American who had bedded his bride-to-be—and hatred for the woman who had left him at the altar with the entire world looking on.

Yet he didn't hate Granger or Emmaline.

Remi wasn't in love with her, nor had he ever, for one moment, believed that she was in love with him.

She claimed that she wasn't in love with Granger Lockwood, either. But Remi had seen the longing in her gaze when she spoke his name.

He assumed that it was the same expression that flickered in his own eyes when he thought about Josephine.

Remi sighed.

He knew what he longed to do . . .

Just as he knew what he *must* do.

He supposed that Emmaline would be grateful for his wise, selfless decision. And that Josephine would understand that they must all put their personal desires aside for the greater good, as generations of royals had done before them.

Remi glanced at his watch.

It was half past eight o'clock in the morning. He would reach the palace in Chimera before nine.

He and Emmaline could be married in the king's private study before noon.

Granger's breath caught in his throat at the sight of Emmaline in the doorway of the hotel suite. Several palace security guards hovered in the corridor behind her.

Mere days had passed since he had seen Emmaline, yet her appearance was drastically altered. He took in her elegant, dark, figure-hugging dress, her upswept hair, her fully made-up features. She was a princess once again—regal, sophisticated, beautiful.

Only the slightly noticeable protrusion where the fabric hugged her tummy confirmed that Granger had ever been in her life at all.

"Emmie!" Brynn swept her into a hug before she could glimpse Granger standing across the room. "It's so wonderful to see you."

"It is, but . . . what are you doing here in Chimera?" Emmaline asked as Brynn released her.

"I told you when we spoke on the phone last night—I came to see you," Brynn said, closing the door, leaving the guards stationed outside. "You left so abruptly, Emmie. I didn't even get to say goodbye. And there's one more little thing . . ."

As she looked past Brynn, her gaze sweeping the elegant suite, Emmaline spotted Granger. She gasped.

"Hello, Emmaline." He walked toward her.

"Granger! I didn't realize that you were—"

"I know." He halted a few feet from her, so close that he could smell her perfume. His eyes swept over her, taking in the details—the tendril of hair that had escaped a pin just above her left ear, the unusual pendant she wore around her neck. "I knew that if Brynn told you I was here, you wouldn't come."

"That's not—"

"Of course it's true. Come on, Emmaline. Would you really be here if you knew that you were going to see me?"

"I don't know," she said quietly.

"Well, I do know. You want to avoid me. You'd probably be happy if I'd leave an ocean between us forever. But we have to talk," he told her.

On cue, Brynn started to slip into the next room.

"Brynn, don't go," Emmaline ordered. To Granger, she said, "There's nothing to talk about."

"Of course there is. You can't shut me out of your life. We're having a child together."

"Granger, when I told you about the baby, you made it perfectly clear that you'd be more than happy if the baby—and I—just disappeared."

He thought back to that day in his bedroom. Okay, she was right. But things had changed.

"I wasn't thrilled about the baby at first," he admitted, watching Brynn edge toward the door out of the corner of his eye. "But now—"

"Now you're thrilled?" Emmaline shook her head. "Granger, the last thing you need is the burden of a child."

"How do you know what I need?"

A door closed quietly as Brynn left the room. Emmaline didn't notice.

"I know what you need because you told me," she said. "You told me—more than once—that you need freedom. That you don't want to go back to work for Lockwood Enterprises."

"You're right. I don't."

"Yet you were willing to do so for the baby. I can't allow you to—"

"And for you," he said softly, capturing her trembling hands in his own. "I was willing to do it for you."

Debi Hanson gasped.

It was her third or fourth gasp in the space of the last sixty seconds. Sinking to the nearest chair in her elegant hotel suite, she pressed her earpiece so hard that it pinched her ear, but she barely noticed the pain.

This was extraordinary.

Utterly extraordinary.

Princess Emmaline was pregnant . . .

And the baby didn't belong to Prince Remi . . .

The prim Verdunian royal had apparently had a raging affair with one of America's most eligible—and supposedly perennial—bachelors . . .

And the luscious cherry topping this delectable scandal sundae: Granger Lockwood had fallen head-over-heels in love with the pregnant princess. That much was obvious. Even Debi's near-deaf Grandma Gretl could have detected the passion in Lockwood's voice just now when he declared, *I was willing to do it for you.*

What else was he willing to do for Princess Emmaline?

And just what, Debi wondered, was the princess willing to do for Granger Lockwood?

Ditch her royal groom at the altar and run off to New York, for one thing.

That didn't last long, Debi reminded herself.

Yet it sounded as though Granger Lockwood wasn't going to let her go without a fight.

Never in her wildest dreams had Debi imagined so sensational a scoop.

And for once, everything had fallen into place so easily. Almost too easily.

All it had taken were some strategic feminine wiles—and of course, cold hard cash—to convince Dolph to convince his trainer, Jean Paul, to convince Jean Paul's brother Pierre to give Princess Josephine the bugged pendant for her sister.

Even then, there was no guarantee that the princess would wear it.

But wear it she had, and now Debi found herself privy to the scoop of the millennium—directly on the heels of what she had thought would be her ultimate coup de grâce: the exclusive interview with Prince Remi.

To make matters most convenient, the confrontation between the princess and her playboy lover was taking place in this very hotel, in a suite just down the hall from Debi's. She took that coincidence as a sign—a cosmic thumbs-up.

"I didn't ask you to do that—or anything else—for me," Princess Emmaline was saying in her ear.

"Oh really? Look, I didn't blindly call up and offer to land a helicopter on the palace grounds and rescue you from your wedding. If you recall, that was *your* idea."

Debi gasped again. The helicopter! Of course! She had seen it that day, while she was doing her live feed in front of the palace.

And to think she had believed that it was a news chopper, perhaps with Naomi Finkelmeyer on board.

Just wait, Naomi Finkelmeyer. Just wait until I drop this bombshell. You'll be history.

Move over, Naomi.

Move over, Barbara and Diane and Katie . . .

Here comes Debi Hanson, full speed ahead!

Emmaline deeply regretted the day she had ever laid eyes on Granger Lockwood.

She regretted the day she had ever asked him to help her escape from Verdunia.

Most of all, she regretted the night they had shared in his hotel room . . .

Or did she?

If it weren't for that night, she would be married to Remi . . . and she wouldn't be pregnant.

Somewhere along the way, the unplanned pregnancy had already turned into a baby. *Her* baby. And she wanted this baby more than she had ever wanted anything in her life.

Even more than she wanted Granger Lockwood out of it.

She glared at him. "You can't resist throwing that

in my face, can you? You repeatedly remind me of how you came to my rescue. And I am grateful, Granger, really I am. But I never should have asked you for help, and I certainly don't expect anything else from you."

"What kind of man do you think I am, Emmaline? Do you think I don't intend to take responsibility for the baby—and for you? I'm willing to do whatever it takes to support you. I'm willing—hell, Emmaline, I'm willing to marry you and give the baby a name."

Willing?

He was *willing* to marry her?

A jagged shard of pain ripped into her heart as his words sunk in.

She realized that a proposal was what she had waited to hear from him all along.

But this wasn't how it was supposed to be. He was supposed to want to marry her. Not merely be *willing*. He was supposed to get down on one knee, and take her hand, and tell her that he loved her and always would.

"Forget it," she said grimly. "I don't want you to marry me. I want you to go back to your life so that I can go back to—"

"To what? To your gilded cage?" he asked darkly, his face inches from hers. "Or to Remi?"

"Perhaps." She turned away, unwilling to let him glimpse her true feelings—feelings for him.

It was tempting—oh, so tempting—to throw caution to the wind and tell him that she would return to New York with him. That she would marry him.

If only he could offer her more than a mere arrangement.

Here he was, asking her to do the very thing he had condemned mere months earlier: enter into a loveless marriage for a selfless cause.

"And what will you tell Remi about the pregnancy?" Granger asked.

"I've already told him."

"And he's willing to take you back, and marry you, and raise my child as his own?"

She hesitated only briefly before nodding. "Yes. He is. It would be the best thing for everyone involved."

He was silent for so long that at last she had to turn back to look at him.

To her shock, his gaze betrayed sharp regret.

"All right, then," he said quietly. "If that's the best thing, then I wish you and Remi—and my child—well."

No! she wanted to scream. *No, I lied. About Remi. About not wanting anything from you. And about my marrying Remi being the best thing. The best thing would be for you to ask me to marry you again, and this time, tell me that you love me. Because . . .*

Because . . .

Because I love you.

There.

There it was, the stunning truth.

She loved him.

She had to tell him. Telling him might make a difference. It might allow him to realize that—

"Goodbye, Emmaline," Granger said gruffly, turning his back.

"Granger . . ."

"Just go. Get out of here. That's what I want, okay? And for once, all I care about is what *I* want. So go."

She nodded. Somehow she found her voice. "All right. I'll go. Goodbye, Granger."

Thirteen

....

The throng of reporters at the palace gate had thickened considerably when Emmaline's chauffeured car returned from the Traviata Hotel shortly after nine A.M.

She was grateful for the tinted windows that masked her tearstained face from the gaping crowd as the car slowed and passed through the entrance.

She was grateful, too, for her security team's professional, detached silence. Neither the uniformed driver nor the two burly men sharing the backseat with her had so much as glanced at Emmaline as she sobbed quietly into a soggy linen handkerchief.

Toying with the so-called good luck pendant around her neck, she stared dully out the window as the car pulled to a stop beside the familiar side entrance, well out of view of the media circus. It wasn't until she had stepped out into the warm September sunshine that she saw the shiny black Rolls Royce parked nearby, its hood marked by two Buironese flags.

Startled, she jerked the pendant so hard that the chain snapped.

A chill slithered over her.

Remi was the last person she wanted to see now.

She gazed from the car to the broken necklace in her hand.

So much for that.

She hurled it into the bushes with a muttered curse.

A guard was holding the side door open for her.

She couldn't stand out there all day.

Emmaline forced her wobbly legs to carry her inside. She was immediately met by Tabitha, who had been alerted to her arrival.

"Prince Remi is waiting in the front drawing room with your parents, Your Highness," the lady-in-waiting announced. In a whisper, she added, "Are you all right? Have you been crying?"

"I'm fine, thank you, Tabitha." Emmaline resisted the overwhelming urge to flee.

She took a deep breath to steady herself and walked slowly toward the drawing room. A maid scurried ahead to open the door for her.

The trio—Prince Remi, King Jasper, and Queen Yvette—were seated before the fireplace. All three rose when she entered.

"We'll leave you two alone," Queen Yvette said, hurrying to the door.

"I'll see to it that those phone calls are made,"

King Jasper said, exchanging a meaningful glance with Remi as he strode past.

"Which phone calls?" Emmaline asked.

Her parents were already out of the room.

"Why don't we sit down?" Remi asked.

She gladly sank onto the sofa, desperately wishing that she were alone.

Remi sat beside her, his expression betraying nothing. She noticed that for a weekday morning, he was overdressed—even for him. He wore a well-cut suit with an ascot.

"You're looking a bit shaken, Emmaline," Remi said.

"It's just . . . I'm quite surprised to see you here."

"And I was quite surprised to arrive and find that you *weren't* here. I was told that you had gone to the Traviata Hotel to visit a friend who was staying there."

"Yes, and she had arrived in Chimera quite unexpectedly the night before." Emmaline stressed the female pronoun, lest Remi inquire further, having assumed that the friend had been Granger Lockwood.

She wasn't about to share the fact that Granger had used Brynn's visit to ambush her. This strained tête-a-tête with her former fiancé was complicated enough.

"It must have been an urgent visit," Remi pressed, "if you were so willing to brave the press outside."

She remained silent. Perhaps she owed Remi an explanation, but she was too emotionally drained to provide further detail now.

Remi waited a moment. Then, mercifully, he shrugged and went on, "I've given great thought to our situation, Emmaline. I'm sure that you've done the same."

"Of course I have."

But they both knew that it didn't matter what she thought. The verdict lay in Remi's hands. He could choose to move on, or he could choose to go ahead with the marriage.

If his decision was the former, she wouldn't blame him.

And if it was the latter . . .

Well, at least her lie to Granger would be validated.

She would marry Remi. He would raise the child as his own. Someday, Granger Lockwood's illegitimate son or daughter would inherit the throne to Buiron, and nobody would be the wiser.

"What is it that you want, Emmaline?" Remi asked, surprising her with his gentle tone.

"I don't know . . ." She shook her head, wishing she could tell him the truth. That she wanted Granger to love her. "I don't know what I want, Remi. And I don't think it matters."

"It matters to me," Remi said, taking her hand.

To her surprise, she believed him. Tears sprang to her eyes. "Oh please . . . Don't, Remi . . ."

"I beg your pardon?"

"Don't be kind. I don't deserve your kindness. And you didn't deserve what I did to you."

"No," he agreed, "I didn't. But we've no choice other than to move on, Emmaline."

"Move on?" Did he mean—

"Move on," he repeated. "Put the past behind us . . . and get married."

Oh. Move on *together*.

Was that the answer she wanted to hear?

Or was it the answer she had been dreading?

Suddenly Emmaline was so confused that all she could manage was a faint "You want to marry me?"

"Yes. I've concluded that marriage is the simplest solution to our dilemma."

She wanted to cry—or laugh—or both simultaneously—at the irony. Here she was, receiving her second perfunctory marriage proposal in a matter of minutes.

Remi went on briskly, "I've discussed the situation with King Jasper and—"

"You didn't tell Papa about my pregnancy!" she asked in horror.

"Of course not. Emmaline, nobody must ever know."

"Nobody ever will." She pushed aside a twinge of guilt about Tabitha. And Brynn. But both had sworn that they would carry the secret to the grave. As for Granger . . .

"What about Lockwood?" Remi asked ominously, as though reading her thoughts. "How do we know that he won't step forward someday to claim paternity?"

"He won't," she said. "He has never wanted anything to do with this baby, or with me."

Heart pounding, she forced herself to hold Remi's gaze.

Never? she asked herself.

"Never" wasn't exactly the truth. Granger had offered to take care of both her and the baby. A hollow offer, sans loving commitment, but a legitimate offer just the same.

"Just to be sure, I'll have an attorney draw up a legal document for Lockwood to sign," Remi said. "Now, assuming that the palace is contacting the abbey as we speak, the minister should be here shortly to marry us."

"Here?" she asked in dread. "Now?"

"Of course. At this stage, a public affair will only become a media circus," Remi pointed out.

"It was a media circus in the first place," Emmaline murmured. "I suppose you're right. There's no point in waiting for . . ."

"For . . . ?" he prompted, when she trailed off.

For Granger to come to his senses and realize he loves me.

"No point in waiting forever," Emmaline said, wishing her heart didn't ache so.

"Precisely." Remi mustered a smile. "We'll announce the marriage in an official statement to the press this afternoon. Your father is contacting his press secretary now to make arrangements."

"Good," she managed to say around the lump in her throat.

Remi leaned toward her and pressed a chaste kiss to her cheek. "I'm glad it's settled, then."

She nodded, unable to speak.

Staring morosely into space, Granger had taken only a sip of the first of three glasses of scotch he'd had sent up from room service when the suite's telephone rang.

"Who can that be?" Brynn asked, lowering her martini.

That was what Granger loved about Brynn—she wasn't one to let a man drink alone.

"Who cares who it is? We're busy," he growled.

"I'd better pick it up. It might be Emmaline," Brynn said.

That was one thing he couldn't stand about Brynn. The woman was prone to delusions.

Granger snorted. "Yes, it might be Emmaline— and that glass you're holding might be filled with fruit punch."

"She might have had a change of heart," Brynn told him. "Or maybe, if you would at least speak to her again, *you* will."

"What's that supposed to mean?"

"Oh come on, Granger," Brynn said, walking toward the ringing phone. "You can do better than you did when she was here."

"Meaning . . . ?"

"Meaning I couldn't help overhearing your conversation through the bedroom door . . ."

He snorted again, and took another gulp of scotch.

". . . and I must say, your proposal left a lot to be desired. You didn't even tell Emmaline that you love her."

"Love her?" he sputtered, as Brynn, distracted, lifted the telephone receiver.

He didn't love . . .

Oh yes he did.

You do?

I do.

I love Emmaline.

His jaw dropped.

He *loved* Emmaline?

He went absolutely still as the truth enveloped him, welcome as a dryer-warmed comforter on a chilly winter night.

He loved Emmaline.

He plunked the glass on the table so hard that the amber liquid sloshed over his fingertips. Heedless, he stood and paced to the window, gazing absently at the cobblestone street several stories below.

He loved Emmaline.

Then he had to do something.

Before it was too late.

"Hello?" Brynn was saying into the phone. "Yes, this is . . . Excuse me? . . . Excuse me? I don't know what you're talking about. No, I don't . . . No, he isn't. Goodbye."

She slammed down the receiver.

Granger barely noticed, caught up in the wonder of his discovery.

He knew nothing about love. Nobody had ever

loved him before—or at least not in a very long time. He supposed his parents might have loved him, but they hadn't shown it.

Nor had Granger ever loved anybody. Not in decades. There was a time when he might have felt more than occasional affection for Grandfather, but the old man had long since succeeded in transforming their relationship from familial to professional.

As for the women who had come and gone . . .

He certainly hadn't loved any of them. Some he had even disliked.

But Emmaline didn't belong in that category. How could he ever have assumed—

"Granger!" Brynn's tone alerted him that she had been trying to get his attention.

Dazed, he murmured, "What is it?"

Everything happened at once.

The phone rang shrilly again . . .

Just as Granger noticed the chaos on the street below . . .

Just as Brynn said, "They know. The whole world knows about you and Emmie."

"Are you ready, Your Highness?" Tabitha asked, hovering nearby as Emmaline surveyed her reflection in the full-length mirror in her dressing room.

No. No, I'm not ready. I'll never be ready for this.

"Yes, I'm ready."

Lies. When had her whole life become about lies?

She turned away from the mirror, not caring that there was an almost noticeable gap between two midsection buttons on the simple ivory suit her wardrobe mistress had hastily prepared for her impromptu wedding.

Tabitha cleared her throat. "Your Highness, the buttons—"

"Are straining across my stomach. I am quite aware of that, Tabitha, thank you."

"Would you like me to locate a seamstress to—"

"No, thank you." Emmaline sighed. "The palace florist is sending a bouquet from the greenhouse— I can hold it so that it will conceal the gap. Besides, it will be a five-minute ceremony at most. No photographers, and I'll change my clothes right afterward."

"All right, then. The minister is here. They're waiting downstairs in your father's study."

Emmaline nodded and began walking toward the door, and her future.

It's going to be all right, she silently told the baby. *I'm doing this for you. So that you'll have a future . . .*

Her own future be damned.

Ensconced in her top floor suite at the Traviata Hotel, Debi Hanson was on the telephone with Jack in New York when she heard an abrupt knock on her door.

Not just a knock. More a violent pounding.

She ignored it, but Jack broke off in midsentence to ask, "What the hell was that?"

"Just a chambermaid. Go on, Jack."

"Where was I?"

She said, over another eruption of door banging, "You were congratulating me on my—"

"Debi Hanson?" A male voice boomed in the hallway.

"That doesn't sound like a chambermaid," Jack informed her.

Debi sighed. "Hang on a moment."

She set down the receiver and stalked to the door, not bothering with the peephole. After all, rapists and murderers didn't knock. It must be another fruit basket or bucket of champagne being sent up from management.

Still, even a newly sought-after person such as herself should be able to have an uninterrupted conversation with her boss.

Debi yanked the door open and demanded, "Just what is so urgent that—"

A handsome stranger she immediately recognized as Granger Lockwood stood in the corridor.

"I need you," he said abruptly. "You and your camera crew. Right away."

Emmaline stood facing Remi before the fireplace in her father's study, flanked by her parents, her sisters, and Tabitha, whom Emmaline had insisted be allowed to stay.

She looked down at the bouquet clutched in her quaking hands.

Roses. The florist had sent roses.

"All right then," the minister said, and cleared his throat. "Shall we begin?"

Emmaline looked up at Remi.

He nodded slightly, his expression benign; resigned.

Emmaline looked at her parents. They were beaming.

So was Genevieve.

Not Josephine. Her eyes glistened with tears.

Emmaline was startled by the sight. She had never considered Josephine the type to cry at weddings. Perhaps her sister had been concealing a sentimental side all these years.

The minister began speaking.

Emmaline didn't hear him.

She heard only Granger's voice, echoing in her head.

It's my baby, too. I want to support it. I want it to have the best of everything . . .

She inhaled deeply, and her nostrils filled with the scent of roses.

Roses . . .

"I can't do this," she blurted, just as a sharp knock sounded on the study door.

The others gaped at her.

"I'm sorry, Remi." Emmaline shook her head. "I can't marry you. I can't."

There was another knock at the door.

"Yes?" the king asked impatiently.

The door opened.

His press secretary breathlessly announced, "Your

Majesty, I'm sorry to interrupt, but I'm afraid . . . I'm afraid all hell is breaking loose. You must turn on a television."

"Are you ready, Granger?" Debi Hanson asked, facing the cameraman who stood poised before them.

Granger nodded. He was ready. He had been ready for this for much longer than he'd realized. Now he only hoped that it wasn't too late.

"Just remember our agreement," he warned Debi Hanson. "No personal questions about anything else."

"And you remember your end of the bargain," she replied. "When and if you decide to do a sit-down interview, you'll do it with me. I get the exclusive."

"Of course."

Yeah, right.

This was a one-shot deal. He would never again be willing to speak to the press about his personal life. He had turned to her out of sheer desperation.

"All right, then. Let's roll, Lenny," Debi ordered the cameraman.

A spotlight went on, nearly blinding Granger.

Better get used to it, he told himself. Whether it worked or not, he had been thrust squarely into the limelight.

He hated this. He hated giving this artificial blond barracuda exactly what she wanted. But this was his only option—his only chance. And if it didn't work . . .

No. It has to work.

Granger took a deep breath and prepared to take the biggest gamble of his life.

Emmaline stared at the television screen in disbelief.

There, an emaciated supermodel named Millicent was being interviewed in a live feed from Paris.

"I had no idea that my beloved Granger was involved with the princess," Millicent said, weeping suspiciously artificial tears. "And now, to discover that he is the reason that she abandoned her fiancé at the altar—and that she is carrying Granger's baby . . ."

Emmaline felt sick inside.

It was all over.

The media knew. Her parents and her sisters and the minister and the press secretary knew. The world knew.

The news about her pregnancy—and the fact that Granger Lockwood was the father—was being beamed around the world.

"Emmaline . . . ?" Queen Yvette turned away from the TV to stare at her daughter in disbelief.

"I'm sorry, Mother. And . . . everyone." Somehow, she maintained her composure, even as her mother put her arms around her.

"Oh, Emmaline, I wish you had told us," her mother said. "When I think of all you put us through when you vanished—"

"I left a note," she said feebly, looking from her mother to her father.

They were stunned, yes. Stunned and dismayed. But miraculously, they hadn't condemned or disowned her.

Yet.

"I'd have told you if I could," she said, her voice wavering. "But we—Remi and I—we thought it would be best if—"

"How on earth did this get out?" Remi cut in, his eyes glued to the television. "It has to be Lockwood. He must have—"

"Granger would never go to the press!" Emmaline protested.

"No, but he clearly told his supermodel girlfriend."

Emmaline didn't know what to think. "He swore to me that—"

"Shh!"

Startled, she broke off to look at the press secretary, who had belatedly remembered protocol and appeared mortified. "I apologize for the interruption, Your Highness, it's just . . . Look! Listen! Something is happening!"

Emmaline followed his gaze.

The televised interview with the allegedly heartbroken Millicent had given way to an anchorman announcing a breaking news bulletin.

Then the screen shifted to a live shot from Chimera and a vaguely familiar blond reporter wearing a smug expression.

"Good morning again," she said. "I'm Debi Hanson, and I'm live in Chimera with Mr. Granger Lockwood, the American tycoon whose name is suddenly on everyone's lips."

"You see?" Remi snapped. "I should have known better than to—"

This time it was the king who said, "Shhh!"

"Mr. Lockwood, let's cut to the chase. Following in the footsteps of Prince Remi of Buiron, you have contacted *me* . . ." Brimming with self-importance, Debi Hanson paused to bring greater emphasis to the word before continuing, ". . . because you have a special message that you wish to send to Princess Emmaline. What is it?"

The camera zeroed in on Granger. He looked directly into the lens. Emmaline felt as though he were looking directly at her.

"Emmaline, I hope you'll forgive me," he said. "For this. And for everything else. For not telling you how I feel."

Emmaline held her breath, trembling all over.

"I have so much to say to you . . ." Granger cleared his throat and added, "In *private*. But right here, right now, in public, for the whole world to hear, there's only this: I love you."

Emmaline gasped.

He loved her.

He loved her!

The camera cut back to Debi Hanson.

Emmaline didn't wait to hear what she had to say. She was already headed for the door.

The room erupted behind her in a chorus of dismay.

"Emmaline!"

"Emmaline, come back here!"

"Your Highness . . ."

"Emmaline, where are you going?"

"To find Granger," she tossed over her shoulder—along with the bouquet of roses, which landed in Josephine's ready hands.

Back in Brynn's suite, Granger paced the floor.

He ignored the repeated bleating of the telephone receiver, which he had taken off the hook. It was better to listen to this than to incessant ringing.

Brynn didn't agree. Declaring that she had a violent headache, she had left the suite in search of ibuprofen, promising to return momentarily.

"Will you be all right without me?" she had asked.

"I'll be fine."

But he wouldn't be fine without Emmaline.

He would go on, yes. He would survive. But he wouldn't be fine.

If only . . .

If only something would happen.

He couldn't stand the waiting.

He didn't even know what he was waiting for . . .

For Princess Emmaline to burst through the door and tell him that she loved him, too.

Which meant that he was waiting for the impossible.

Even if, by some miracle, she had seen him on television just now, there was little likelihood that she felt the same way.

Or that she would be willing to tell him if she did.

Or that it wasn't already too late for that.

Debi Hanson had informed him that Prince Remi had been seen arriving at the palace that morning, followed shortly by a minister from the abbey.

His official reply to that news had been "No comment."

His unofficial one had been a colorful curse.

Unless he was mistaken, Emmaline and Remi were already married, and he had just bared his soul to the masses.

Should he turn on the television and replace the telephone in its cradle so that he could receive the latest update?

No.

He decided he didn't want to see, yet again, a blow-by-blow account of his personal life, and Emmaline's.

Anything was better than that.

And anyway, the longer he kept himself in the dark, the longer he could cling to hope . . .

If Emmaline had stopped to think, she might have done things differently.

For example, she might not have raced out of the palace still wearing the ill-fitting ivory suit. The exertion caused the button to pop off and roll under a shrub as she dashed toward the gate.

Which was where one of her bodyguards caught up with her.

"Your Highness—"

"I have to get to the Traviata Hotel."

He opened his mouth to protest.

"Nothing is going to stop me," she informed him with all the deadly conviction of a pregnant runaway bride.

"All right," the bodyguard conceded. "But we'll drive you."

She hesitated.

And then one look at the mobbed street beyond the gate convinced her that he was right.

As the car drove through the crowded streets, trailed by a caravan of reporters, a royal motorcade, and Prince Remi's limousine, she fought against the wave of panic that repeatedly rose within her.

She knew that Granger loved her.

She knew that she loved him.

After she found him, and told him . . .

Then what?

Love wouldn't solve everything. In fact, it wouldn't solve anything.

As far as she knew, Granger was still penniless, and Emmaline had all but turned her back on her family—and her kingdom—just now.

She and Granger would have nobody to turn to but each other.

Would that be enough?

As the car pulled up in front of the mobbed hotel—trailed by more security, her family, Prince Remi, and a media posse—Emmaline wished that she had taken the time to think things through.

"We'll escort you inside," one of her guards said.

She hesitated. "Maybe we should call the desk first and let them know that I'm coming."

"Oh, they know."

She followed his gaze, past the bloodthirsty reporters—and saw the entire hotel staff lined up expectantly inside the lobby.

Outside there were police officers, and countless reporters, and throngs of curious onlookers. The crowd threatened to swarm the car, and the law enforcement officials were hastily setting up barricades.

It dawned on her that the world was of course following her every move—live on television.

Did Granger know, then, that she was coming?

She scanned the crowded lobby for his face.

He wasn't there.

Her heart sinking, she looked at the police officers and her own security officers keeping the hordes of people back from her car. She felt like a zoo animal, gazing through the glass at the strangers who gaped and pointed and took pictures of her.

Granger's words haunted her.

Don't you think it's time we found out what we're made of?

Don't you think it's time we found out how regular people live?

Yes.

Yes, it was time.

She knew then that it was going to be all right.

Maybe it didn't matter if all they had was each other.

Maybe Granger—and the baby—were all she had ever needed in the first place.

"Granger!" Brynn burst into the suite. "You'll never believe who's—"

"I know. I know!" He rushed past her, leaving behind the television set and the surreal image of the princess getting out of her car several stories below.

He dashed down the carpeted hallway to the elevator bank with Brynn trailing behind him.

"Granger, it's a madhouse down there!" she said. "At least wait here for—"

"I can't wait another second." He jammed his hand on the Down button.

It lit up.

He waited, beating a staccato rhythm on his thigh with his jittery hand.

"Come on come on *come on*!" he said.

"There's a mob scene down there. At least let me go first and create some kind of distraction to divert attention from—"

"No, Brynn, it's okay," he said, punching the button again in frustration. "If I could just get to her . . ."

But damned if he was going to wait all day for the elevator.

He spun around, searching for—and finding—the exit door to the stairwell.

"Where are you going?"

"I'm taking the stairs!"

"Fourteen flights? But that'll take—"

The door swung closed behind him, cutting her off.

He was halfway to the ninth floor, nearly tripping over his own feet in his haste, when he heard a door open somewhere below, followed by the echoed tap-tapping of heels on the stairs.

Somebody—a female somebody—was coming up.

Running up.

A female somebody was in as much a hurry as he was.

If it's her, I'll take it as a sign that everything is going to be all right.

Granger started to fly down another flight . . .

And nearly fell, his foot twisting beneath his weight as he caught himself on the banister.

He cursed as pain exploded in his ankle.

The tap-tapping heels were coming closer, faster.

If it's her, it'll be a sign that we're meant to be together. That we'll work things out, no matter what.

Gritting his teeth, he limped down another flight . . .

If it's her—please let it be her—I'll never wish for another thing as long as I live.

And then she came into view.

"Emmaline!"

Relief washed over him.

"Granger!"

They met on the landing in a joyous embrace.

The phrase spilled from their lips simultaneously.

"*I love you.*"

They laughed, kissed, laughed again.

"Where's your entourage?" he asked. "And the press?"

"I gave them the slip in all the commotion in the lobby," Emmaline said.

"Commotion?"

"My sister Josephine fainted. I'm certain she's all right. Remi stepped forward quickly and caught her before she hit the floor. I'm sure that she's come to by now, and that she's enjoying her moment in the spotlight. But we have about two minutes before they find us," Emmaline said. "We'd better go back up to your suite and barricade ourselves inside."

"I hope I can make it that far. I twisted my ankle."

"Oh, Granger . . ."

"I'll be okay."

"But can you make it up all those flights?"

"That depends on how many there are," he said. "I lost count."

They looked around.

He spotted a sign on the landing door.

"Looks like we're at the seventh floor," he said. "And my suite is on the fourteenth."

"You know what that means, don't you?"

"That you'll have to carry me up piggyback?" he asked, wincing as he tested his weight on his injured foot.

"No. It means we finally met each other halfway, Granger."

"I was willing to come all the way down for you, Emmaline."

"And I was willing to come all the way up for you."

"Then from now on, it won't be my way or your way. Just halfway. Deal?"

Flashing a delighted grin, she agreed, "Deal."

They sealed it with a kiss.

Then they began their long journey—side by side, one step at a time.

Epilogue

 "So . . . congratulations, Mrs. Lockwood."

"Same to you, Mr. Lockwood."

They smiled at each other over the sleeping blue-blanketed bundle cradled in Granger's arms.

Alone together at last, just the three of them, they had endured a torturous twenty-two-hour labor and an excruciating delivery. Granger had held Emmaline's hand throughout the ordeal, compassionately coaching her and occasionally shedding tears of empathy for her pain.

Yet somehow, a mere couple of hours after the birth, the grueling vigil had already taken on a surreal morning-after haze.

"I can't believe he's really here at last," Granger said softly. His fingertip looked enormous with the baby's impossibly small pink fist grasping it.

"Neither can I," Emmaline said contentedly.

"And I'll bet you can't believe he's a he."

"Hmm?"

"You thought he was a she—remember? You told me that when we were living back on Eldridge Street."

"Yes, but I didn't really mean it," she told him. "I had no idea what the gender would be."

"But you said—"

"I said a lot of things back then that weren't true," she told him.

"Like when you told me that you hated my guts?"

"I never said that!" She grinned and reached out to swat him playfully, then winced. "Ouch!"

"What's wrong, Em?"

"Nothing, just . . . ouch." With a grimace, she reached for the button that would raise the hospital bed a bit higher, the better to watch her husband beaming over their newborn son. "Do you think they'll give me something stronger for the pain if I beg them?"

"They didn't when you were in labor," he said wryly. "And luckily they didn't just shoot you and put you out of your misery when you begged them to do that, either. Although I'll bet that one nurse, Elvira, was tempted when you kicked her in the stomach."

"You'd have kicked her in the stomach, too, if she were shoving your knees over your ears."

"She was trying to help you push," Granger said mildly. "And I think she was quite surprised to hear such unladylike language coming from a princess's mouth."

"Yes, well, she'd be surprised about a lot of things

this princess does," Emmaline said, making another futile attempt to reach the bedside switch. "I wonder how long it will be before the stitches don't hurt every time I—ouch!"

"Here, let me help you." Carefully balancing the sleeping baby's cheek against the burp cloth draped across his chest, Granger reached over and raised the bed. "Comfortable now?"

"Yes, thanks." She sighed and looked at the bedside tray. "Now if only they'd give me something to eat other than that horrid bright pink meat—"

"It's called corned beef—"

"—yes, and soggy cabbage, and slimy green Jell-O . . ."

"Well, what do you expect, having a baby on Saint Patrick's Day?" Granger asked with a grin. "You have to get used to our American customs."

"I thought it was an Irish custom," she grumbled. "And anyway, you know that I adore American food. After all I've been through, the least they could do is send up a Big Mac."

"I'll run out and get you one," he immediately offered.

She sighed, glancing at the rain-spattered windowpane high above the Manhattan street. The sill was lined with vases of flowers—roses, dozens of roses—and all of them from Granger.

"No, darling, don't go," she said. "It's pouring out, and besides, I want you here with—"

"Mrs. Lockwood?"

She looked up to see an unfamiliar nurse peering

into the room, wearing a strange expression. She seemed to be either blocking the doorway or cautiously keeping her distance from the patient. Perhaps she'd been warned by the bruised Elvira.

"Yes?" Emmaline asked sweetly.

"You have a visitor, if you're feeling up to it."

A visitor? Hmm.

She certainly wasn't feeling up to small talk, but she couldn't wait to show off the baby to someone other than his proud papa.

She looked at Granger. "It must be Brynn. Nobody else would know where to find us. Is she back in town already?"

"I doubt it. When I reached her on her cell phone to tell her that you were in labor yesterday, she was still in Verdunia, helping your sister with her trousseau."

Josephine, of course, was preparing to marry Remi next month in what promised to be the royal wedding of the century, joining the two families together after all.

The coastal access road was already nearing completion—with no thanks to Granger's vindictive grandfather. Lockwood Enterprises had cut all ties with the project last September, after the scandal broke.

Emmaline's one regret was that she and Granger hadn't been able to travel overseas for her sister and Remi's formal engagement announcement in Buiron on Valentine's Day. Her doctor forbade it. But they had watched the television coverage. Josephine looked radiant, as always, and Remi was positively beaming.

They didn't even seem to mind when that pushy television reporter Debi Hanson—who was now anchoring her own wildly successful afternoon talk show—had ambushed them with a camera crew on their way to the engagement party in their honor. Of course it was Brynn who stole the spotlight—on the well-sculpted arm of Dolph Schumer, whom she had since decided was a halitosis-plagued narcissist.

Emmaline frowned and asked Granger, "If Brynn isn't here, then who else can the visitor possibly—?"

Emmaline broke off midsentence, noticing that Granger's face had gone whiter than the cloth diaper on his shoulder.

She followed Granger's stunned gaze to the doorway, where an enormous bird hovered.

That pain medication must be causing hallucinations . . .

Emmaline blinked.

The bird was still there.

Furthermore, it was speaking.

A blustery, unfamiliar voice—not a squawk, but a voice—filled the hallway. "Please step aside, Nurse. My hip is bothering me. I can't stand here all day."

All right, it wasn't the drugs—and it wasn't a bird.

It was a man. An old man.

An old man who had lowered the enormous stuffed parrot he was holding and stepped into the room—then stopped just inside the doorway.

He was staring at Granger. And the baby.

Emmaline could swear she saw a tear glisten in

the visitor's eye, but it had vanished by the time he had cleared his throat noisily and turned his attention to her. "Your Highness, it's a pleasure to make your acquaintance at last. I'm Granger Lockwood. The other Granger Lockwood. And now there are three of us once again."

"Grandfather—" Granger began.

Emmaline cut him off with a warning look. This wasn't the time. The old man had shown up there out of the blue, clearly ready to make amends.

"It's a pleasure to meet you, too, Mr. Lockwood. And I'm Emmaline. You don't have to call me Your Highness."

"And you don't have to call me mister," he replied, gesturing at the stuffed bird he held. "I brought this for the baby."

"That's so sweet of you. It's his first gift," Emmaline said, truly touched.

"Please sit down, Grandfather." Granger regained his composure and spoke stiffly for the first time, rising from the chair.

"No, you sit with that baby." His grandfather plunked the stuffed bird on the foot of the bed.

"But your hip—"

"My hip is good as new. I just said that to get that nosy nurse out of my way so that I could see my new namesake—"

"Grandfather—"

"He's already three hours old," the old man went on, either hard of hearing or deliberately ignoring Granger's attempted interruption, "and he hasn't even seen his great-grandfather yet."

Emmaline's thoughts whirled. How had Granger's grandfather found out about the baby? Had the press somehow gotten wind of the delivery already, despite their elaborate efforts to avoid a news leak?

The initial furor of headlines had long since died down, but the media refused to leave Emmaline and Granger alone—even now that they were mere private citizens living a boring married life in a two-bedroom co-op on the East Side.

Granted, the place was a far cry from the studio on Eldridge Street. Her parents, who had purchased the co-op as a wedding gift for Emmaline and Granger, had insisted on an elevator building with a doorman. And a terrace, so that their grandchild would have access to fresh air.

The king and queen—and of course, the royal aunties—were currently winging their way across the Atlantic, eager to greet the baby.

As for the paternal side of the family . . .

"How did you hear about the birth, Grandfather?" Granger asked. "Was it on the radio, or in the paper, or—?"

"Not yet, but I'm sure it will be."

"Then how did you—"

"I have my sources," the old man said mysteriously, taking a step closer to Granger and peering down at the sleeping infant.

For a moment the room was silent.

Then Granger's grandfather cleared his throat. Several times. "He's a handsome little thing, isn't he?" he asked gruffly. "Looks like he's got the Lockwood eyebrows. But I think that's his mother's pretty nose."

Emmaline smiled, touched. "Do you want to hold him?"

"No, that's his father's job," came the brusque—but not unpleasant—reply. "But if his father would like another job . . . I've got a position that I think might interest him."

Granger looked up, a shadow crossing his face. "Grandfather—"

"Before you turn me down, let me tell you that I've been thinking, and it's about time I took some time off. An extended leave of absence, if you will."

"How long a leave of absence?" Granger asked dubiously.

"A permanent one," the old man said. "Doctor's orders. It seems that the stress of running my business is going to kill me if I don't slow down. I used to think retiring was the worst thing that could happen, but now . . ." He shrugged. "Now I know that there are other things. Worse things."

"Like dying?" Granger asked dryly.

"That's one of them. Being a lonely old man with nobody to talk to except a couple of birds is another."

Granger's jaw dropped.

"So I'll make a deal with you," his grandfather went on. "You come back to Lockwood Enterprises, and I'll clear out."

"I . . . I'd have to think about it."

"Don't be silly. You can't support your wife and son forever on handouts from the royal in-laws."

"We haven't taken handouts," Granger protested, a dangerous gleam in his eye. "And I'm quite capable of supporting my family. I've raised nearly all the capital I need to launch my business plan—without Anderson Lowell's support, I might add."

"I know," his grandfather said quietly. "Regardless, you would be a fool not to consider my offer."

Emmaline held her breath, willing Granger to swallow his ferocious pride and do the right thing.

"As I said, Grandfather, I'm quite capable—"

"You are capable," his grandfather interrupted. "Far more capable than I ever realized. But sooner or later, Granger, you need something you can be proud of. Something you can someday hand down to Granger Lockwood the fifth."

"I'm going to build—"

"That will take decades. I'm offering you something that is already established. Something that is your birthright. And his."

Granger and Emmaline looked at each other.

"Don't be stubborn. Accept the offer," she said. "He's right."

"I'll do it," Granger told his grandfather.

Emmaline broke into a wide grin.

Then her husband said, "But about Granger Lockwood the fifth . . ."

Uh-oh.

"What about him?" The old man reached out a gnarled, tentative finger and gently stroked the baby's fuzzy dark head.

"He doesn't exist. Grandfather, meet Eldridge Lockwood the first."

"Eldridge?" the old man echoed, scowling. "What kind of a name is Eldridge?"

"An old family name," Granger said with a grin.

"Her family?" Grandfather asked, looking at Emmaline.

"No. Our family." Granger indicated himself, Emmaline and the baby. He added firmly, "We're going to do things our way."

"And we wanted him to have a one-of-a-kind name," Emmaline added.

"That's a one-of-a-kind name, all right," the old man said. "Eldridge, hmm? Granger Lockwood the fifth would have been better. But I suppose it could have been worse . . ."

"Here—you can hold him, while I hold my wife," Granger said, and thrust the baby into his grandfather's arms before he could protest.

Granger settled on the edge of the bed and wrapped Emmaline in an embrace. She leaned her head contentedly against his chest as they watched Granger Lockwood II lose every ounce of his dignity as he cooed and made faces at their newborn.

"Do you know what I'm thinking?" Emmaline asked in a voice only her husband could hear.

"That my grandfather's utterly lost his mind?"

"That, too, perhaps . . . but I'm thinking that this princess has found her fairy-tale ending after all."

They smiled.

They kissed.

And they lived happily ever after.

Lose yourself in enchanting love stories from Avon Books.
Check out what's coming in December:

HOW TO TREAT A LADY by Karen Hawkins
An Avon Romantic Treasure

Harriet Ward invented a fiance to save her family from ruin, but when the bank wants proof, fate drops a mysterious stranger into her arms, a man she believes has no idea of his own identity. And so she announces that he is her long-awaited betrothed!

A GREEK GOD AT THE LADIES' CLUB by Jenna McKnight
An Avon Contemporary Romance

What if you had created the perfect replica of a gorgeous Greek god, and right before you're about to unveil it to a group of ladies, it comes alive in all its naked glory? What if your creation wanted to reward you by fulfilling your every desire? What if you're tempted to let him . . .

ALMOST PERFECT by Denise Hampton
An Avon Romance

Cassandra wagered a kiss in a card game with rake Lucien Hollier and willingly paid her debt when she lost. Then, desperate for funds, she challenges him again . . . and wins! Taking Lucien's money and fleeing into the night, the surprisingly sweet taste of his kiss still on her lips, Cassie is certain she's seen the last of him . . .

THE DUCHESS DIARIES by Mia Ryan
An Avon Romance

Armed with advice from her late grandmother's diaries, Lady Lara Darling is ready for her first Season. But before she even reaches London, the independent beauty breaks all the rules set forth in the Duchess Diaries when she meets the distractingly handsome Griff Hallsbury.

REL 1103

Discover Contemporary Romances
at Their Sizzling Hot Best
from Avon Books

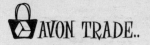

Avon Romantic Treasures

*Unforgettable, enthralling love stories,
sparkling with passion and adventure
from Romance's bestselling authors*